ALL'S FAIR IN LOVE AND WINE

RAISE A GLASS, BOOK NINE

MARY E THOMPSON

1

———————

LEO YOUNG WIPED UP THE BAR AND CHECKED IN WITH THE few guests lingering. He offered advice to a couple at the end who were debating between two wines, unsure which one to purchase. They thanked him and moved to the gift shop, grabbing two bottles of wine before heading to check out.

Leo grinned to himself and went through what he had open and available. His favorite Sangiovese was always popular when he was there to sell it. Kristen, his cousin and partner in the tasting room, wasn't as big of a fan as he was, but Leo could drink it by the gallon.

He poured himself a glass, enjoying the sharp bite and tangy kick of the wine. He closed his eyes for a second, savoring the flavor. He didn't normally drink during the day, but it was the kind of day that required a little extra fortification.

When Leo opened his eyes, there was a curvy blonde smiling at him. "What will your boss think?"

Leo almost admitted he was the boss, but he held back.

It sounded like a line, and he didn't want to put her off. "I think it'll be okay. Are you here for a tasting?"

She glanced around then looked back at him with her head cocked to the side. Her amber eyes sparkled, a hint of green in the middle. "Is that what people do when they come to a vineyard?"

He pursed his lips in a smile. He liked a woman who wasn't afraid to spar with him. "Well, some people just come for the scenery." He added a wink and gestured to himself.

She scoffed. "Well, then I better head out. If *that* scenery and day drinking is all you have to offer..." She stood and made a move to the door.

"Ouch," Leo said with a laugh. "You sure know how to wound a guy."

She smirked. "Something tells me a guy like you can take it."

"Is that so?"

She laughed and move back to her stool, sliding onto the edge. "Yeah. I think you can handle just about anything."

Leo drained his glass and set it in the dirty rack. "Well, I can definitely handle one woman sitting at my bar on a Thursday afternoon. I bet I can even tell what you like to drink."

She raised an eyebrow and grinned. "Is that so?"

Leo nodded confidently. "Absolutely. It's my superpower. To look at someone and know what they like."

She grinned even wider. "Wow. A lot of people claim to know me, but very few actually do. I find it hard to believe a man I've never met before today will know me better than friends I've had for years."

Leo grabbed the list of wines and one of the small pencils. He circled five wines that he knew she would love and turned over the list. "This is what you're drinking today."

She narrowed her gaze and shook her head. "No. I don't drink any of these wines."

Leo smiled. "Maybe not yet, but you will."

"If this is how you treat all your customers, I guess I'm not surprised the bar is empty today."

A surprised laugh burst out of Leo. He shook his head as he grabbed the first bottle, the newest Riesling. It was good, and if you were tasting wine in the Finger Lakes Region of Central New York, you had to try the Riesling.

"What is that?" she asked, her voice hinting at apprehension.

"I'll tell you what," Leo said, pouring a bit into a clean glass. "If you don't like all five wines, your tasting is on the house. If you do, then you admit I really do have superpowers."

She smirked, her brown eyes darkening. She was a gambler, and she couldn't pass up a challenge. He could see it in that little twinkle and the excitement.

She reached across the bar and waited for him to slide his hand into hers. She gave his a firm shake, alerting every one of his senses to the woman captivating him. She smelled like a woman should smell, fresh and clean, but not flowery or fruity. She was simple with her blonde hair tied back into a loose ponytail, her face dotted with minimal makeup. His mouth watered at the idea of tasting the wine his family produced on her tongue, or other parts of her body. He stirred in his shorts at the thought, and nodded at the agreement between him and the woman.

She released his hand and lifted the wine glass. She examined the color then swirled it like an expert, and Leo lost a little bit of his confidence. She looked like she knew what she was doing. Was she an employee of another vineyard? There to check out the competition? It wouldn't be the first time it had happened, but if Perry hired a beautiful woman to spy on them, he was getting smarter.

All his fear vanished when the woman locked eyes with him and lifted the glass to her lips. Her eyes widened at the first sip, and Leo could almost taste the dry Riesling coating his own tongue. He swallowed with her, then waited as she examined the glass again and took another sip.

"Damn it. I really thought you were going to screw it up on the first one. How is it possible I like this?"

Leo grinned and went to grab the next bottle. "I told you, I know people. Also, Riesling is a staple in the area. The grapes grow like crazy, so every vineyard has Riesling, but I'm partial to ours. It's dry, but the lightness and strong grape flavor make it taste a little sweet."

"That's exactly it," she said after emptying the glass. "It's really good."

Leo nodded and rinsed her glass, then poured her second tasting, a chardonnay. While she swirled, he grabbed some cheese and chocolate from the mini-fridge under the bar and set them on a plate for her.

"This is good, too," she said. "I didn't plan to spend my whole paycheck here today."

"You work in the area?" Leo asked, knowing the answer before she spoke.

Then she nodded. "Yeah, I just moved here. I start work tomorrow."

"Really?" he asked, surprised. "I wouldn't have pegged you as a local."

She shrugged. "I'm not. I grew up in Montana."

"What brought you out here?" Leo poured her third tasting, pinot noir.

She swirled and sipped and groaned. "Are all the vineyards this good?"

Leo smiled, ignoring the fact that she didn't answer his question. "Of course not. We're the best. Best wines on Cayuga Lake. We sure think so."

She nodded. "I planned to spend my summer tasting a bunch of different wines, but it's going to be hard for me to avoid coming back here. This is so good."

"I told you I knew what you would like."

She rolled her eyes. "Yeah, yeah, you have superpowers."

Leo laughed. "Oh, come on. Say it like you mean it."

She stood next to her chair and slapped her hand on the bar. She peered at his name tag and cleared her throat. "Attention, everyone. Leo here is the most amazing bartender there ever was. He has superpowers! But don't tell anyone. You know you can't tell people about that. Just use it to your advantage and try the best wines on Cayuga Lake. Right here, people!"

Leo's cheeks heated under the watchful eye of the handful of customers and his relatives who came over to see what was going on. His sister, Andie, winked at him then waddled back to her desk, taking his future niece or nephew with her.

"Thanks for that," Leo said when the woman finally took her seat.

"Any time," she said with a smirk. "What's next?"

Merlot went next, then a glass of the Sangiovese. She swirled both and loved them. "Okay, I give. How did you do it?"

Leo chuckled. "You looked like someone willing to try something new. It really isn't hard to read people. I guessed you were a sweet fan, but it's hard to come to a vineyard and not try new things. What is typically your favorite wine?"

"Moscato or Gewurtztraminer."

"We have a Gewurtztraminer if you want to try it. I'm happy to let you try whatever we have."

"How much? I haven't started work yet, so I'm trying to stick to my budget, and tasting is not nearly as much fun as buying a whole bottle."

Leo shook his head with a smile. "No charge. Just don't tell everyone about the deal you got."

She slid off her stool again and took a deep breath like she was about to shout her deal to the room. He froze. It wasn't like he'd get in trouble for an extra tasting, but he'd feel bad that he didn't give it to all his customers.

She smirked at him and eased back onto the stool. "I wouldn't do that to you."

He laughed. "Thanks. You'll give me a heart attack, though."

She grinned. "I don't have any medical training so you might want to save that for some big burly dude who knows CPR. He can give you mouth-to-mouth."

Leo laughed. He couldn't remember the last time he enjoyed a woman's company as much. Or anyone's for that matter. He'd been letting everything get to him lately, and he hadn't been able to shake the feeling that something was wrong.

"Okay, I need to get out of here before I really do spend my entire savings. I think I have a list of eight wines."

"If you buy ten, you get two free," Leo said.

She groaned. "Maybe I can ask for a raise. On my first day. Or maybe I can bribe my boss with a bottle of wine."

Leo laughed again.

"Thank you, Leo. This was a great way to start my summer in Bereton."

"I hope you enjoy it," he said. "And hopefully you'll be

back sometime."

She nodded. "I definitely will be. Bye."

He waved and watched as she moved to the gift shop. She chose her wines and added a few other small items, then was heading for the door with a wave and a grin.

He should have asked her name.

Leo added her glass to the dirty rack and pulled his buzzing phone out of his pocket. He closed his eyes when he saw his brother Dillon's name on the screen.

"Yeah?"

"You got a few minutes?"

Leo looked around. "I'm working."

"Is anyone there?"

Leo sighed. "No."

"Okay, good. Come to the office for a minute. I want to show you something. Let them know in the gift shop so we don't lose customers."

"Yes, sir," Leo said before ending the call and slipping his phone into his pocket again. He closed his eyes and followed instructions, like he'd always done.

SARA DONOVAN MUSCLED the box of wine she bought into her tiny apartment and knew she was going to regret the choice to buy so much. She barely had enough space for herself in her new home, and adding a box of wine on day one was not good planning.

But really, what did she need in life? Wine was always a good addition to a room.

She set the box on the floor near her fridge and opened it. She grabbed bottles until she found the one she was looking for and put it in the fridge. It was the only thing in there, but that was okay. She'd do some shopping eventually.

Her new apartment was furnished, which was the only way she could live there, and it was clean. It was considered a one bedroom, but the bedroom was behind a temporary wall, so it barely counted. Still, she didn't mind. It was all hers for a few months.

And then she'd move on again.

Her landlord, Tom, left an envelope of menus with places that would deliver on the kitchen table, so Sara sat down and flipped through it. She was debating between Thai and pizza when her phone rang.

"Hi, Dad," she said without looking at the screen.

"Hi, honey. How are you?"

"I'm good. How are you, Dad?"

"Good, good. What time are you going to be home?"

Sara sighed. "It's not going to be for a while, Dad. What do you need?"

"I lost my glasses again. You always know where they are."

Sara smiled. Her father was amazing, but he was forgetful. Like losing his glasses, and forgetting his daughter moved out the day she turned eighteen. Almost twelve years ago. She hadn't stayed in one place for longer than two years since, and none of them were in the same town, let alone the same house, as her father.

"Have you looked in the kitchen, on the table?"

His solid footsteps thundered through the phone. Papers shuffled, no doubt bills he was behind on. She made a mental note to check his accounts later and pay what she could.

"They're not here."

"How about the night stand?"

More thundering footsteps, faster this time. The bed squeaked when he sat on the edge. "Nope, not here either."

Sara sighed. "Dad. Did you check your head?"

He laughed. "I told you you always know. They were right there all along. Thanks, honey. See you soon."

He hung up without another word and Sara stared at the blank screen. She loved her father, but he never paid attention to anything. His glasses weren't the only thing he lost.

Sara shook off the melancholy thoughts and went back to her menus. She couldn't decide between them because both meant she'd be alone in her new apartment that didn't feel like hers yet.

She grabbed her keys and headed for the door. There was a diner not far from her apartment and greasy food sounded good. Maybe a cheeseburger. Or grilled cheese. Or really anything with lots of cheese.

She stepped inside and breathed deep, enjoying the scent of meat sizzling on the grill and grease filling the customers. The din of silverware on plates and conversation made her smile. She wasn't alone. Not for the moment.

"Table for one?" the waitress asked.

Sara nodded, but someone stepped up next to her and said, "Make that two."

Sara took a step away from the guy. He was cute, but she wasn't accustomed to having dinner with complete strangers. Sleeping with them was okay once in a while, but that didn't involve questions and talking and someone trying to get to know her. That was just naked skin slapping together and letting the beast out once in a while.

"I'm Peter. And I hate eating alone. I'll buy your dinner, and Denise can seat us in her section so you know someone is watching my every move."

Denise lifted an eyebrow at them then focused on Sara.

"He's as harmless as they come, but I will be watching. I'm friends with his mom, and trust me when I say if he steps out of line, he'll regret it."

Sara looked at Peter and smiled. "Fine. And thank you. I don't plan to order a salad, though."

Peter scoffed. "As if you could get a salad here."

Denise whacked him with a menu. "Hey, we have salads."

"Yeah, taco salads. It hardly counts."

Denise rolled her eyes and turned to lead them to a table. Peter gestured for Sara to go first then followed her. She felt oddly comfortable with him, even though it'd only been a few seconds. She didn't get the feeling he was staring at her ass, which was good. And she didn't think he was hitting on her. Another good.

How was it possible she met two nice guys in one day?

Denise took their drink orders and left. Sara watched Peter from under her lashes, hoping he didn't notice. He was cute with blond hair and matching eyebrows. His eyes were a moss green color that made him look a little exotic. His gray shirt stretched across a broad chest and curved over wide shoulders and strong biceps.

"So, are you going to tell me your name or just stare at me all night?" Peter asked, lifting his gaze to hers.

Her cheeks heated, but she shook it off. "I was thinking about just staring at you all night."

Peter chuckled and went back to his menu. "Well, then, enjoy the view."

His words reminded her of Leo. It wasn't fair to Peter to be thinking about Leo, but they weren't on a date.

"Obviously, you live around here. Do you still live with your mother?"

Peter smirked. "No, I don't. Although, I'm close to my

mom. My whole family, actually. They're insane, but I love them."

"So, what do you do?"

Denise interrupted them with drinks before Peter could answer. She took their orders and was gone again in seconds.

Sara took a sip of her sweet tea and shook her head. Not nearly sweet enough. She grabbed the sugar on the table and added three packets, stirring quickly and taking another sip.

"We don't really know how to do sweet tea around here. Are you from the south?"

Sara shook her head. "I lived there for a while. Got hooked on sweet tea. And you're right. This is not sweet tea."

Peter sipped his water and studied her. "Not from the south, likes sweet tea, no accent, beautiful and funny, and I'm guessing just moved to town."

"What are you doing?"

"Listing all the things I know about you. Since you won't tell me your name, I have to keep track of everything else."

Sara grinned. She smoothed a hand down her plain white tee and debated sharing more of herself with Peter. He reminded her a lot of Mark. Mark was her best friend growing up. They dated for a week and realized it was weird because they knew too much about each other. Besides her father, he was the only person she kept in touch with from home. Mark had a ranch and a wife and a few kids and was living his dream.

Everything Sara didn't have.

And didn't want.

"My name is Sara," she finally admitted.

"Well, now, was that so hard?"

Sara smiled. If he only knew.

2

THE NEXT DAY, SARA SMILED ON HER WAY TO HER NEW JOB.
She already had a friend, and she was excited to start her
new job. So far, it was a great start to living in Bereton.

She always loved the first day. Getting to know new
people, figuring out new tasks. Even though she was only
going to be there for a few months, she always had a goal of
leaving the place a little better than when she started. If she
could make some small improvement, she considered her
job a success.

She'd only ever spoken to her new boss over the phone.
Megan Shepherd was insanely talented, but she admitted
she needed help in the gift shop and as a personal assistant.
Sara was clear up front that she wasn't staying longer than
the three months they agreed on, and Megan was prepared
to hire someone else for the winter when everything slowed
down in the area.

Sara walked into Lakeside Glass and stopped. Wow. It
was stunning to see the different sculptures created using
glass. Sculptures that defied the laws of gravity and amazed
her. The colors helped to tell the story, from the reds and

oranges of a vase that looked like fire to the blues and purples of a bowl that she wanted to reach out and touch to see if it was wet. Everything was arranged nicely, but Sara immediately saw a few things she would change.

Probably not on day one, though.

"Hello?" she called out, wondering if she was late or early. Megan never really said what time she should start working, so Sara looked up the shop's hours online and decided to show up just after opening.

"Hang on a second!" came a voice from the back.

Sara moved closer to a door behind the counter and waited for someone to walk through it.

And waited.

And waited.

She glanced at her phone and finally someone walked out.

"Hi," the guy said with a warm smile. He wore jeans and a black tee and heavy boots that thumped the ground as he walked toward her. "I'm Adam. How can I help you?"

"Hi, it's nice to meet you, Adam. I'm Sara Donovan. I'm supposed to start working here today."

Adam's russet colored eyebrows tugged together. His matching hair flopped to the side, giving him a lost puppy look. "Um, doing what?"

"I'm Megan's new assistant and I'll be working out here in the gift shop."

His features relaxed and he grinned. He was cute when he smiled. And appeared close to Sara's age. *Why had I never visited this town before?* It was a gold mine for hot guys.

"I think she mentioned something about you. Sorry about that. Um, well, this is the gift shop." He glanced around, his light brown eyes lighting on some of the pieces. "Enjoy."

He turned to go back through the door.

"Wait!"

Adam spun around again. "Yeah?"

"What am I supposed to do?"

He shrugged. "I don't know. Sell stuff. Do you know how to use a cash register and a computer?"

"Of course," she said.

He nodded and slid his hand through his messy hair. "Good. When Megan can take a break, I'm sure she'll come introduce herself."

Sara opened her mouth to say something else, but he was already gone.

"What the hell?" she wondered aloud.

Sara thought about following Adam through the door, but she wasn't brave enough. There was no way to know what was on the other side, and she was smart enough to know it could be dangerous.

She looked around the gift shop and decided to make the most of it. If the job was a bust, she could try to find something else. The promised pay was good, but she had no idea if she'd ever see any of it if her boss couldn't even pull her shit together long enough to say hi.

It wasn't long before the bell above the door rang and two customers walked in.

"Hi," Sara said. "Welcome to Lakefront Glass."

"Thank you," the woman said. "This place is stunning."

Sara nodded. "It really is. Are you looking for anything in particular?"

"Mostly browsing."

Sara grinned, understanding customer code for back off. "Let me know if I can help you with anything."

The woman nodded and Sara backed away, leaving the couple to explore. Sara did the same on the other side of the store, looking at every piece so she would know what was available in case a customer asked for anything specific.

"This is gorgeous," the woman said a minute later, catching Sara's attention with her awed tone. "It would be perfect in our living room. Don't you think?"

Her husband nodded. "It would. You've been looking for something with these colors."

Sara grinned as the woman ran a finger over the smooth, green glass. Then her smile fell as she noticed the price. "It's a bit out of price range, though."

The husband shrugged. "If it's what you want, we'll get it."

The woman glanced at Sara and caught her watching them. Sara pasted on what she hoped was a friendly smile.

"Can you tell me a little more about this piece?"

Sara walked closer to them, trying to figure out how she could get out of the situation. "Um, it's beautiful." She grinned and admitted the truth, knowing that was her only option. "I actually just started working here. About an hour ago. I don't know anything about it. I'm so sorry."

The woman's hopeful expression fell. She looked at the piece wistfully, then pressed her lips together in a grin. "Thank you."

Sara edged away again, knowing she'd just blown a sale. She was frustrated and annoyed. The only way she'd keep her job was if she could do it well, and she didn't know a damn thing about what she was doing. She hadn't even met her new boss, let alone gotten any instruction about what in the hell her job was.

She watched as the couple made their way to the door a few minutes later, empty-handed, and vowed to get some answers.

Sara stomped to the door Adam disappeared through earlier and pushed her way inside.

The first thing that hit her was the heat, followed quickly by the sound, like an airplane flying overhead. She looked around the open space and found two people covered head-to-toe in heavy clothing, one of them holding on to a thick rod, blowing on the end, the other supporting the fire-red orb of molten glass.

Holy shit.

Sara froze in place, knowing immediately that she was in danger if she took another step into the workspace. She backed up, stopping when her back hit the door. She pushed through it, keeping her eyes on the molten glass until the door swung shut with her safely on the other side.

She sucked in a ragged breath and tried to calm her pounding pulse. She knew glass blowing was dangerous, but coming face-to-face with it, wearing shorts and flip flops, was not a good thing.

Sara busied herself by getting familiar with the cash register and the computer it was linked to. Most people paid with cards, but Sara wanted to make sure she wasn't fumbling around with the register if she needed to make change.

Three more customers came in and she managed to make a sale. They bought a small glass dish that looked like a flower floating in water. It was stunning, and Sara was a little disappointed she didn't see it and snatch it up first. It was going to be hard to choose one thing from Lakeside Glass. She always bought something from wherever she settled, a tiny memento of the time she spent at every new place. She would be elevating her collection by choosing one of the beautiful pieces her new boss created.

"Sara!" a woman said from behind her, catching Sara browsing again. "It's so nice to meet you."

Sara recognized the voice as Megan's and turned to her new boss. Megan was short, an inch or two shorter than Sara's own five-four, with curly, gray hair. Her dark skin was a rich, smooth brown. Her eyes were a bright and vibrant amber. The overalls she wore, now rolled up to her knees, and her white tank top gave her a casual look.

"Hi, Megan," Sara said automatically extending her hand.

Megan pushed right past Sara's outstretched hand and wrapped her in a hug. "I don't shake hands. I hug. We're all a family here, and families hug. How are you? Did you get all settled in?"

Sara nodded. "I'm good. Thanks so much for helping me find the apartment."

"Tom's a good guy. He wasn't sure if he wanted to rent the apartment, but when I told him you were only here a few months, he agreed. Of course, I didn't tell him I'm going to try to talk you into staying longer."

Panic lifted up and tightened Sara's throat. First a family and now staying? Sara wasn't sure she could handle it.

"Oh, calm down. I know you want to leave. But good help is hard to find."

"I just started."

Megan laughed. "Yes, and you already sold something."

Sara opened and closed her mouth.

"I get an alert on my phone when a sale goes through. Unfortunately, I don't have enough of those sales, so I get excited with each one."

"There was another couple in here, but they didn't buy anything," Sara admitted. She hated that she didn't help out. It was her job to sell things.

"It happens all the time. I price my work where it deserves to be, but not everyone likes that. If they don't come back, they weren't meant to take a piece of me home with them."

Sara smiled, loving Megan's mindset. She needed a little of that confidence. Maybe it would rub off.

"Have you had lunch yet?" Megan asked.

Sara shook her head. "No. I wasn't sure when I should take a break."

Megan waved her hand. "We're pretty laidback around here. Adam and I are the only ones here most of the time. We had a young mom working for us for a while, but her kids are busy this time of year and she always takes the summer off. She told us before she left that she isn't coming back this fall. It was perfect timing for you to start."

Sara grinned. "It was perfect timing for me, too."

"Good," Megan said, looping her arm through Sara's. "Let's go see what Adam brought us for lunch and we can get to know each other. After lunch, I'll be in the shop with you for the day so you can ask me questions and find out more about the pieces we have available."

Sara nodded and let Megan drag her back through the door to the workshop. The furnace was closed, but the heat was still there, making Sara sweat instantly.

"It gets warm in here. We'll just grab Adam then head back up front. We have a small office off the showroom where we eat and relax when we aren't creating."

They walked past the furnace to where Adam was stripping off his protective gear. His black tee and jeans fit snugly over a fit male form. Sara licked her lips unconsciously, tugging the bottom one between her teeth.

"He's nice to look at, isn't he?" Megan asked quietly.

"Even more frustrating, he's a damn nice man. If only he wasn't so young." She stopped and looked at Sara, narrowing her eyes. "You two are actually close to the same age."

Sara shook her head. "I'm not looking to get involved with anyone."

Was that relief in Megan's eyes? She grinned. "Probably just as well. Adam will be done with his apprenticeship at the end of summer."

"What does that mean?"

Megan's gaze drifted to Adam and slid down his form. Sara's followed, her lips curling up when she realized her boss was checking out his ass.

"It means Adam won't work here much longer. He'll be a certified glassblower, and probably start his own business. He's talked about leaving the area."

Adam looked up and caught them watching him. He smiled at Sara, but his eyes went dark and needy when they eased over to Megan. Sara almost had to fan herself, but Megan looked away and didn't even notice the scorching look.

Adam shook his head once, then walked over to them. "Showing Sara around?"

Megan nodded. "I am. And we're hungry."

Adam smiled, his eyes going soft. "You're always hungry."

Megan nodded again. "True. And you're always feeding me amazing things."

Adam glowed under the praise, and Sara felt like she was intruding on a private moment. "Um, I can just go out and grab something."

"No, no, eat with us. We should all get to know each other. Adam always has more than enough food."

Adam gave Sara a forced smile and nodded. "Always. You should join us."

Sara finally nodded, and the three of them made their way back to the front. A door to the side that she hadn't paid any attention to earlier revealed a small room that was half office and half kitchen. A table for four sat in the middle with a fridge, microwave, and two cabinets along the wall. The other side of the room had a desk with a computer and a raised shelf with a bank of black and white screens.

"Security system," Megan explained. "We don't have many issues, but I like knowing it's here."

"She keeps strange hours, so it's necessary. We need to know if someone is here," Adam said firmly, going to the fridge in the corner. He pulled out a covered glass dish and put it in the microwave.

"He worries about me," Megan said with a grin for Sara.

She just smiled. She couldn't tell what their relationship was, but it didn't seem purely colleagues. She wanted to ask, but she learned long ago that if she started asking questions, people would expect that she would answer them also. That wasn't going to happen, so Sara kept her mouth shut.

The microwave beeped and Adam removed a steaming container of something that smelled amazing.

"You've outdone yourself again, Adam," Megan gushed. "I don't know how you do it. Some woman is going to snatch you up."

Adam glanced at Sara, then avoided meeting either of their eyes. She felt bad for him. It was obvious he had a major crush on their boss, but Megan was obviously not willing to do anything about it. Then again, Megan was probably fifteen years older than him, so maybe she was married.

"You're single?" Sara blurted.

Adam glanced at her, then looked at Megan. Finally, he pressed his lips together and nodded. "I am. Unfortunately."

Sara nodded, wishing she'd kept her big mouth shut.

"How about you, Sara? Ever been married?" Megan asked.

Sara shook her head. "No, never. No kids. No real ties to anywhere. I love seeing the country and getting to do different things, and being on my own makes that possible."

She'd recited the same thing so many times, she almost believed every word of it. Almost.

"Having ties is what makes a place special. There hasn't ever been a place you wanted to settle down? Dig some roots. Stay?" Megan asked.

Sara shook her head and lied, "Nope. Never."

"What about your parents? Are they nomads like you?" Megan pushed.

Sara shook her head, always ready to answer questions about her parents. They were quick and easy, and no one pried once she said, "My mom died when I was in college. My dad still lives in Montana where I grew up."

"Montana? Wow. I've never been there. What was it like to grow up in Montana?" Megan asked.

Sara took the plate of food Adam offered her, along with the understanding smile. Sara almost laughed out loud, but she clamped her lips shut and accept that she had an ally who wouldn't push her for more details than she was comfortable sharing.

"Montana is nice, but it wasn't for me. I wanted to see the country. That's what I'm doing."

"Do you see yourself ever going back there?" Megan asked.

Sara shook her head automatically. "No."

Hearing the finality in her tone, Megan nodded.

Before Megan dove into a new round of questioning, Sara asked her own question. "How did you get into glass-blowing?"

Sara read Megan's bio on her website and knew a little about her, but she was always curious what made people tick. What drove someone to do one thing instead of another? Why did someone pick one life and not another?

She let herself get lost in Megan's story about discovering glass blowing in college and falling in love with not only the beauty of it, but the danger. She didn't want to play it safe with any part of her life, so she started glassblowing. When she got pregnant at nineteen and dropped out of school, she took whatever jobs she could, but as soon as she had enough money saved up, she went back to school and got not only her art degree, but a business degree, too. Megan wasn't willing to give up on her dream, and she taught her daughter to always go after hers, too.

"Are you married?" Sara asked.

Megan shook her head. "No, never. Anna's father is a good man, but we weren't meant to be together forever. He's there for Anna, but he has another family, too. It's been mostly Anna and I."

Sara's heart clenched at Megan's casual words, as though having a second family was no big deal. She wished she felt the same. Instead, a second family was what tore her world apart. A second family destroyed her. A second family ruined the one she had.

A second family killed her mother.

3

———————

"DUDE," PETER SHOUTED AS HE LET HIMSELF INTO LEO'S house. "I met the woman of my dreams last night. I've never been so thankful that you blew me off in my whole life."

Leo smirked and shook his head. He and Peter grew up together. They'd been friends off and on, but they'd gotten closer over the last year to where Leo thought Peter as his closest friend.

"Oh, yeah? I think I heard something similar last week," Leo teased. Peter was constantly falling in love.

He shook his head and helped himself to a glass of Leo's wine. "No way, dude. This woman, she's beautiful and smart and funny. She's going to be my wife one day. I promise you that."

"What's her name?"

Peter shook his head. "Sara, and she's amazing so don't tell me anything bad about her."

Leo grinned. "I don't think I know a Sara."

"Really? You know everyone in town."

Leo shrugged. "I guess not. Are you sure she lives here?"

Peter nodded. "Positive. I walked her home after we had dinner."

Leo nodded and took a sip of his wine. He had a long day and was promised another one, so he was going to enjoy his break. "When are you going to see her again?"

"I don't know. I didn't get her number, but I know where she works."

"Where does she work? Maybe I know her and don't realize it."

Peter shook his head. "No. If you don't know her name, I'm not taking any more chances. If you know who she is, you're going to tell me something I don't want to hear. And you're not going to mess this up for me by going to see her at work. She's perfect, and you can meet her at our wedding."

Leo snorted and raised his glass. "Congratulations then. To your future bride. May she not be smart enough to run the other way before you get her down the aisle."

Peter flipped him off and finished his wine. "I gotta go, but are we still on for this weekend?"

Leo nodded. "Definitely." He wasn't sure how he was going to fit their Saturday morning fishing trip into his schedule, but he'd make it work. He always did.

Peter was gone in seconds, leaving Leo to a quiet house. He took a deep breath and considered going out, but he was too tired. Working full time in the tasting room plus training under Dillon was exhausting.

He knew his brother meant well, but Dillon didn't listen when Leo said he wasn't interested in filling in for him. Dillon's girlfriend, and soon to be wife, was busy, and they wanted a life together, which meant long months away from Amavita Estates. Dillon said he wanted Leo to take over, but Leo really didn't want to do it.

What he wanted didn't really matter.

Dillon was training Leo to be the CEO, and Leo had no choice but to suck it up and play nice. It was his family's heritage to run Amavita Estates. Their grandparents came over from Italy and made a home at the vineyard. Leo and his siblings and cousins had only been in charge for two years. He wasn't going to risk it all falling apart because he'd rather spend his days pouring drinks than kissing ass.

Leo was dozing on the couch when the front door opened again. He jerked upright, tipping his wine glass over. He caught it just before it spilled on the dark blue fabric.

"Are you already asleep?" Ryan asked. Ryan was the youngest of the nine Richliano cousins and Leo's roommate. He worked more hours than anyone Leo knew between cultivating the grapes on the seventy-three acres of Amavita Estates and his volunteer position with the Bereton Fire Department.

"I'm exhausted," Leo said.

"Dillon?"

Leo nodded. "Yeah, another early morning tomorrow. I should head up."

Ryan turned away, but not before Leo saw the eye roll.

"What?"

"I thought you were going to tell Dillon where to stick it? You always said you loved the tasting room."

"I'm wasting my talents in there. I have a business degree and should be doing more with myself than pouring drinks all day. The family needs me," Leo said. His anger bubbled right under the surface. He and Ryan had the same discussion for months, ever since Dillon approached Leo about filling in. Ryan encouraged him to do it at first, but then he switched sides and started giving Leo shit.

"You're right. Sorry. I wasn't thinking. I guess I'm just too tired," Ryan said. His words were flat and his tone accusatory.

Leo didn't feel like arguing, so he ignored it and headed upstairs. He crashed hard, not waking up until his alarm went off far too early.

The inn was still quiet when he made his way to Dillon's office. Dillon looked up with a grin when Leo let himself in. The only other person happy to be awake that early was Zach, and that was usually because no one bothered him.

"Good morning. I have coffee already here so we can jump right in. Let's go over budgets today," Dillon said happily.

Leo bit back his groan and grabbed the cup of coffee waiting for him. It wasn't going to be long before he needed a refill. Maybe an IV would keep him awake.

DILLON LET Leo out of the office for lunch. Katherine was in town, so Dillon went home to spend some private time with her. Leo really didn't need to know about his big brother's sex life, but apparently that was part of the job description.

"How's it going?" Andie asked Leo as Dillon rushed out the front door.

"Good," Leo said with a forced grin. He loved his sister, but she was married to Dillon's best friend. If he admitted to her that he hated working with their brother, Andie would tell Cody, and Cody would tell Dillon. Leo knew how the Amavita grapevine worked.

"You don't look like it's that good. Are you sure this is what you want?" Andie pressed.

Leo nodded. "Of course. Why wouldn't I?"

Andie rubbed her round belly, massaging the left side.

"This baby is a pain in my ass today. I'm so ready to give birth."

Leo jumped on the subject change knowing Andie would happily talk about her pregnancy and new baby forever if he'd let her. "You only have just over two more months."

"Yeah," Andie groaned, "don't remind me."

"Is Cody rubbing your feet or something? Aren't guys supposed to do that for their pregnant wives?"

Andie smiled, soft and sweet and lost in memories. Even worse than hearing about his brother's sex life was hearing about his sister's. Leo needed an escape before whatever put that look on Andie's face was shared.

"Are you here to take me to lunch?" Nonna asked from behind Leo.

Leo turned to face his grandmother. She was his favorite person in the world, and seeing her walking toward him made him forget how tiring his morning had been. He ached to get back behind the bar and talk to customers, but he would happily join his grandmother for lunch.

She was in a light blue dress with shoes that looked like slippers on her feet. Her gray hair was short, curling around her ears, and made her look like she was twenty years younger than she was.

"I'd love to take you to lunch. Where should we go?" Leo teased.

Nonna laughed and swatted his arm, slipping her hand around his elbow. "If you're paying, we can go anywhere you want, but if I'm paying, we're staying right here."

"Well, I have another meeting with Dillon after lunch, so we should probably stay put."

"How is that going?" Nonna asked.

"Great," Leo lied.

Nonna narrowed her eyes briefly, seeing the lie on his face. She didn't call him on it, though. It was only a matter of time before she would.

"Can you join us, Andie?" Nonna asked his sister.

She shook her head. "Not today. I have a doctor's appointment. Cody'll be here in a few minutes."

"Make sure you eat something. You need more calories to help the baby grow."

Andie snorted. "Trust me, this baby is getting enough calories. I've gained thirty pounds."

Nonna shrugged. "Most of that is the baby. It means you're healthy, and so is my new great-grandchild."

Andie grinned, her eyes misting. "Crap. These hormones are killing me. You can't say things that'll make me cry, Nonna."

Nonna left Leo's side and hugged Andie. They spoke softly to each other until Andie stopped crying. "I really hope this goes back to normal after the baby comes. But I'd love to keep my boobs."

Nonna shook her head. "Those will go away, too, sadly. You'll have to get pregnant again. That's what I did."

Nope, Leo was wrong. He'd listen to his brother and sister talk about their sex lives every day if it meant he never had to hear about his grandmother's sex life. That was definitely the worst one.

"Nonna!"

She turned to him and shrugged. "What? Did you think the aunts just appeared one day? Did your parents never talk to you about where babies come from?"

"Jeez, Nonna, I don't need to hear about this." Leo cringed. "It's bad enough that Dillon's home with Katherine and Andie's pregnant. I don't want to hear about you, too."

She dismissed him with a wave of her hand. "You're such a prude. We need to find you a woman."

Leo was silent, thinking about the customer from the other day. She was beautiful and funny. He knew she lived in Bereton, so it was only a matter of time before he saw her again, but he couldn't help hoping it would be sooner rather than later.

"It looks like he already found a woman," Andie said with a snicker.

"It does." Nonna slipped her hand through his arm again. "Come and tell me all about her."

"There's no woman, and there's nothing to tell," Leo protested.

Nonna glanced back at Andie and shook her head. "I'll fill you in later," she said.

"Good!" Andie replied.

That was why he never told anyone anything.

They found an empty table at The Drunken Grape, the restaurant inside the inn. Leo's cousin Zach was the cook, and he made amazing food. Leo enjoyed cooking once in a while, but Zach was a master. As was his assistant, Michele. Between the two of them, Leo was well fed.

One of the waitresses they hired for the summer greeted them with glasses of water and menus.

"We don't need those, Kelly," Nonna said. "Just tell Zach we're here and he'll make something for us."

Kelly nodded. "Okay. Sorry about that."

Nonna shook her head. "Not to worry, Kelly. And bring me a glass of wine when you get a chance. Red. Zach knows what I like."

Kelly nodded again and took the menus away. She rushed to the kitchen, looking like her ass was on fire.

"Why do you do that?" Leo asked.

"Do what?" Nonna asked, full of innocence.

"You scared that poor girl. She's terrified because she's not doing things the right way."

Nonna waved her hand. "She's fine. You'll leave her a really good tip and she'll be fine."

Leo laughed. "Oh, I'll leave her a good tip? I think the tip I should leave you is to bring your own money."

Nonna shook her head. "All my money went into making this place something you and your siblings and cousins could live off of forever. A beautiful place to raise families and be a part of the community."

"And it is. Alyssa and Andie have babies. Sean and Zach have the older girls. I'm sure Dillon and Katherine will start sometime soon, too. I wouldn't be surprised if Sean and Zach had more, or Andie and Alyssa. This place will be full of kids before long."

"And what about you? Are you going to bring some kids to the party?" Nonna asked pointedly.

Before Leo could answer, Kelly returned with a glass of wine for each of them.

"I'm going back to work after this," Leo said. "I can't drink."

Kelly, flustered once again, apologized and reached for the glass.

Nonna beat her to it. "I'm not. I'll take care of it for you."

Leo shook his head and smiled up at Kelly. She eased away, probably scared of what they'd come up with next.

"Who's the girl?"

"There is no girl," Leo said firmly.

Nonna shook her head. "Fine. Who's the woman?"

"She's no one. I don't know her."

"But there is someone."

Leo sighed. "She came into the tasting room the other

day. I don't know her, Nonna. She's not anyone. She didn't even tell me her name."

"But you liked her."

He shrugged. "She made me laugh."

Nonna stared him in the eyes, holding his hazel eyes captive with her brown ones. "You haven't done enough of that lately. She's a keeper if she can make you smile, but if she can make you laugh, you need to find a way to hold on tight."

Leo shook his head. "I don't know her, Nonna. I don't know anything about her. She just moved to town. There are so many summer workers. Hell, she could be working here and I wouldn't know it."

"You'd know. As much time as you've been spending on the business side of things, you'd know."

Leo grimaced. "I don't leave the office. The woman could be cleaning, and I'd never see her because I'm locked in with Dillon."

"How is that going?"

Leo realized what he admitted and dialed it back quickly. "It's good. Dillon's showing me everything I'll need to know about running things while he's gone."

"And you like it?" Nonna asked pointedly.

"Um, yeah. Sure. Why not? I have a degree in business, and my job can easily be hired out. I'm wasted in the tasting room. Kristen needs to stay there for outreach and connection to the community, but there's no reason for me to be there."

Nonna looked at him closely again. "Did Dillon shove his hand up your ass, Leo?"

Leo snorted. "What?"

"You sound like his puppet. This isn't you."

Leo shook his head. "No, it's good. It's what's best for

Amavita, and that's what matters. Like you said, you spent all your money making sure this family had a place to call theirs. I'm not going to screw that up for everyone."

"How would you screw it up?" Nonna asked.

"I wouldn't. I won't. I just meant this is the best solution. Dillon needs to hand things over to someone who's here all the time, and that's me. Everyone else has jobs that can't be replaced so easily. It's good, though. Really good."

Nonna sipped her wine and studied him. He sat silently, knowing his best bet was not to give her anything more to sink him with. Dillon wanted his help, and he'd help his brother. Dillon was the boss. He was the person in charge. Of course he'd do whatever Dillon said.

"You know if you don't want to do this, you don't have to, right?" Nonna said after a minute.

Leo shrugged. "I want to. It's a good job. A new challenge. Something for me to sink my teeth into."

Nonna turned around in her seat. She looked back at him, then leaned over and peeked under the table. She looked over her other shoulder, then scanned the ceiling.

"What are you looking for?" Leo asked.

"The puppet strings, because we both know those aren't your words. You've never wanted to be CEO."

"I have a business degree," Leo argued.

Nonna shrugged. "I never had a business degree and did just fine running this place for a couple decades."

Nonna was right, but that wasn't the point. Dillon asked him to help. He needed him. He had to do it. His brother was smarter than he would ever be. He understood things Leo could barely begin to try to understand. If Dillon said it was for the best, then it was for the best. Leo didn't have to like it, but he did have to shut up and do it.

"It's the best option, Nonna." Leo looked up and saw Zach heading toward them. "Hey, look. Zach has our food."

Leo nodded at his cousin and thanked him for their lunch. "Any time. Dillon's not with you today?"

Leo shook his head, ignoring the daggers his grandmother was shooting him. "He went home to spend some time with Katherine."

"Aw, dude! I didn't need to know that."

Leo chuckled. "Trust me, I didn't either."

"Listen, let me know what you guys think of this. It's a new recipe I'm trying out. If you think it's good, I might add it to the menu as a weekly special. But I need to get some opinions. Gianna says everything is good."

"Funny how your wife isn't all that partial," Nonna said. "That's exactly how she should be."

"Oh, please," Zach said. "There's no way you agreed with everything Nonno said."

Nonna laughed. "No, I definitely didn't. But we only had each other. If I let him make all the decisions, we wouldn't be where we are today."

"It sounds like you two were a good team," Zach said.

"We were. Just like you and Gianna. And all of you kids with your spouses or significant others."

Zach narrowed his gaze at Leo. "You have a significant other?"

Leo shook his head. "No."

"He met a woman in the tasting room," Nonna said.

Leo groaned. "I...She just came in. It's not like we're together."

"No, but you met someone. That's good. You need to find someone."

"Excuse me, but weren't you the cousin who always said he would never get married?" Leo asked.

Zach shrugged. "Things change when you meet the right person. When you find someone you can't imagine your life without. You'll find her. Usually when you stop looking and don't have time for her in your life. That's how you know she's worth it. Because you'll make time."

"He's right," Nonna said softly. "You always make time for the ones you love."

4

———————

Nonna and Zach's words stayed with Leo the rest of the day and into the weekend. He was looking for someone. He wanted to find love. He'd gotten to where he was ready to settle down. He just hadn't found the woman who was going to settle with him.

Leo was up early Saturday morning to meet Peter. It was the only time they could get together to go fishing. Dillon wanted to talk more that afternoon, but Leo needed a break first. Some way to distance himself from being the next CEO and just be himself for a few hours.

Peter let himself in to Leo and Ryan's house before the sun was up. Leo had a cup of coffee ready for each of them and handed one over, then followed Peter back outside. Ryan got called to a fire late the night before, so they were quiet as they made their escape.

After a few sips of coffee, Peter spoke. "That's better."

Leo smiled and nodded. "Yeah. The fresh air helps, too."

They walked the rest of the way to the dock in silence, both of them drinking coffee and watching their steps in the fading moonlight.

The boat was ready for their trip with fishing rods and a cooler in case they caught anything they wanted to keep. The boat was a new purchase for Amavita, a partnership between the vineyard and InZane's, the local adventure company run by Leo's cousin Kristen's boyfriend Zane. Zane didn't mind the vineyard using the boat whenever any of them wanted to, as long as there wasn't an adventure planned.

Leo loved getting outside, enjoying the water. As they motored quietly away from the dock, he felt all his stress fade into the wake, leaving him at peace.

"Are you working today?" Peter asked when they anchored and had their lines in the water.

Leo nodded, his tension creeping back into his shoulders. "With Dillon."

"Who's running the tasting room these days? With Kristen spending her time with Zane and networking with the community, and you taking over for Dillon, who's there?"

Leo gritted his teeth. "Whoever can cover. Sometimes it's Alyssa, sometimes one of the waitresses, sometimes Andie. It depends."

"Wow. Doesn't that hurt business?"

Leo nodded. "Yep. Dillon is working on hiring someone full time in there so there's consistency. I'll be there today some, but he wants me up to speed on everything else soon."

"When do they leave for Nashville?"

"Three weeks."

"Shit. I guess it's time for us to grow up."

Leo snorted. "Something like that." He hated the idea of growing up. His whole life, he'd been the baby. Youngest of four kids, he was always the one everyone else felt they had to take care of. When he was a kid, he didn't mind it, but he was twenty-nine and hadn't needed anyone to do his laundry, or anything else, in more than a decade.

Leo and Peter were quiet for a while, casting their lines and watching for bites. The sun rose over them slowly until the reflection off the water was blinding and Leo knew it was time to head back.

"I have to meet Dillon soon," he said reluctantly.

"Shit, I didn't realize it was so late. No wonder I'm starving."

"You're always starving," Leo said as he reeled in his line.

Peter nodded. "True. But today I have a lunch date."

"No shit? With your future wife?"

Peter flashed him a shit-eating grin. "Yep. She's going to tell me about her first few days at her new job. She doesn't really know anyone yet."

"So you're going to snatch her up before anyone else can?" Leo teased.

"Hell, yeah. I'm not dumb enough to let this one go."

Leo started the boat with a shake of his head and drove slowly back to the dock. Peter helped him tie up the boat and they carried their poles and the empty cooler back to Leo and Ryan's house.

Ryan was in the kitchen when they walked in. "Did you catch anything?"

Leo shook his head. "Nope."

Ryan laughed. "I don't know why you two do that. It makes no sense at all."

Leo grinned. "Because not all of us get to spend our days outside and our nights saving the town. Some of us have to get fresh air in other ways."

"Open a window," Ryan said with a straight face.

Peter chuckled. "Not the same. Besides, Leo's getting stressed about being CEO. He needed some time away from the desk."

"You mean away from his brother," Ryan said with a sly grin. "I never thought you'd sell out. Did you buy a suit yet?"

Leo avoided his cousin's eyes, which made both men laugh.

"You did? Oh, wow, you really are becoming Dillon. Of course, you did hit on Katherine when she first came here. I never knew you aspired to be your older brother," Ryan teased.

Leo scowled at his cousin, hating how close to the truth his words were. Ever since he was young, Leo looked up to Dillon. He got a degree in business because it was what Dillon did. He came back to Amavita because that's what Dillon did. He liked the same kind of women, even Dillon's girlfriend.

It was the moment he realized he was trying to pick up a woman his brother laid claim on that Leo knew he had to make some changes in his life. A year later, he was back where he'd always been, following Dillon's advice and doing everything his brother said he needed to do.

"Being the younger brother sucks," Peter said, a fact all three of them could agree with. Ryan worked side-by-side with his older brother, but Leo knew it wasn't always easy for Ryan. Peter left for years, but when he came back, he thought he'd be out of his brother's shadow. Unfortunately, his brother had everything, and Peter felt like his life paled in comparison. All three of them knew how difficult it was to grow up in someone else's bigger, better shadow.

"I'm not Dillon. I'm just helping him out," Leo argued.

"You do know Dillon is grooming you to replace him. He isn't asking you to fill in. You're going to be the CEO."

Leo shook his head. "No. He's not leaving. He'll still be here. He wouldn't leave."

Ryan shrugged. "Katherine's career is big. Why would he stick around when she's doing so well? You're going to be the next CEO."

Leo shook his head. It couldn't be. Dillon talked about Leo filling in, not taking over. Dillon was the CEO. He'd been in charge for years, and he worked with their dad even more years before that. He was the one who knew how to make everything run. He was the one everyone went to when they needed something. Not Leo. Never Leo. The place would fall apart with Leo in charge.

"Did Dillon say he's leaving?" Leo asked.

Ryan shook his head. "No, but he will. Just give it time." Ryan guzzled the last of his water and put the cup in the dishwasher. "I gotta go. My grapes need me. And you need to shower before you kiss your brother's ass."

Leo flipped off his cousin and said bye to Peter, who walked out with Ryan. He headed upstairs to take a quick shower and was back at the inn, walking into Dillon's office, twenty minutes later.

"I was about to call you," Dillon said as a greeting. "I thought you were going to be here earlier."

Leo shook his head. "I went fishing this morning. I told you that."

Dillon nodded. "Right, I forgot. Do you have any questions for me? We've covered a lot over the last month. I just want to make sure you're ready to go forward."

Leo sat across the desk from his brother and watched him for a moment. Dillon shuffled papers on the desk that belonged to their father and before him their grandfather.

Dillon was the oldest of all the cousins, and the only one alive when their grandfather died. Dillon didn't remember Nonno, but Leo was still jealous that his brother met their grandfather. Dillon was groomed forever to follow in his footsteps. Nonno started working on the vineyard in the field, but eventually bought the property when the owners decided to retire. He taught himself how to run a business using the knowledge he picked up from his boss, and he grew the vineyard into what it was, a seventy-three acre estate with a restaurant, an inn, and almost fifty employees.

Just the thought of being responsible for all that made Leo anxious. Everyone was convinced he was afraid to let people down, but the reality was, he would. No matter what, someone would always be disappointed. Dillon handled it. He could look at the full picture and know what the right decision was. Even if he was wrong, he owned his decision and knew he made the best one at the time.

Leo didn't want to have to deal with that. He liked working in the tasting room. He was the face of the vineyard, the person customers went to when they had questions. He knew some of their regular customers, and he made sure the travelers felt like they were just as important. His job mattered. But it wasn't flashy. It wasn't big. It wasn't CEO.

And it wasn't worthy of his big brother.

"Questions? You're looking at me like you have no idea what I'm talking about," Dillon said after a minute. His head tilted to the side and his dark eyebrows pulled together. His gaze was sharp, not missing anything.

"When's the last time you talked to one of our customers?" Leo blurted.

Dillon looked out the window and shrugged. "Sunday. At the picnic. I always talk to people at the picnic. Why?"

Sunday, almost a week ago. Could Leo handle that? "Just curious. Are you leaving for good?"

"What?" Dillon asked with a laugh. "For good?"

Leo nodded. "Yeah. Quitting. Retiring. Whatever. Are you moving to Nashville with Katherine and only coming back for vacation?"

Dillon shook his head but didn't meet Leo's eyes. "Of course not. I'm just going to be gone for a while and need you to fill in for me."

"But you'll be back."

Dillon nodded, still avoiding Leo's gaze. Leo knew there was more to the story, but he could only push so hard. Something else was going on. Why was Dillon leaving? And why didn't he want anyone to know?

"Okay, so you're good on budgets and all the financial stuff. I know you understand how the vineyard works. We need to talk about ordering. Making sure everyone has everything they need. Everyone has their own department budget, which you will need to approve, and they are all responsible for their own orders, but everything will come through you. You'll need to make sure little things don't fall through the cracks and big things are delivered on time." Dillon pulled out a binder. "This is a master list of our vendors. Contact information, personal information, everything you need to reach anyone you need to. Any time you need them."

Leo bit back his groan. What century were they living in? Dillon could digitize that book and make things so much easier. It would take Leo a month to find anything in there.

"Are you ready?" Dillon asked.

Leo rose from his seat and walked around the desk so he was in front of the massive book. He glared at it, as though the book was to blame, and nodded. "Ready."

Sara walked into Dine In The Vines at twelve-oh-two. She hated being late, but her dad called and she lost track of time.

Peter was already at a table and waved to her when she stopped to let the hostess know she didn't need help. She wove her way through the other patrons until she reached him. He stood and kissed her cheek, then gestured for her to sit first.

"This place is so cute," Sara said, looking around. The cafe was quaint and had a small town feel to it that made Sara feel like she'd been there forever and belonged. She liked that feeling.

Peter nodded. "Yeah, it's great. It's been here forever, but they've updated it regularly so it doesn't feel as old as it is."

"I almost feel like I'm underdressed."

Peter shook his head. "You're perfect."

Sara's cheeks warmed at the compliment. His eyes blazed with heat and desire, but she ignored the look and focused on her menu. Getting involved with Peter wasn't a good idea. Sara liked him, but she didn't know him. Not that she had to know someone before she slept with him, but Peter was a nice guy. Nice guys liked women who stuck around. They wanted to build lives and stay in their tiny towns and never leave.

Sara wasn't built that way.

"So, what's good here?" Sara asked, hoping she could change the subject.

Peter leaned back and picked up his menu again. "Everything really. They make this great marinara sauce that's a little sweet, but also has a kick to it. Their pastas are all good. Chicken, steak, seafood. You really can't go wrong at all."

Sara scanned the menu as her mouth watered. Everything looked good. It was a little heavy for a lunch, but she was starving, and she'd rather have a long lunch that felt too much like a date than eat another meal by herself.

The waiter came over and took their orders, and Sara was left with Peter staring at her.

"How was your first week?"

She smiled thinking about her new boss and coworker. "It was good. A little strange, but good."

"Strange?"

Sara shrugged. "I'm not used to people being so trusting. I mean, day one, I walked in and said I was starting there, and then left alone with the cash register. I could have been anyone and stolen anything."

Peter grinned. "It's a small town. Things like that happen. Not saying there isn't crime or anything, but people tend to be trusting. My friend's family owns one of the vineyards and they leave their doors unlocked all the time. They figure no one is going to drive into the middle of the vineyard to try to break into one of their houses."

Sara shook her head. "I just can't imagine it. I mean, where I grew up in Montana, people were trusting like that, but I guess I've gotten jaded over the years."

"I know what you mean. I lock my door when I'm just running out to my car to grab something. After living in a city for a few years, you forget how to trust people."

Sara chuckled and nodded. "Exactly. That's both the good and bad about city living. You can disappear easily and no one will bug you about who you brought home or why you changed your hair, but you can't trust anyone because you don't know anyone."

Peter laughed, his green eyes lighting up. His blond hair shook as he nodded, agreeing with her statement. He reached for his glass, his strong forearm catching her attention. She had a thing for arms. His were lean and tan with thick, blond hair. Sexy arms.

He was definitely the kind of guy she would normally go home with. But she wasn't there yet. He could be a friend, and she definitely needed a few of those.

"Have you met anyone else since you've been here?" Peter asked after a second.

Sara tore her gaze from his sexy arm and looked up at him. His eyes studied her, trying to figure her out. She didn't want to lead him on, so she had to tread carefully. "Not really. Megan is great, and Adam seems really nice. I like working there. I've mostly just worked and tried to settle in. I've been unpacking and trying to learn where everything is. Like the grocery store and the liquor store. The most important places."

Peter tipped his head back and laughed, a loud sound that drew the attention of a few customers near them. She grinned. He was comfortable in his skin. Sure of himself. He didn't care that he was making a little bit of a scene. He was enjoying himself. She could take a few hints from him.

"Well, if you need help finding your way around town, I'm happy to show you were a few more important places are. Like the best ice cream in town and the movie theater and my favorite hang out."

Sara nodded and ducked her head to avoid his gaze again. He was definitely hinting at more dates.

"Um, I'm only here a few months."

"I know."

"And I'm not sticking around after that."

"Yeah?"

"I'm...um...I'm just saying that I don't intend to get involved with anyone while I'm here."

Peter nodded. "I know. But you can always use a friend, right?"

She forced a smile and nodded. "Absolutely. A friend."

5

———

Once Sara stopped telling herself Peter was after something other than friendship, she was able to relax and enjoy their lunch.

"What's the best place you've ever been?" Peter asked her.

"Visited or lived?" Sara clarified as she took a bite of her Caprese pasta.

"Both." Peter grinned at her.

She spent most of lunch telling him about herself. He insisted he wasn't that interesting of a guy, but she had a feeling that was just a line so she'd talk about herself.

"Best place I've lived is definitely Sanibel Island in Florida. It's on the Gulf Coast, not far from Fort Myers Beach. It's beautiful. There's this huge bridge you drive to get to the island, one way on or off. The white sand beaches are stunning, and the crystal clear water is calm and perfect. It was hard to leave there."

Sara loved it in Florida. It was one of the first places she went after she finished college. The dive company she worked for only needed someone for a few months while one of their employees was on bed rest then maternity leave. The guys she worked for were a lot of fun, and their families were amazing.

It almost made her rethink her decision not to settle anywhere. But that was exactly why she made that choice. Because emotions got messy and getting attached meant listening to what someone else wanted instead of what she wanted. She lived too many years for other people.

"I love the Gulf Coast," Peter said. "I spent some time in Alabama, but I never made it down to Sanibel Island. I might have to check it out."

"You'll love it. It's stunning."

"Maybe we can go there one day. You can show me around there in exchange for me showing you around Bereton."

Sara grinned. Her eyes scanned Peter's arms again, and she knew she could have fun with him. He was attractive, but her blood didn't heat when she met him. It hadn't even warmed through lunch. She could appreciate he was good looking, but she didn't want him. Not like that.

Leo, though? She still thought about the hot, funny guy who made her laugh and talked her into buying a case of wine her first full day in town.

"Where'd you go?" Peter asked after a few seconds.

Sara shook her head and focused on him again. It wasn't fair she was thinking about Leo when she was at lunch with Peter.

"Sorry. I thought we were friends."

Peter shrugged. "Friends can't go on vacation together?"

"How many rooms are we going to get?"

His grin was wolfish and exposed his true intentions. She laughed in spite of herself. "Can't hate a guy for trying."

She just shook her head.

"What about your favorite place to visit?"

Sara hoped he'd forgotten about that part of the question. Her breath hitched with the truth, but she wasn't sure she could get it out. The truth was the place she thought was the most beautiful place, the nicest place on earth, the place she'd go back to again and again if she had the courage, was the one place she couldn't bring herself to ever go back to.

Because she lost her mother there. And as much as she loved it, she hated it with equal passion. Just like she hated the family her mother had there, the step-children she claimed as her own, the husband Sara didn't know about until after her mother died. On her way home from the grocery store. Like a normal mom in a normal town with a normal family.

It just wasn't the family Sara thought she had.

"Um, Hawaii," she lied. Who didn't like Hawaii? "It was gorgeous, of course, but the food was delicious and the people were wonderful."

"Why didn't you ever work there?"

Sara shrugged. "Since the weather is the same year round, there aren't as many seasonal opportunities. Plus, they don't have many vineyards."

"Is that how you pick where you go? By the vineyards?"

Sara grinned and nodded. "Yeah, didn't I tell you that? I'm working my way through the country going to different areas that are known for good wine."

"You've been to Napa and Sonoma, I'm guessing?"

Sara nodded. "Of course."

"That's really cool. How did you come up with that?"

Sara again forced her lips into a smile and lied, "I really like wine."

It wasn't a total lie. She did like wine, but it wasn't the full truth either. No one knew why she did what she did.

Some days, she didn't even know. But she couldn't stop. She had to keep going, searching wine towns until she understood why her mom hated living on a farm in Montana but found a home on a vineyard in Portland.

"Ooh, you know where you should go? My favorite wine is pinot. You should really go to Portland. They're known for it there. You'd love it."

And just like that, lunch was over.

LEO WAS dead on his feet, but still smiling. After Dillon made him look up no less than a hundred contacts in that massive book of his, he went over everything they kept in stock in all areas and how frequently they reordered each item. Just in case someone else forgot to do their job and ran out of something.

When he was done, Leo took over in the tasting room and schmoozed with customers for a few hours. Now, he was ready for a break, some food, and if he had it his way, a woman.

He'd have to settle for two out of three.

Leo put the rest of the bottles in the fridge behind the bar and started the dishwasher. He turned on the low lights that stayed on all night and flipped the switch to turn off the overhead lights in the tasting room. The gift shop was still open for another hour, but he was done and ready to go.

Zach had his dinner ready and waiting when he got to The Drunken Grape. Leo carried his food back up front so he could check in on Andie before he left. She worked way too many hours and needed to hand over more of her duties before she delivered his niece or nephew during the work day. There were limits to what he would do for his siblings, and staring at his sister's vagina while she pushed a baby out definitely went far beyond those limits.

"Are you going home yet?" Leo asked as he approached Andie's desk. He heard her talking and felt bad for shouting at her.

"Oh, here's Leo. He can give you some recommendations. Obviously, I haven't been doing much drinking lately," Andie said.

Leo grinned and finally got a look at the person his sister was talking to. "Hey," he said, surprised to see the woman from a few days earlier. "Out of wine already?"

She rolled her eyes. "Not quite. I was hoping I could try a few more, though. But it looks like I'm too late."

Andie stepped out from behind her desk and kissed his cheek. "I'm leaving, baby brother. I'll see you tomorrow at the picnic. Will I see you also?" she asked the blonde.

"Um, at what?"

"Leo didn't invite you? We need to work on him. We have a picnic every Sunday. Starts at eleven. Tickets are sold at the door, and it's a buffet lunch. The tasting room is open. Half the community will be here. It's a great party." Andie rubbed her belly. "At least, if you can move it's a great party. I sit in the corner so I don't have to slap a Wide Load sign to my ass."

Leo rolled his eyes. "Please, you're growing a human. Besides, Cody hasn't let you do anything since you two got together. The man waits on you hand and foot."

Andie grinned. "Yeah, I have a pretty amazing husband."

"You do. So stop complaining."

"Okay, fine," Andie said with a groan. "Anyway," she turned back to the blonde, "will I see you there?"

"Um, yeah, maybe. I don't think I have to do anything tomorrow."

"Excellent. Be good, baby brother."

Andie winked at him as she left, and Leo just shook his head. "My sister likes to meddle. She thinks if she's blissfully happy, everyone else is stupid for not being the same."

"She's sweet."

He grinned. "She's going to be an amazing mom."

"Um, so you work with your sister?"

Leo hesitated. He couldn't keep the truth from her any longer. Which meant one of two things was going to happen. Either she'd be intrigued and possibly push a little more or she wouldn't care. It was possible she'd be pissed, but he didn't even know her name, so it wasn't likely she'd be too mad at him for keeping the truth from her that his family owned the vineyard they were in the middle of.

"I do," he said. "And the rest of my family. We own this vineyard."

"What?"

He shrugged. "My grandparents came here from Italy and started their family here. My mom is one of four girls, and now us cousins are in charge."

"Are you kidding me?"

He shook his head, waiting for the reaction. He didn't get the feeling it was going to be a good reaction.

"Um, wow. Okay, I didn't see that coming. How old are you?"

"Twenty-nine."

"And you're the owner of a successful vineyard?"

"Part owner," Leo clarified. "There are nine of us, and we all work here together."

"Why didn't you tell me that when I was here the other day?"

He smiled. "Probably for the same reason you never told me your name."

Her eyebrows drew together, and she tilted her head. "You don't know my name?"

He shook his head.

"I gave you my credit card."

He chuckled. "No, you didn't. You paid at the gift shop."

She tilted her head again, then her brown eyes brightened and she laughed. "Yeah, you're right. We're strangers. And it would have been pretty weird if you started the conversation telling me you owned the place."

Leo nodded. "You either would have thought I was hitting on you or lying. Or both."

"Since you were hitting on me, I would have assumed lying."

Leo laughed and shook his head. "True. So, now that my secret is out, are you going to tell me yours?"

Panic flashed across her face, eyes wide with fear. She tried to recover, but it wasn't before he realized she had a few secrets.

"Your name," Leo said, hoping to calm her.

She visibly relaxed, her shoulders falling and her breath coming out in a relieved sigh. "Oh, sorry. Sara. Sara Donovan."

"Wow, I get a last name, too? That's impressive."

She laughed again. "Yeah, well, I know where you work and I met your sister, so I guess we're even."

He shook his head. "Hardly. Are you hungry?"

Her eyebrows drew together.

"I have dinner, and it's too much for me to eat. We can sit outside and share. I figure that's more likely to get a *yes* out of you than inviting you back to my place."

Her wide eyes and lustful look told him he might have gotten a hell of a lot more than a yes out of her if he'd gone for door number two.

"Sounds good," Sara said.

Leo grabbed his dinner and guided Sara through the inn with a hand on the small of her back. She pressed closer to him as they moved through the other diners on their way to the back door.

It was a beautiful night, early and still quiet outside. It wouldn't be long before the patio was packed and you couldn't find a seat, but Leo led Sara to an empty table in a section that wasn't staffed until six.

"Are you sure it's okay if we sit here?" she asked.

Leo nodded and pulled out her chair. She sat and scooted up for him to push the chair back in. He took the seat next to her instead of across the four person table. "Do you like lasagna?"

She grinned. "I love it."

"Good. I can get you something else, but we'd have to wait a little while."

She shook her head. "Nope. This is perfect. Wow, I can already smell it."

Leo grinned and opened the to-go container. The super-sized slice of thick lasagna was covered in sauce and accented with a three large meatballs. Mixed into the lasagna were vegetables as well as the typical meat and cheese, giving it a custom flavor that only The Drunken Grape delivered.

Sara unwrapped the silverware at her place setting and had her fork poised and ready when she looked up at him. "Are you sure you can't eat all this?"

Leo grinned. "I have before, but I don't usually. It's a great breakfast."

"As good as it smells, I don't think it would last until breakfast at my place."

Leo grinned, thinking neither would he. But that had

nothing to do with food and everything to do with the beautiful woman smiling at the food between them, her knee pressing against his.

She stabbed her fork into the lasagna. It sank through the soft pasta and tore at the piece. She slid it into her mouth and her eyes closed on a moan.

He was hard instantly.

"Wow, that's good," she said after a moment. "I don't think I've ever had anything that good."

The dirty comments were stacking up in his mind, but he kept them locked up tight. He definitely didn't know Sara Donovan well enough to offer up something else she could have that might be even better than his cousin's lasagna.

"Did you make this?"

Leo shook his head. "No, my cousin did."

"Is he single?"

Leo shook his head again. "Sorry. Married with a kid. And crazy in love with his wife."

"Damn. Well, I guess I'll have to stick to my plan of not getting attached. It makes it easier to leave in a few months."

He felt a pang at the idea of her leaving. "Getting attached doesn't work well when you have one foot out the door. Is your job temporary?"

She nodded as she chewed another bite. Leo finally forked a bite for himself while she ate hers.

"All my jobs are temporary. I have to write a resume based on my skills instead of jobs because I scare off most bosses."

Leo chuckled. "Really?"

"Yeah. I move every three to four months. I like to see new places and do new things. I get bored doing the same thing over and over again."

And the dirty thoughts kept coming.

"I don't know if I could imagine that. I love my job."

She grinned. "You do have a pretty amazing job." She rolled her eyes and laughed. "And I just realized why you weren't worried about your boss getting mad at you when you were drinking the other day."

Leo laughed with her. "I'm not going to fire myself."

"I can't believe I didn't pick up on that," Sara admitted. "I'm usually pretty good about seeing things. At least, sometimes I am."

Her eyes drifted away and her smile slipped.

Leo wanted to bring her back, to see the light in her eyes again. He didn't know anything about her, though. He had no clue what would make her laugh, or what put that look in her eyes.

Leo nudged her with his knee, drawing her gaze back to his. "I didn't want you to know. Not everyone takes it well."

She smiled, accepting his answer with a nod. "Yeah, that makes sense."

"I also threw myself pretty hard into flirting with you. I'd had a...challenging day. Your pretty, smiling face made it better."

She blushed a sexy shade of pink and ducked her head. When she met his gaze after a few seconds, heat filled her eyes and warmed him up. "You made my day better, too."

Leo smiled and dug in to the lasagna. They barely knew each other, and getting too close wasn't going to be good. Especially since she already said she had no intention of sticking around. She was beautiful and funny and amazing, but she wasn't the woman for him. Not if she was only there for a few months.

They finished dinner, and Leo asked if she wanted to walk down to the lake. The darkening sky cast long shadows over them as they walked the familiar path to the dock at the edge of the property.

"You grew up here?" she asked when they stood at the end of the dock.

Leo nodded. "Lived on this property my whole life."

"Except college."

He nodded again. "True. But I went to college in Ithaca, so not far away. I was home almost every weekend."

"That had to be a boring college career."

He laughed. "At times, but I managed to have fun, too. Plenty of parties and girls and opportunities to screw up my grades."

"I bet your parents loved that," she teased.

"They weren't too worried about me. My oldest brother, though? He was the stick in the mud for me."

"How much older is he?"

"Nine years."

"It's you, Andie, and your brother?"

He shook his head. "I have another brother, Sean. He's between Andie and me."

"Four? Wow. And you're the baby? No wonder your parents left it to your older brother, oldest brother, to kick your ass if you didn't stay in line."

Leo laughed and nodded. "Probably a fair point. What about you? Siblings?"

That haunted look flashed on her face, but it was gone quickly, replaced by a smile that didn't meet her chocolate eyes. She shook her head. "Nope. I'm an only child."

6

———

There was a part of Sara that wanted to tell Leo the truth. That she had two step-sisters, two women she didn't know who weren't really her step-sisters but thought of themselves that way. Two women her mother claimed and helped raise for nearly a decade before she died.

Sara didn't like to think about them. She never talked about them. Once she and her dad learned about her mother's accident, and the family she had a few states away, they stopped talking about her mom. It was like she never existed, and to Sara, she didn't.

Neither did the daughters her mother chose over her.

"I can't imagine not having my crazy family to grow up with," Leo said, oblivious to Sara's discomfort. "I'm not just the youngest of four, but I'm the second youngest of nine if you count my cousins. We all grew up here, on Amavita, so it was like we were one big family. I got yelled at by my aunts just as much as my parents."

Sara forced a smile. "My house was quiet. My mom traveled a lot, so it was just me and my dad most of the time."

"It had to be so quiet."

Sara nodded. "It was. I liked it."

Leo nodded, looking out at the water. Sara wondered if he was perceptive or just lost in his own world. Either way, it was good for her to have a minute to breathe.

"How was your new job? Are you enjoying it?"

Sara smiled at the subject change. "I am. Have you heard of Lakeside Glass?"

Leo turned to look at her. "No shit? Megan makes amazing sculptures. She's ridiculously talented."

Sara laughed. "Do you know everyone in town?"

He nodded. "Pretty much. That's what happens when you grow up in a small town and are one of nine cousins. Everyone knew me by the time I went to school, which wasn't always a good thing. But working in the tasting room means I get to know a lot of other people, people I didn't know as a kid. Megan's great. I know Anna a little better, though. She's only seven years younger than me."

Sara shook her head. "I haven't met Anna yet."

"She has one more semester of college and is student teaching. She wants to stay in the area, but there aren't many schools so she's not sure where she's going to end up."

The topic of staying put Sara on edge. She understood people liked to be around their families, but she didn't know that feeling. Even when she was in high school, she couldn't wait to get out of Montana and explore the rest of the world. See big cities and meet boys she hadn't known her whole life. Being trapped in a small town forever didn't hold any appeal to her.

Even with the spectacular scenery in front of her.

"I should head out," Sara said abruptly.

Leo reached for her, lightly grasping her arm. "Did I upset you?"

She shook her head. "No, but I need to go. I still have some unpacking to do."

Leo nodded, but it was clear he thought she was lying. He released her arm and said, "I'll walk you up."

"You don't have to."

He smiled. "I'd like to. If that's okay."

Sara nodded and led the way off the dock onto solid ground. She still felt like she was rocking, the impact of everything already shaking up her life.

They walked in silence to her car, and Leo opened the door for her. She turned back to thank him and found him right there. Her chest brushed his, drawing a gasp from her lungs.

She stepped closer, needing to feel his solid strength for just a moment. She looked up at him, his hazel eyes questioning and curious. She tilted her chin up in invitation, and he answered her, slowly easing closer, giving her plenty of time to say no.

Sara pushed herself up on her toes and pressed her lips to his. Surprise had him momentarily stilled before he tilted his head and kissed her back.

And dear God, did he ever kiss her back. His tongue slicked over her lips, imploring her to open for him. She had no choice in the matter and parted, welcoming him in for her first taste.

As their tongues slid together, his arm threaded around her waist and tightened her body to his, pressing all of her to all of him. Her hands landed on his chest and slid up, wrapping around his neck. She took another step, ensuring she felt every inch of him, from knees to nose.

He rose against her soft belly, but he made no move to push for anything more than a kiss. He tilted his head and thrust his tongue deeper into her mouth, then tilted the other way and teased her with soft kisses. She chased him, needing deep, powerful, mind-numbing kisses before reality raced in and told her what a bad idea it was to be kissing a man she had no intention of getting involved with.

Leo eventually gentled their kiss, easing back with his body before he let up with his lips. Sara wasn't ready to stop, but she said she had to go.

"Wow," he said. "That was...damn."

She chuckled. "Yeah, pretty much."

"Will I see you tomorrow?" Leo asked.

"Tomorrow?"

"The picnic. Andie mentioned it earlier."

"Oh, yeah. Um, I'll see."

He nodded. "I hope you come, Sara Donovan."

She smiled and finally got into her car. "I'll do my best."

He stepped back and nodded, then waited until she pulled away. She watched him in her rearview mirror until he disappeared from her view.

Bereton was going to be a hard place to leave.

LEO WATCHED the door for Sara the entire picnic. He really thought she was going to show up, but as it approached the end, he knew she wouldn't. But he knew where she worked, so he could go see her.

Or he could let her have her space.

That wasn't likely to happen, though.

The crowd had thinned and Leo was the only one left behind the bar, so he cleaned up and consolidated open bottles to one bin. The vineyard was closed on Mondays, so he was planning to spend another day with Dillon, which really made him want to take one of the bottles home. Or two.

"What do you have left?" Nonna asked, sauntering up to the bar and setting her glass on the top.

Leo glanced at the bottles. "All you're favorites."

"They're all my favorites," Nonna said.

Leo grinned. "I know. And for you, we have anything."

"You're too good to me. I don't know how I ended up with so many sweet grandchildren, but I'm a lucky woman."

"Don't forget all those great-grandchildren."

She nodded, her brown eyes lighting up. "I'd never forget them."

Leo smiled and poured her a glass of merlot. It was her favorite at the moment, but Nonna drank everything and didn't ever turn down wine, no matter what flavor it was.

"Did the woman you were kissing outside yesterday show up?" Nonna asked as she took her first sip. "Ooh, that's so good."

"Are you a ninja?" Leo asked. He knew no one was outside when he kissed Sara. After she left, he looked around and made sure he was alone. Not only that, but it was late, barely light enough to see, and there's no way Nonna could have seen him from the inn.

"I'm not so light on my feet anymore."

"Who told you?"

She shook her head. "You just did, dear."

"What?"

She shrugged. "I saw the two of you walking to the dock and just assumed. Since your cheeks aren't red, I know you didn't do something more than kiss her out there, but since you're asking how I know, I was just guessing there was a kiss. Maybe a few. Who is she?"

Leo shook his head and laughed. Only his grandmother

could catch him with something like that. She was a fire-cracker who always kept him on his toes. He credited her with his ability to tell a joke and make people laugh.

"Her name is Sara, and no, she didn't come today."

"She's good enough for tonsil hockey but not for a family event?"

A surprised laugh puffed out of him. "You have a way with words."

"Stop avoiding the question."

Leo sighed. "No. I invited her. Well, Andie invited her. She came to the tasting room last week and we talked and flirted, but I didn't think I'd see her again. She showed up yesterday after I'd closed up for the day and was talking to Andie when I was about to leave."

"And?"

"And nothing. We had dinner and talked."

"And kissed."

Leo breathed a laugh. "Yes, that, too."

"She didn't show up." It wasn't a question. It was a fact laced with pity of the truth.

"Nope. But that's fine. She's only here for the summer, and she isn't looking to get attached."

"She told you that?"

He nodded. "Yeah, it came up. But not in a weird way. She just...She's not the one for me."

"Oh, my sweet boy. You were always the most naive. You saw the good in everyone and you wanted to believe people told the truth, even when you weren't willing to."

"Hey!"

She patted his cheek. "Don't get offended. You were always afraid to rock the boat. I'm sure it was because you were the youngest. You weren't like most youngest who wanted attention. You wanted everyone else to be okay.

That's why Dillon wants you to take over for him. He knows he's leaving this place in the best hands possible if you're in charge."

Leo shook his head. "Dillon needs a puppet. Someone who will do exactly what he says. That's what you said the other day."

Nonna thumped him on the shoulder. "I only said that because I know it's not what you want, not because you can't do it. You know better. Your brother isn't setting you up to fail, and he's not using you. He wants to make sure you don't screw up, sure, but he doesn't think you will. He has eight people to choose from. Do you really think he picked you because you're the only one who will do what he says?"

Leo thought about it and had to admit Nonna was right. All of them went to Dillon. Every single one of his cousins and siblings looked up to Dillon, and not just because he was the oldest. He was steady, reliable, and confident. He had answers, and if he didn't, he would talk them through the problem until the answer became obvious.

Leo shouldn't be pissed that Dillon wanted him to fill in. He should be honored.

"I never thought about it like that," Leo said.

"Well, it's time you start. You're smart and capable, and you should give Dillon a real chance at teaching you the things you don't know. You could be an amazing CEO."

Leo nodded, feeling better than he had all day. Sara wasn't his, and the fact that she didn't show up didn't take anything away from him. If she wasn't interested, he still had an amazing life full of family, friends, and a job he loved. There was no reason for him to get down on himself for it.

"Thanks, Nonna," Leo said. He grabbed the bottle of merlot from under the counter. "You should take the rest of this home. We're closed until Tuesday, and it won't be any good by them."

She grinned. "You're sweet. And I was already planning to do that."

It was the end of Sara's second week of work when Megan knew she was ready to experiment. Sara was asking more and more questions about the glass they made and how it was done. Megan knew the best way for Sara to sell the pieces was to experience it herself.

"Adam is going to cover the store for a few hours," Megan said, walking into her showroom.

She'd always loved her showroom, but in just over a week, Sara had changed things to where it was a place that everyone loved. Megan had already seen the increase in revenue, and it was all thanks to Sara's ideas and changes to the layout.

"Um, okay. But I'm not done yet. Is there something wrong with my work? I can change it all back," Sara said, her voice full of panic and her eyes darting around the room.

Megan laughed. "Not at all. You've sold more in the time you've been here than I sold all of last month. You're a genius with a great eye. But I want you to experience a little bit of the glass magic."

"Oh, no, you don't have to do that," Sara protested.

Megan gripped Sara's arm and tugged her toward the door to the studio. "I promise, you can't screw it up."

"Didn't you and Adam break something the other day? A piece you'd been working on?"

Megan's heart ached at the loss of that piece. It was one

of the biggest ones she'd ever attempted, the kind of thing she'd only try with a partner she trusted. They did everything right, but working with glass wasn't always perfectly predictable. The piece got too big and drooped off the end of the blowpipe, shattering as it hit the ground.

"Yes, but you and I won't be working on anything nearly that big. We're going to do something simple. Something you design. What's your favorite piece here?"

Sara's eyes drifted to the cool section. How genius. Megan never thought to organize the store like a color wheel. She had everything by size and use or style. Sara asked if she could shift things around a little. The first thing she did was turn the mermaid tail vase into a centerpiece and add more pieces that were similar colors to the display around it.

Megan was starting to wonder if she'd ever sell that mermaid tail, but with Sara's shift, it sold in a day. It had been there for six months. After that, Megan encouraged Sara to rearrange anything else she wanted to. What came out of it was a color wheel, giving customers a chance to see all the pieces available that would match their home's decor instead of having to hunt for things. It was brilliant.

"I loved the mermaid tail. I was seriously thinking of getting that. But I think my favorite piece is the blue wave vase."

Megan went to it, pointing to the piece. "This one?"

Sara nodded. "I love the turquoise color, but also the movement of it. Like the ocean is flowing right there on the shelf. It's stunning."

"Is turquoise your favorite color?"

Sara shook her head. "It never has been, but after seeing this vase, I keep looking at all kinds of things with that color in them. I'm drawn to it."

"What other colors do you like?"

"I've always been a fan of pink. Like bright, hot pink, not a dull or pastel pink."

Megan nodded, creating the piece in her mind. She always visualized her work before she began. It never came out exactly how she thought it would, but almost every time she loved the actual artwork more than her vision.

"I think we're ready to get started," Megan said. "Adam will be in here soon. He's just cleaning up."

"I'm right here," Adam said from behind her. "Just listening to your process."

Megan waved, dismissing the heat she felt every time she looked at her apprentice. "You know my process inside and out."

Adam shrugged. "I still like to listen to you."

The man could set a woman on fire just by standing nearby. Being between him and a furnace nearly had Megan passing out on more than one occasion, but she managed to hold it together. Not only would it be wrong to hit on her student, but he was fourteen years younger than her. He was closer to her daughter's age than her own.

There were times Megan tricked herself into thinking Adam was looking at her with something other than respect in his eyes, but he'd never said anything. Her overactive imagination was no good for her. She just turned forty-two and with her daughter almost on her own, Megan was starting to consider dating again. She needed to get a handle on how men looked at women or she'd end up in bed with the wrong man. Again.

"You're going to develop your own process soon. It's hard to believe you're almost finished with your apprenticeship."

Adam nodded, his gaze holding hers for a long moment. "Then I won't be your student anymore."

Megan's breath caught in her throat. She nodded, but couldn't get any words out. He couldn't possibly mean what she thought he meant. Could he?

She forced a smile and dragged Sara out of the showroom into the studio. Once the door swung behind them, separating her from Adam, she could breathe again.

"Wow," Sara gasped. "That was seriously hot."

Megan gawked at her.

Sara clapped a hand over her mouth. "I'm so sorry," she mumbled. "That was really inappropriate of me to say."

"Did it sound like he was flirting with me?"

Sara chuckled and nodded.

"Shit."

"Is that a bad thing?"

"Yes. No? I don't know. He's my student. And he's almost young enough to be my child. He should be dating someone like you, someone young with her entire life ahead of her."

Sara shook her head. "First of all, he only has eyes for you. And second, I'm not dating anyone. At all. Not here."

Megan set her hands on her hips and grinned. "There's a story there, and you're going to tell it to me."

Sara shook her head. "No story. Nothing to tell."

"Why don't I believe you?"

Sara snorted. "Maybe because we're both lying about the men we want?"

Megan glanced back at the door where Adam was and nodded. "Big, fat liars."

7

———

Sara couldn't believe how amazing the vase she and Megan made turned out. It was stunning, and she could truly appreciate all the work that went in to the pieces Megan was selling.

She stripped off her protective gear and sat back. They'd been at work for a couple hours, but her piece was in the annealer to cool overnight. Megan said they would look at it in the morning and probably be able to take it out before she left work the following night.

"I never knew it took this long to make one piece," Sara said.

Megan handed over a bottle of water and nodded. "That's why it's so expensive. I know people come through and look at my prices and leave, but I'd be doing myself a disservice if I didn't price my work where it needs to be."

Sara shook her head, blonde strands sticking to the back of her neck. She brushed them up to cool her heated skin. "You deserve every penny you get. The work you do is amazing, and I'm even more impressed after watching you do this."

Megan shook her head, her gray curls dancing. The smile on her face was enough to tell Sara how happy she was that they'd had a chance to work together. "You did this. You can take it home and be proud of what you created."

"I am proud. I'm pumped. I want to celebrate or something."

Megan slid off the edge of the table and spun to her, grinning. "Maybe go see that guy?"

Sara chuckled. "I don't know if that's a good idea."

"Why not?"

Sara shrugged. "He's the kind of guy who sticks. He's lived at the same place forever, he has a job he loves, and he's really close to his family. I'm only here a few months."

"Well, maybe you'll change your mind," Megan suggested.

Sara immediately shook her head. "I won't. People always tell me I'll want to settle down eventually, but I won't. I like moving around. I like doing new things and seeing new places. I can't imagine being stuck in one place forever."

It was her canned speech, the one she recited everywhere she went, but after almost two weeks in Bereton, it felt flat. She'd already gotten used to her new home. And not just used to it, but she loved it. The people were friendly, and the food was amazing. She was still working her way through the box of wine she'd bought from Amavita Estates, but she explored a few more vineyards also, although none were as good as Amavita.

But none of those were reasons to stick around. At least not big enough reasons. She had a home before, and it was destroyed by lies and deception. She couldn't trust that the same thing wouldn't happen again.

"Even though my life hasn't always been easy, I love it here. My daughter is still here, so I can't imagine leaving as long as she's close. Even then, this is my home. My friends are here. My work. My life. I love having roots," Megan said.

"Can I ask you a personal question?" Sara finally asked.

Megan nodded. "Absolutely."

"Have you ever thought about having more kids?"

Megan sighed. "A long time ago, but not now. I'm too old. It wouldn't be safe. At forty-two, I'd be putting a baby and myself at risk. I'd consider adoption, though. Or I'd happily be with someone who had his own kids. They could be my family, too."

Sara's breath caught in her throat. That was why she didn't get close to people. They always said something that hurt, even though they didn't intend to. Megan had no way of knowing Sara's mom did exactly that, but it still hurt for her to say how easily she'd bring other kids into her world.

"Would Anna be okay with that?"

"I don't know. But it's not likely to happen. I haven't been out on a date since I found out I was pregnant. I don't see that changing any time soon."

Sara gave her boss a devilish grin. "I think if Adam has his way, he'll change that."

Megan dismissed the thought with a wave. "Please. That man should be out having fun. Enjoying life. Not getting tied down to an old woman."

"Oh, please," Sara scoffed, "you're not old. And I think he might like the idea of being tied down."

Megan laughed, and her cheeks darkened. "You're bad, Sara."

"Bad can be good."

"Well, how about you tell me about the man you're running from."

Sara stood up and finished her water, dropping the

bottle into the recycling bin. "I think it's time for me to go back to work."

"Chicken!" Megan called after her.

"I'll go see mine when you say something to yours."

Megan didn't say another word.

LEO WAS LAUGHING at something Adam said when Sara walked into the showroom. Her hair was stuck to her neck and her face was flushed. A smile curled her lips up at the sound of their laughter.

Until she saw him standing there.

"What are you doing here?" she blurted.

"I came to see you," Leo answered honestly.

"Why?"

Leo glanced at Adam, who leaned back on the counter and did nothing to hide the fact that he was watching them and listening to their conversation. The door behind Sara opened and Megan followed her out. Megan's face brightened with the smile she flashed Leo.

"Leo Young. I haven't seen you in here in a long time. How are you? How're your grandmother and the aunts?"

Leo nodded, his manners taking over from his frustration. He grinned at Megan and brushed past Sara to give Megan a hug. "Everyone's good. They're all enjoying their retirement and bossing us around."

"They've always enjoyed that," Megan teased.

Leo laughed.

"What brings you out here? Are you looking for a piece for the inn?"

The hopeful look in Megan's eyes had Leo feeling like an ass. He should have thought his plan through before he jumped in his SUV and took off across town to track down the woman who'd kept him up all week. He told himself countless times to put her out of his mind, but she kept reappearing, stealing his ability to sleep or function until he found out why she ditched him after the scorching kiss they shared.

"He's looking for a piece for himself," Adam said cheekily.

Leo glared at him, then grinned at Megan. "Andie does the shopping for the inn, but I thought I'd look around a little bit."

"Oh, excellent. Let me know if there's something special you're looking for," Megan said happily.

Leo's gaze slid to Sara and he nodded. "I will."

"Apologies, Leo. This is Sara. She's my new assistant. She's here for the summer. Sara, Leo's family owns Amavita Estates. His grandmother and her four daughters were always very kind to me and not only gave me advice on running a business, but on raising a child. They're wonderful people."

Sara nodded, a forced grin on her lips.

Leo couldn't stop staring at her. She looked different, guarded.

"I think they already know each other," Adam said after a minute, when neither Sara nor Leo made a move to shake hands or even say hello. "And something tells me he didn't come here for a sculpture."

Leo glared at his friend again. "Shut it, Adam."

Adam grinned. Megan looked between Sara and Leo, recognition dawning in her pretty, amber eyes. "Is he the guy?" she asked.

That finally snapped Sara out of her trance. She glanced at Megan but didn't answer her question, instead moving back behind the desk and scrolling through something on the tablet used to record sales.

"I should head out," Sara said, her eyes darting around the room, not landing on the others.

Megan snickered. "He is, isn't he? Leo Young."

"What guy?" Leo asked.

Sara glared at him.

"Ouch," Adam whispered.

"What guy?" Leo asked again.

"Sara could use a night out," Megan said. "I think you should take her to dinner. She's staying at Tom's, that room above his garage. You should pick her up at seven? Does that work for you?"

Leo nodded.

"Good. She'll be ready to go," Megan said. "It was so nice to see you again, Leo."

Leo turned and headed for the door, wondering what in the world just happened.

~

"Why did you do that?" Sara blurted as soon as Leo was outside.

Megan grinned. "Because he's the guy. You don't just let a guy like Leo Young walk out of your life. You have fun with him."

"Have fun? Is he that kind of guy?" The idea had promise, but Sara saw Leo as a serious guy who was looking for a family. Not a casual hook up.

Megan laughed. "Aren't they all? Yeah, he wants a family, but he hasn't been a monk his whole life."

For some reason, the idea of Leo with someone else lit a

fire in Sara's gut. She didn't want to think about him with anyone else.

"That look? That's why you need to go out with him tonight. He knows you're leaving. He knows you're not getting attached. He came here to find you anyway. Go have fun."

Sara took a deep breath and nodded. Fun. She could have fun. She liked Leo. He was a nice guy, and he made her laugh. She could definitely have fun.

Three hours later, Sara was sure she was going to throw up. Leo took her to a small restaurant, and they'd shared the best Thai food she'd ever had in her life. She was stuffed and laughing so hard, she wasn't sure it was all going to stay down.

"Stop making me laugh," she chastised him. "I'm going to be sick."

He picked up his empty bowl and held it out to her. "Make sure you hit the bowl."

She laughed again, gasping for breath.

Leo laughed with her. His eyes crinkled at the edges when he laughed. His lips curled up, revealing mostly straight teeth, except that one that was a little twisted. A scar split the stubble on his jaw. Black ink peeked out from the collar of his green shirt, an olive green that changed his hazel eyes to match.

Their laughter faded as they looked at each other. Heat slid into his eyes, turning them a forest green. Her pulse kicked up, anticipating another one of his hot kisses.

He reached into his wallet and grabbed a stack of bills, throwing them on the table then tugging her out of her seat and outside.

The cool air of the summer night tried to chill her out,

but the sexy man grasping her hand and dragging her toward his SUV eliminated the possibility.

They reached his SUV and Leo stopped. His hands came up and cupped her cheeks, holding her face steady, inches from his. "Tell me not to kiss you, Sara."

She tilted her chin up. "Why?"

"Because if I kiss you again, I'm not sure I'm going to be able to stop with a kiss."

"Then don't," she breathed.

His lips were on hers before the words were all the way out, prying his way inside and demanding she go along for the ride with him. She wrapped her arms around his neck, dragging him closer and closer until he pressed her back to the door and covered her body with his.

He hitched her leg up, spreading her thighs wide, and settled against her. His lips slid wet kisses down her neck before returning to her parted lips and delving inside all over again.

Sara reached for his shirt, needing to feel his heated skin under her palms. His back twitched at her touch, but he groaned and thrust against her.

Her head fell back on a gasp, giving him access to her throat. He devoured her, dragging his tongue over her flesh until she was panting and on the edge of coming from just his kisses and his body pressed to hers.

"Let's go to my place," Sara whispered into the night, her eyes closed against the darkness and the truth. She wanted him, but she knew he was the kind of guy she could lose herself over. He wasn't safe, but she couldn't resist. And that scared the hell out of her.

"Fuck, yeah," he replied, sealing their lips together again. He kissed her until her head spun and her thighs ached. Her breasts were heavy, sending need spiraling through her with every brush of his body against hers.

Then he pulled back, letting the cool air bring clarity to what she'd just done. What she was about to do.

He opened the door for her, waiting until she was inside before shutting it and running around to the driver's door. He was inside, with the vehicle cranked, and on his way to her place before he looked over at her.

"Shit," he murmured.

Shit was definitely right. She chewed on her lower lip and told herself she could do this. It wasn't like she was a virgin. Far from it. She's slept with all kinds of guys. Men whose names she didn't know, men she'd never seen again, men she thought of as friends, men she really didn't like that much. But she'd never slept with a guy she knew she could fall for if she let herself.

He pulled up in front of her apartment and shut off his SUV, then turned to her. "I shouldn't have shown up at Lakeside today."

"Why not?" she asked, finally looking at him.

"Because if I hadn't, you wouldn't be feeling like you are right now. Like you have to tell me you aren't really that interested, but you didn't know how to say so in front of other people."

She laughed. She actually laughed at him. And when she caught sight of his confused face, she laughed harder. She laughed until he joined in with her, even though he had no idea why she was laughing, which only made her laugh harder still.

Her laughter finally slowed when she realized Leo hadn't touched her since he put her in the car. He stayed on his side of the vehicle. Every other time they laughed together, he touched her hand or grabbed her arm or made some kind of contact with her. But this time, he kept his distance. It was sobering.

"I'm glad you came to Lakeside today," she said softly. "I wanted to see you again."

"You have a funny way of showing it," he teased.

"See, that right there. That's why I didn't want to see you."

"Um, what?" he asked.

Sara shook her head. "You're sweet, and you're sexy and funny and smart and I can't get involved with someone like you. You'll make me want to stay here."

"So, you're avoiding me because you think you're going to fall in love with me? Wow. I mean, I've dated some whackos before, but you might take the cake with that one."

His words were laced with humor, and his lips were curled up in one of his sexy smiles that made her body hum. He was danger in a hot as fuck package, and Sara knew she wouldn't be able to resist him forever. Hell, she couldn't resist him at all.

"You're so funny."

"Yes, I know. You already said so."

She slapped his shoulder. "I'm trying to be serious here."

He sobered and grabbed her hand. "All right. Let's talk this through. You're here for what? Two more months?"

"Yes."

"And you know you're moving on after that, no matter what."

"Yes."

"And you don't want to get involved with me because you're going to end up madly in love with me and want to stay, but you can't stay because you really don't want to be stuck in one place. Does that about cover it?"

She screwed up her lips and nodded, not giving him the satisfaction of saying the words.

He smirked in victory anyway. "So, all we have to do is make sure we don't fall in love. Sex only. Lots of hot, sweaty, screaming sex. No love."

"And how do you think we're going to manage that?"

"Have you ever been in love before?" he asked.

She shook her head.

"Good. Neither have I. So it should be easy. Neither of us have been in love, so we obviously know how to handle not falling in love. You're worrying over nothing."

Sara chewed on her lip and tried to decide if she agreed with him. It sounded reasonable that if neither of them had fallen for any of the other people they were with then the odds were in their favor, but she was worried.

"No more dates?" she asked.

Leo shrugged. "How about all dates include sex. That way we can still eat together, if it works out, but sex is always on the table. Or the floor. Do you have a couch?"

She laughed with him, shaking her head. Leave it to him to lighten the mood and convince her that her fears were nothing to worry about.

"Does that mean sex is on the table tonight?"

"That depends," Leo said.

"On?"

He gave her a wolfish grin. "On how sturdy your table is."

She laughed and scrambled out of the SUV, wondering where she could buy a table. Immediately.

8

———

Leo chased Sara up the stairs to her apartment. She giggled the whole way, then shushed him when he caught up to her and pressed his cock against her back.

And moaned. She definitely moaned, too.

She finally managed to get them inside and he slammed the door and pressed her against it, not willing to wait another second to have another taste of her.

He thought the night was over when he saw her panicking in the front seat. Thankfully, she was just having a meltdown about her future. It was risky promising her they'd keep their relationship to just sex, but it was the only promise he could think of that would get her to open up to him.

Her phone dinged, a happy, bright tune that had her pulling away from him to get the phone. "Sorry," she mumbled, digging into her purse. She spun away, shielding the screen from his view.

A smile tilted her lips up and had him instantly jealous. He wanted to be the only person who could make her smile, but she didn't smile like that for him. She gave him other grins, the sexy, turned on one. The sassy, smart ass one. The you're ridiculous one. Even the damn, that was good one. But she didn't give him the you're so sweet and I really like you one.

He didn't like that.

"Is everything okay?" Leo asked, unable to stop himself.

She nodded and turned the phone off. "Yeah, sorry. Just a friend of mine. He wondered if I'm free tonight for a late dinner."

"Did you tell him you're about to be dessert?"

She laughed, her eyes melting the way they did when he kissed her long and hard. "No, I didn't. He doesn't need to know about that."

Leo reeled her back in slowly, kissing his way up her arm. "Would he be jealous?"

She didn't answer right away, and he finally looked up at her. "Are you?"

"What? No. Of your friend? Why?"

She smirked. "I think I kind of like you a little jealous. It's kind of sexy that you want me to be all yours. For a few months."

"For a few months," he repeated, resuming his kisses so she didn't see the look in his eyes. He couldn't let her know he was already regretting the promise he made to her. Hell, he regretted it the second the words were out. He knew better. He wanted her, and the only reason he wanted her was because...

Well, hell. There was more than one. She was smart, sexy, and funny. She kept him on his toes. He hated that she didn't show up when he thought she would. She kissed like a fantasy come to life. He hadn't been able to stop thinking about her. And, oh yeah, he was a glutton for punishment.

Leo spent his week shadowing Dillon. He had no time in

the tasting room, and he felt off. He loved talking to people and figuring out a new wine they would like. He enjoyed the challenge of delighting people with something they normally wouldn't try. But he didn't get to do that all week. Instead, he was doing his best to become the next CEO.

There was a part of him that still didn't want the job, but after talking to his grandmother, he knew he had to give it a real shot. So he was, reassigning his shifts in the tasting room and going with Dillon to meet with local restaurant owners who had contracts with Amavita Estates. Dillon mentioned trying to get Amavita Estates wine stocked in one of the largest area liquor stores, but so far, he hadn't been able to secure a deal with the distribution management company.

Through all of it, his whole week, the only thing that helped him feel like he wasn't losing himself entirely was the thought of Sara. Seeing her again, being able to listen to her laugh.

He didn't go to Lakeside Glass with the hope he'd end up in her bed, or on her table, but he wasn't going to complain either.

"Did you change your mind?" Sara asked softly.

Leo looked at her and realized he'd been quiet for a minute. He grinned and shook his head. "I'm just trying to find your table."

She laughed, her eyes going dark and rich. "I don't have one, but it's on my shopping list now."

"Damn. I guess sex isn't on the table after all. How about on the counter?"

"Ew. I make my breakfast there. I don't want my bare ass there," Sara said with a wrinkled nose. So cute.

Leo chuckled. "Couch?"

She nodded. "The couch works. I just got it yesterday."

"Seriously? You're going to christen your couch with me? I'm so honored."

She laughed and pulled him by the collar toward the couch. Before she sat down, he slid his hand down her side and stopped her. He tipped her chin up with his other hand, holding her gaze for a moment. He needed to know she was with him. That she wanted him as badly as he wanted her.

The desire in her gaze had him hard and throbbing. He captured her lips as passion blazed between them. He tugged her shirt up and over her head as she pulled at his. He cupped her breasts, loving the scratchy feel of her lace bra. Their tongues dueled for dominance, both of them needing something only the other could give.

She slid her hand into his shorts and wrapped her fingers around him, and he gave up control of their kiss. She could have whatever she wanted as long as she kept stroking him like that.

Leo tugged her bra cup to the side and rasped him thumb over her peaked nipple. She gasped, breaking their kiss. He kissed his way down her throat, not stopping until he wrapped his lips around her perfect pink nipple.

Her stroke faltered, letting him think again. Her pulled the other cup to the side and thumbed over her other nipple. Her entire body trembled, her breath coming out in gasps and pants.

"Oh, God, Leo. That feels so good."

He nipped her flesh, then laved over the bite with the flat of his tongue. She moaned and pressed his head tighter to her breast, stopping him from even thinking about moving.

He was happy right where he was.

Every so often, she stroked him again. He teased her

until she stopped. He tugged her hand out of his shorts and sat on the couch, bringing her down onto his lap.

"That's better," he said to her breasts, now at eye level. "So perfect."

He used one hand to serve her breast to himself and set the other on her hip, encouraging her to move over him. She whimpered with her first stroke, rubbing herself on his cock, but it wasn't long before she was grabbing his shoulders and throwing her head back in pleasure.

"Fuck me, you're beautiful," Leo said, leaning back just to watch her make herself come.

"Don't stop," she whimpered. "Please."

He lifted her breasts together and alternated between them, nibbling and sucking and grazing them until her back bowed and she shuddered through a gentle release.

"God, you're sexy when you come," he breathed against her chest. He loved how completely she gave herself to him, trusting him with her pleasure, knowing he'd take her where she needed to go without even taking her clothes off.

"Sorry I didn't wait for you," she said with a grin.

"No need. That was amazing."

"Hell, yeah, it was," she said.

He laughed, bringing her lips to his for a kiss that had him pulsing against her sex and dying to sink into her. She wrapped her tongue around his, stroking right with him in long, gentle strokes. Then she pulsed her tongue into his mouth and devoured him, pressing her entire body against his and kissing him with every inch of her.

He'd never been kissed like that in his life.

She reached back and removed her bra while they kissed. His hands roamed her body in a caress, learning where her sensitive spots were. Her skin was smooth, soft, and he wanted to taste all of her.

He pulled back from their kiss and slid his mouth to her ear, leaving open-mouthed kisses and goosebumps in his wake. She shivered against him. He kissed down her neck and across her collarbones to her shoulders. He tasted her skin, soaking in her flavor. The salty perspiration from her efforts, the hint of woman beneath, her soap from her earlier shower. All of it made him drunk on her, needing more of her.

He feasted on her skin as she shivered against him, gently rocking her body along his.

"I want you inside me," she whispered, dragging his lips back to hers.

He kissed her hard, leaving no room for her to doubt he wanted the same thing. She clawed at his back, pulling him closer and demanding more of him. They pulled apart on a gasp, fumbling to strip off the rest of their clothes.

He got his shorts to his knees before she was lowering herself on him again. "Condom. Wait," he gasped, barely holding her at bay while he found and rolled on a condom.

Then she was there, straddling him with her curvy thighs and teasing him with the peek he got of her before his cock disappeared inside her.

"Oh, fuck, you feel good," he groaned as she sank onto him.

"Yeah, me, too. So good," she murmured, positioning herself just right.

Then she moved, her hands on his shoulders, her thighs gripping his. She lifted herself up, peering down to watch where they came together. He stared at his cock vanishing inside her as she lowered herself onto him again.

"That's hot," she whispered.

Leo grunted in agreement. His hands rested gently on

her hips, but as she tortured him with her slow strokes, he tightened his fingers and urged her to hurry.

"Can't wait?" she teased.

"For you? No. Fuck, no."

Her eyes darkened at his words, and she repositioned herself, then increased her pace. Up and down. A little twist. A roll of her hips. Up and down.

It didn't take long for a tingling to start in the back of his throat. He guided her, slamming her down on his cock until he could barely hold back.

Her fingers tightened on his shoulders, silently begging him to help. He slid his hand across her hip to her center and pressed his thumb to her clit. She moaned and instantly clamped down on him, releasing a long yell as she came hard.

Her body, worn from doing all the work, fell limply against his, vibrating through her orgasm as his raced up to meet her. He shifted his weight beneath her, stroking again, and lifted her just enough to get the friction he needed to let go of his own release. He came with a grunt and a shake that had him already wishing for more of her.

They sat like that, on her couch wrapped around each other, until their bodies cooled and Leo had to take care of the condom. She pointed to the bathroom door, and he closed it softly, unsure where the boundaries were with a woman he slept with but wasn't attached to.

Leo loved women, but he didn't love casual hook ups. He wished he was more like Ryan and could sleep with a woman and walk away, but Leo always felt guilty. It was rare he slept with a woman he wasn't involved with already. But he'd take whatever he could get with Sara whatever way he could get it.

When he left the bathroom, she was already getting

dressed. He tugged his shorts up in the bathroom, since they were still around his ankles, but he wasn't ready for their connection to be over yet.

Too bad she was.

"Thanks," she said softly. "That was amazing."

He smiled. "Yeah, it was. Maybe we can do it again sometime?"

She grinned. "Just sex, right?"

He nodded, choking back the bad taste in his mouth. "Absolutely."

"Then I'm sure I'll see you soon."

Leo nodded and grabbed his shirt, understanding he was being dismissed. She wanted her space, or just wanted him out of her space. Either way, he wasn't going to force her to put up with him being there.

He was almost out the door when she called out, "Wait!"

"Yeah?" he asked, turning with a grin. He knew she'd change her mind and ask him to stay a little longer.

"I forgot to get your number."

Disappointed, he took her outstretched phone. He quickly keyed in his number then sent himself a text so he had hers also.

"Thanks," she said quietly.

"No problem. I'll see you soon."

She nodded and let him walk out the door, down to his car, and drive away.

He tried not to let it bother him that she really only wanted sex from him, but when he got home, he had a text that made him smile.

> I had a great time. All night. Thank you for chasing away a little bit of my loneliness.

He couldn't help but smile, or reply.

She texted back a smiley face.

Maybe it wasn't just sex.

~

ADAM WALKED into the studio and stopped. Megan was standing by the work table, tying her long curls into a ponytail. She hated how they framed her face and made her cheeks look puffy, but he loved it. He thought it made her look youthful and stunning. But when she tied her hair back, exposing her long neck, he nearly lost it.

She hadn't noticed him yet, so he stayed where he was and watched her. She moved around the studio with grace and fluidity. He was often surprised she wasn't a dancer. The way she floated around was enough to hypnotize any man with a pulse, not that she ever noticed.

Adam had been trying to hold back his desire for his boss for years, but as the end of his apprenticeship drew closer, he had more and more trouble not saying something to her.

Megan looked up and caught him staring at her. She lifted her hand to wave, a curious look on her face. He forced a grin and walked across the room to her side.

"What are we working on today?" Adam asked.

"I had this idea last night. I was thinking about Sara and Leo, and I want to do a piece that looks like two people embracing. Complimentary colors, very abstract, but something that clearly looks like a lovers' embrace."

Adam's blood heated at the thought. He could see it in his mind, the way they would fit together, the passion reflected in the colors of the glass. Two opposites drawn to each other, wound so tightly you couldn't tell where one began and the other ended.

Except he was thinking about himself and Megan, not Sara and Leo.

"Stunning. I love it. How can I help?"

She shook her head. "I don't know. That's what I'm trying to figure out now. Where to start. How to do this. Can I do this?"

"You can do it," Adam said, and he knew it was true. Megan was the most amazing glass blower he'd ever heard of. When he finished his schooling, he knew he wanted to work with someone who would show him how to do unique and special things. Someone who would push the boundaries of what was possible. Someone who wasn't afraid to take risks and fail, because that was how you learned.

Megan did that. All the time, in her work, she stretched the limits. She went for things that seemed impossible. And she nailed them every time.

Adam wished she carried some of that over to her personal life. Instead, she was afraid of everything that bordered on real feelings. She kept Adam at arm's length, even though they'd known each other for years. Adam tried to tell himself it was because he was her student, but she didn't get close to anyone. She never dated, had very few friends, and didn't share anything about herself.

He tried to draw her out, but so far, it hadn't worked.

"I don't think I've ever done anything like this. It's basically two pieces that are formed together," she said, staring at the drawing she'd done.

"Okay, so let's think it through. If you want two different colors, we can start with two gathers, each of us working with one color. Then we can start to mold them together once they reach the right temperature. Press them together like we would with different colors in a striped vase or something like that, but bigger pieces."

"That will leave us with two rods, though. I don't know if we want two."

Adam nodded. "I think we do. That way each figure can be sculpted and blown on its own, but they can come together."

"I've never used two rods at once," she said, still considering.

"What do you always tell me?" he asked.

She grinned. "Every great idea starts with someone being brave enough to try something they've never done before."

Adam returned her smile. "So, what do you say? Are you going to be brave enough?"

Her grin widened and she nodded. "Hell, yes."

MEGAN SMILED behind her face shield. When she had the idea for the new sculpture, she honestly wasn't sure how she was going to pull it off. Until Adam challenged her, she didn't think she'd be able to.

They worked side-by-side with the glass, sliding it into the glory hole, then rolling and blowing the glass until the shape started to appear.

"Are you ready to merge them?" Adam asked over the roar of the furnace.

Megan nodded. "We're ready."

Megan and Adam took their blowpipes to the glory hole together and opened the door. They slid them in, rolling each tube before they pressed them together and rolled the piece as one.

Adam took the blowpipe from Megan, holding both in his strong hands. She stepped back and watched him work, both fascinated and turned on.

He moved the glass inside the furnace, letting it heat and blend into one piece. He gave her a look before he pulled the large piece out of the furnace, then backed up with it and moved to the bench.

Megan took one blowpipe from Adam and helped him shape and twist the sculpture. She grabbed jacks and pulled the glass to give each figure arms and to add movement to the piece.

Adam took it back to the glory hole to keep the heat level consistent, then they blew the glass.

Eyes locked together, they had to be completely in sync. Megan took a deep breath and watched Adam, exhaling strongly with him.

Her eyes bounced between the piece and the man helping her bring her vision to life. As they worked, what she envisioned appeared before her eyes. Two people wrapped around each other, arms holding, heads tilted in a kiss, hips lined up. It was stunning.

Adam held the blowpipes while Megan finished the last parts of the sculpture. She smoothed her gloves over the surface, then steadied it while she snipped the molten glass and freed her couple. Megan stood them up and looked at her piece. She loved it.

Adam moved behind her, his body close to hers. "It's beautiful. I've never seen anything like it."

Megan nodded. "I agree. I couldn't have done it without you."

Adam shook his head. "It was all you. I just helped

where I could. You were the one who saw this and made it a reality. You're amazing."

Megan smiled, looking up at him from under her lashes. His face was flushed and his hair matted to his head. His coveralls were dirty and he definitely needed a shower.

And Megan really wanted to join him.

Her pulse raced as she stared at him, needing him, wanting him. She licked her lips and told herself no one would know.

He moved closer to her, barely shifting at all, and she panicked. She couldn't sleep with Adam. He was her student. He was fourteen years younger than her. And she didn't have time for a relationship.

She turned away from him and left the studio floor, mumbling an excuse they both knew was just that. An excuse.

9

———————

WHEN SARA MADE IT INTO WORK TUESDAY MORNING, THERE was a stunning, erotic looking sculpture on her desk. Well, not her desk. The desk where she worked.

She looked at the piece, loving the green and pink colors wound together in a way that looked like lovers embracing. Her cheeks heated as she thought of the way she rode Leo the other night after their date. Maybe she was imagining the erotic nature of the piece since she hadn't been able to cool down since Leo left her apartment.

He tried to talk her into joining him at his family's picnic on Sunday, but that was too risky for her. She could get attached to him if she got to know him, and she knew his sister would become a friend. She couldn't chance that. Just because Andie wouldn't sleep with Sara's...whatever Leo was...didn't mean it wasn't a risk for Sara to get involved with both Leo and Andie. Sara learned the hard way that friends, like boyfriends and mothers, couldn't be trusted.

Once Leo realized she wasn't going to give in and go to the picnic, he changed his tactics to flirting with her. Her entire body heated at the text he sent her that had her reaching into her nightstand for her vibrator late that night.

Leo was going to be bad for her health. Or very good, depending on how she looked at it.

"Oh, you're here," Megan said from behind Sara, startling her.

"Yeah, I just got here. This is amazing. Was it a custom piece?"

Megan nodded. "Yeah. Adam and I worked on it Sunday and it came out of the annealer last night. It's for you actually."

Sara's gaze snapped up to Megan's. "For me? Why?"

Megan grinned. "Because you inspired it. I had this idea and had to make it for you."

"Wow. I don't know if I can accept this. It's too amazing."

Megan shook her head. "I want it to be yours. You have to take it."

"Can I ask what it is?"

Megan's brows drew together. "You can't tell? Sorry. I get so wrapped up in my work that sometimes I forget that other people don't actually see what's inside my head. It's an embrace. Two lovers. You're always wearing something pink, and Leo owns a vineyard, full of green. It's the two of you."

Sara gaped at the sculpture. "I...wow." She couldn't form words to accurately depict how she was feeling. She didn't know how she was feeling.

"You hate it," Megan said. "Shit. I'm sorry. I'll put it on a shelf somewhere. Someone will buy it. A wedding gift or something. I'm sorry. I should have asked you."

Sara didn't respond until Megan picked up the sculpture and started to walk away. "Stop. Please. I want it."

Megan turned, her curls bouncing around her head and framing her face. The soft gray offset the dark shade of her skin, but her amber eyes almost glowed. She offered Sara a tentative smile, one Sara returned full force.

"When I walked in, I thought that was what it looked like, but then I thought I was crazy because you don't have anything else like that. Knowing you made it for me and Leo...we're not together. I mean, we're sleeping together, but we're not together, together. You know?"

Megan nodded. "I understand. I hope that changes, but that's for the two of you to decide. You don't have to keep this if you don't want it. I don't want you to be uncomfortable or whatever."

Sara shook her head, her eyes falling to the sculpture. "I want it. It's stunning and erotic and will definitely always remind me of my time here."

Megan grinned and brought the glass couple back to the desk. She set it carefully in the center, then moved around to wrap it up.

While Megan pulled out sheets and foam, a couple came in holding hands. They said hi, then noticed the piece and headed straight for the desk.

"Is this for sale?" the young woman asked.

Megan turned and shook her head. "I'm sorry, but it's not. It's a gift."

"It's stunning. We're on our honeymoon and wanted something to bring home that would remind us of our time here. Wine didn't seem significant enough since we'd drink it and be done. We wanted something like this to look at and remember the time we spent here was some of the best days of our lives."

"I'm so sorry. It's already been promised to someone else," Megan said, flashing them a grin. "But I have plenty of other items that could bring you the same joy."

"Do you have anything else like that?" the wife asked.

Megan looked at the sculpture and shook her head. "I'm sorry, but I don't."

"Would you be willing to sell it to us? We'll pay extra. Or maybe make us one?"

"I'm sor—"

"Excuse us, please," Sara said, tugging Megan away from the counter. She flashed a grin at the couple and pulled Megan to the other side of the shop, where the couple might not hear them talking.

"What is going on?" Megan asked.

"You have to sell the piece to them," Sara said.

Megan shook her head. "I made it for you. Adam and I did. We want it to be yours. Not go to some random strangers."

"Make them another one then. You saw them. They're young and in love and cute and perfect. They should have something like this. I only have it because you're amazing. I'm single and always will be."

Megan grinned. "Not always. One day you'll settle down and know that you've found someone you don't want to spend another day without."

Sara shook her head. "I won't, Megan. I wish I could, but too much shit has happened in my life for me to think love is real. Those two? He'll cheat on her within a few years, and she'll gain a bunch of weight and think that's why, when the reality will be he doesn't know how to keep his dick in his pants. Love isn't real. It doesn't exist. I shouldn't have something like that."

Megan glared at her. "You're dark. And I'm sorry your ex cheated on you—"

"How—"

"You just told me. But that doesn't mean everyone is doomed. It doesn't mean you can't be happy."

"Are you?" Sara spat.

Megan's eyebrow went high and she jerked back.

"I'm sorry," Sara said immediately. "I shouldn't have said that. It wasn't fair to you. I'm sorry."

Megan took a deep breath. "It wasn't, but that's okay. Either way, I don't want anyone else to have that piece. It's for you. If I had time to make the couple another piece, I would, but I don't think I have the time."

"What about Adam?"

"What about Adam?" Adam asked, all of a sudden right behind us.

"Don't do that," Megan urged. "This place is full of glass."

Adam looked around. "Oh, damn. I never noticed that before."

Megan rolled her eyes at him.

"So, what about Adam?" he asked again.

"The couple over there wants Sara's piece—"

"And Megan won't give it to them," Sara interjected.

"Because it's yours. Anyway, they asked if I could make them another one, but I really don't have the time. Sara said you could."

"I can do it," Adam said quickly.

"See? Problem solved," Sara said.

"No," Megan added. "Not solved. We had to work together on that to make it work. I don't think it's something either of us could do alone."

"Then give me one of your other projects and we'll work on this together," Adam said.

"Yes, do that," Sara agreed. She couldn't stand the couple not having the piece, especially given how much it clearly meant to them.

"Can you handle one?"

Adam nodded. "Absolutely. I've been working with you for years. I'll be on my own soon. I might as well push the boundaries of what I can do and prove to both of us that I'm ready."

Sara waited while Megan considered the options and finally agreed.

"Okay, you can do the Parker project," Megan said.

Adam nodded, fighting a grin that told Sara he was hoping for that project. "I won't let you down."

Megan nodded once. "You better not."

"Good news," Sara said to the couple studying her new sculpture. "They've figured it out and will make you one."

"Oh, excellent," the bride said. "Thank you so much. This means a lot to me. You have no idea."

Sara packed her sculpture as Megan and Adam talked to the young couple about the piece. They chose black and white for their sculpture, with a thread of yellow through it.

Sara wanted to text a picture of the piece to Leo to show him the gift she received, but she stopped herself. They were just sex friends. Not anything more. And she needed to remember that if she was going to survive the summer.

Sara was leaving work when she noticed a message from Peter. He wanted to grab dinner and maybe a movie if she was up to it. She called him instead of texting back, since it was late.

"Hey," he answered on the first ring. "I was just going to text you again."

"I'm sorry! I didn't check my phone and just saw your text as I was leaving work. Did you still want to get dinner?"

"Absolutely. I'd never miss a chance to spend time with my favorite new Bereton resident."

Sara laughed. Peter had a way of making her feel good about herself. He was sweet and funny, and she enjoyed spending time with him.

"Don't try to talk me into moving here. It's only temporary," Sara said.

"A guy can try," Peter said with a laugh. "Where are you?"

"I'm in my car at Lakeside Glass. I haven't left work yet."

"Head home. I'll meet you there so you don't have to worry about driving home."

"Do I sound that bad?" Sara teased.

"You sound perfect," Peter said, his voice dropping. "But it's Monday, so alcohol is always a good idea."

Sara agreed and hung up so she could drive. Peter wasn't there when she got home, so she ran upstairs to freshen up and put her new sculpture on her brand new table. She was washing her hands when he knocked on her door.

"Come on in," Sara called out.

Peter opened the door and let himself in. "Hello? I'm coming in."

"Hey," Sara said, drying her hands as she walked out of the bathroom. "How was your day?"

"My day was good. We got started on a few things and my cousins aren't making me too crazy. How about you?"

"Mine was great," Sara gushed. "Do we have a minute? I want to show you what Megan and Adam made for me."

"Absolutely. I'd love to see it. Especially after the vase you and Megan made."

Sara shook her head and lifted the lid on the box. "This is nothing like that. This is amazing. Adam and Megan were working on it without me knowing. It's stunning." She unwrapped it and took it out, holding it up for Peter to see. "What do you think?"

"Wow," he gasped. "That's...kind of erotic. It looks like two lovers wrapped around each other."

Sara grinned. "It is. Isn't it beautiful?"

Peter nodded. "It is, but um, why did they make this for you? It seems a little odd as a gift from your boss."

Sara didn't think about that part of it. She didn't want to hurt his feelings and tell him she was sleeping with someone else. They were friends, but she got the feeling sometimes that Peter wanted it to be more. He said they were friends, but still, she didn't want to hurt him.

If she told him about Leo, it could end the friendship they had. Sara liked having both men in her life. A good friend to go out with and talk to, and a sinful lover to keep her fully stocked up on outstanding orgasms. It was a perfect situation because she didn't get too attached to either.

"Um, yeah, I guess. Megan's hoping I meet someone here and stick around. She keeps talking about me not leaving."

Peter nodded. "I can understand why she'd feel that way. I don't want to see you go either."

Sara ducked her chin and smiled, happy she didn't tell him about Leo. It would just be bad. "Should we go to dinner?"

Peter nodded, brushing off her dismissal of his obvious feelings. "I'm ready when you are."

Sara took in his khaki shorts and golf shirt and her cropped jeans and hot pink tank top and stopped. "Should I change?"

"Nope. You look amazing. We're not going anywhere fancy."

"Are you sure?"

He nodded again. "Absolutely. Let's go."

Peter waited while Sara locked her door, then led the way downstairs. He opened her door to get in his car, then jogged around the front. He turned toward town and was parking along River Street in a few minutes. "It's up ahead, but I thought we could walk from here in case we go to the movies or want ice cream after dinner."

"Yes and yes," Sara said.

Peter laughed and offered her his arm. She slipped her hand in and smiled up at him. The sun bounced off his blond hair, making him look like he was glowing. He could have been a model with his strong jaw and easy smile, but instead he was supplying the world with alcohol. Sara definitely enjoyed that one better.

They walked into All Beef, a burger place with a menu that made Sara's head spin. "Wow, they have a lot of choices."

Peter grinned. "Yep, and they're all amazing. Although I guess I should have asked if you like burgers."

Sara smiled. "I ate a meatball the night we met."

Peter nodded. "Yep, you did. I should have remembered that. I was jealous of a piece of beef."

Sara snorted, but the heat in Peter's gaze told her he wasn't joking. She brushed it off again, telling herself he'd get over her once she left. She wasn't the kind of woman a guy pined over forever. She was the kind of woman a guy forgot about as soon as someone thinner or prettier or funnier or smarter showed an interest. She knew that from experience.

Sara and Peter finally made their choices and ordered burgers. Peter grabbed a table while Sara got her drink. When their order was called, Peter picked it up from the counter, flirting with the woman behind it for a minute.

It bothered Sara that she wasn't the least bit jealous of Peter flirting with another woman. He bought her dinner and was taking her to a movie, and she didn't care if he hit on someone else while they were out. In fact, she almost told him he should get the woman's number when he came back to the table, but she held her tongue.

"I love coming here."

Sara took a bite and groaned. "I can see why. Damn, that's good."

"And now I'm jealous of a burger. First a meatball, now a burger," Peter said, a growl to his voice.

Sara grinned at him. "You just want my meat."

Peter chuckled and mumbled something Sara didn't catch.

They ate and talked about their days. She found herself wanting to share more and more with him, but she didn't get too personal.

By the time they finished dinner, it was too late the catch the only movie they were both interested in, so they opted for ice cream instead.

"I should probably skip the ice cream," Sara admitted. Her shorts were already a little tight, and with the way Peter was feeding her, she'd need new clothes by the end of the summer.

"A little ice cream won't hurt you. Unless you're lactose intolerant or something. Then it might," Peter said with a smirk.

Sara shook her head. "Not lactose intolerant. Just worried about the size of my ass."

Peter stopped walking and looked back, blatantly checking out her ass. "Looks just right to me."

"Stop," she said, flustered and flattered.

"Just calling it like I see it. A woman should have a full

butt. Something to hold on to. If you were just skin and bones, you wouldn't be nearly as hot as you are."

"You sure know how to flatter a girl," Sara deadpanned.

Peter winked at her. "Come on, hot ass, let me buy you some ice cream."

Sara laughed and followed him to Bereton Creamery. The woman inside the shop was round with a full face and rosy cheeks. She was fanning herself when they walked up.

"Hey Peter," she said brightly.

"Holly, how are you tonight?"

"Melting," she said with a grin pushing her glasses up her nose. "I probably look like I belong on a Christmas card."

Sara stifled a laugh, but Peter didn't bother. "You're beautiful as always."

She laughed and nodded toward Sara. "Be careful or your girlfriend is going to start to worry about you."

Sara shook her head. "I'm not his girlfriend."

Holly turned back to Peter. "There's a woman in town who's managed to resist your charms? I didn't think I'd live to see the day."

"Ha ha," Peter said. "I haven't slept with you, have I?"

She laughed. "Nope, but I think that's because I got married before you moved back to town. Lost your opportunity."

Peter snapped his fingers and grinned. "That Tony's a lucky bastard."

Holly rubbed her belly. "We're both pretty damn lucky. But enough of that. What do you want?"

"Chocolate peanut butter for me," Peter said. Then he looked at Sara. "You're not allergic to peanuts, are you?"

Sara grinned. "No. I'm not. Can I have blackberry sorbet, please?"

"Coming right up."

Peter paid for their ice cream then directed Sara down the street away from his car. They walked and enjoyed the warm summer night, neither ready to leave.

"How long have you been back?" Sara asked.

"Almost a year."

"Where were you before that?"

"Georgia. I was working for a hospital in Atlanta, doing general community outreach and fundraising."

"Did you like it?"

He shrugged. "Most of the time. When it came time to do the budget for the following year, I always got a few more phone calls from people who wanted to schedule in an event to raise money because they needed a new piece of equipment or wanted to hire someone, but most of the time, my job was about reaching out to the local community to let them know what our hospital was capable of."

"What made you leave?"

Peter smiled. "I missed home. It sounds wimpy I guess, but I wanted to be near my family. It took me a while to figure out what I was going to do, but I finally decided I'd find something once I got here."

"And you did?"

He nodded. "My cousins were just starting up their vodka distillery and asked if I had an interest in helping out. It's been a good fit for me."

"I haven't been in one place for a full year since I graduated college," Sara heard herself admit.

"Wow. Really? What are you running from?"

10

———

Sara didn't want to answer his question, but Peter was her friend. The only one she really had in Bereton. She liked Megan and Adam, but Megan was her boss. She could hold things against Sara and eliminate her job before Sara was ready to leave if she wanted.

Keeping the truth bottled up wasn't good for her. It was starting to wear on her that she had no one to talk to. Not that she wanted to bring up her mother, but Peter seemed to be a good listener.

"My mom died almost ten years ago," Sara confessed. "It was a bad situation and I've struggled to be in one place since then."

"Oh, shit, Sara. I'm so sorry," Peter breathed.

She nodded. "Thanks. It's silly, but right after she died, I found out my ex was sleeping with my best friend, and it was hard to trust anyone after that."

"I don't blame you. I don't think I'd trust anyone if my best friend was sleeping with my girlfriend. I'd kick his ass."

Sara laughed. "There were times I thought about it, but

it's easier to just move away and try to move on. Even though it's hard to talk about it all."

"I didn't mean...I'm so sorry."

Sara took a deep breath and forced a smile. "It's not your fault. I didn't tell you to make you feel bad about it. I just wanted you to know. That's why I don't stay in one place for long. I move around a lot because attachments are dangerous."

"Not every attachment is going to be like that," Peter tried.

Sara glared at him.

He chuckled. "Okay, yeah, it sucks. No matter how you look at it, it was shitty. But that's on them, not you. He's crazy to have even looked at another woman with you around."

Sara heard the heat in his voice, the dip in tone. She wanted it to do something for her, but she just didn't see Peter that way. He was like a brother. A person she could count on, but not someone she ever wanted to see naked.

She had Leo for naked times.

"Thanks," she finally said. "I didn't mean to unload."

He grinned and pulled her in for a hug. "You can unload on me any time you want to. I'm happy to listen."

"Thanks," Sara said, accepting a kiss on her cheek.

Peter lingered a little too long, forcing Sara to pull back. She didn't look at him for a minute, hating that she felt awkward around him after her confession.

"I should probably head home," she finally said. "I feel like I'm not getting enough sleep lately."

Peter sighed and nodded, letting the obvious lie go. "Thanks for coming out tonight."

She smiled. "Thanks for inviting me. I had fun."

"Until I called you out and made you feel like shit," he deadpanned.

She laughed and shook her head. "It was no big deal. I'm glad I told you."

"Me, too," he said.

He dropped her off at home and told her to have a good night. Sara was sitting in her living room, feeling lonely and wishing she hadn't told Peter not to come up. It wouldn't have been fair to him to do that, but she still hated how silent her apartment was. It was always quiet. Even with a TV, she felt the loneliness like it was a living being in the room. The only time she didn't feel alone was when Leo was there with her.

She thumbed out a quick text, asking what he was doing. When he replied nothing, she invited him over.

On my way.

Loneliness — 0, Orgasms — 1+

LEO WALKED into the business meeting the following Monday wondering what happened to the last week. He heard from Sara once over the weekend, but he hadn't seen her since she texted him a week earlier. The shitty part was he'd barely noticed with all the work he'd been doing with Dillon.

"You're going to run the meeting today," Dillon said when he joined Leo. They were the only ones there, a demand Dillon put on Leo. Leaders should always show up before everyone else. Make sure there's coffee and breakfast ready to go so everyone can concentrate on the meeting instead of worrying about where their food is and how hungry they are.

Leo shook his head at Dillon's statement, pouring his first cup of coffee for the day. He added one cream and three sugars to his cup then turned to face his brother. "Why am I running the meeting?"

"Because I'm leaving this weekend, and you're going to be in charge for the next month. You might as well do it today so we can talk about it," Dillon explained.

Leo understood it made sense, but he didn't want his brother critiquing his performance. It was like having someone evaluate his talents in bed. The end goal was to make a woman scream his name. For the meeting, it was to hear from everyone and make sure they all had what they needed. He didn't need a coach.

"I think you should do it. Show everyone that you're around and not going anywhere."

"But I am," Dillon insisted. "I'm leaving in a few days and I won't be back for a while. They need to know you have my confidence behind you. That I believe in you and know you have it all under control."

"I do."

Dillon nodded. "I know you do, and after today, they'll all know it, too."

Leo took a deep breath and nodded. Fighting his brother was a losing battle. It always had been, his whole life. A part of Leo knew Dillon was right, that being on of the youngest, his cousins would never listen to him if they thought he was just playing boss. With Dillon's support and approval right there in front of them, he had a chance to lead while Dillon was away and not sink the entire vineyard in a month.

The rest of the cousins filtered in, grabbing coffee, breakfast, and seats. When everyone was there, Dillon stood in front of the small crowd and the room fell silent.

"I'm leaving this coming weekend for a month, so Leo's

taking over. He's going to run the meeting today and will be handling everything while Katherine and I are gone."

Leo stood and smoothed a hand down the front of his shirt. He felt like he was going to a funeral in his blue button down shirt and gray slacks. He forced himself to swallow past the lump in his throat. It was his family, the people who loved him. There was no reason for him to be so worried.

But he couldn't stop it.

"Hey...um, hey everyone. Uh, like Dillon said, I'll be taking care of um, everything while he's gone. Um, so this week, Dillon and I are meeting with Finger Lakes Distribution, Inc. We're hoping to convince them to put Amavita Estates wine in the local stores so we can get a little more exposure. I think other than that, um, everything is business as usual."

"We start interviewing harvesters this week," Henry said. "We're going to be using one of the tables in The Drunken Grape through lunch all week."

Zach nodded. "Yep, Michele has a Reserved sign on the table you wanted already. We've talked to all the servers to make sure it stays there every day."

"And I have a full house in the inn, which means a full week in The Drunken Grape," Andie said.

"We're booked up through the weekend, too," Zach said about the restaurant. "We have the tables we always keep empty, but it's not many."

"I'm bringing in a few new pieces to the gift shop, also," Alyssa said. "I've been talking to some local artists, and Kristen and I are looking at hosting something here. Maybe incorporate it into one of the events we're hosting over the summer or next year. We haven't gotten far on the planning, but we're moving forward."

Leo stole a glance at Dillon while everyone talked

around him. Dillon nodded and made notes like he was up on everything they were talking about. Leo just felt overwhelmed and lost. All of his cousins had something going on that he wasn't aware of. He was always able to stay in his lane, keep things going in the tasting room, and not worry about everything else happening. If he was acting CEO, he had to be on top of all of it.

Information swirled around them as conversations happened on top of each other. Leo tried to keep up with it all, but he knew he was missing things. Dillon asked a few questions for clarification and made more notes, but Leo just stood there, sweating and panicking.

When the meeting finally ended, Leo thought his head was going to explode. "How do you keep it all straight?" he asked Dillon.

"Keep what straight?"

"Everything that's going on. That was overwhelming."

Dillon shrugged, his dark shirt pulling tight across his shoulders. Dillon looked the part of a CEO in his neatly pressed shirt and slacks that perfectly matched the suit coat hanging on the back of his office door. Just in case, he always told Leo.

"You'll get to where you know about all of it before you walk into a meeting. They'll all come to you with questions and ask for advice and money and bounce ideas off of you. These meetings have always been more of a way for everyone else to stay informed about what's going on, not for me," Dillon explained.

"So you knew all of that already?"

Dillon nodded.

Leo shook his head. "How do you know what idea is the right one to support?"

Dillon folded up his notebook and clipped the pen to

the front. He smiled at Leo as he stood. "You trust your team."

Leo thought about that for a second and realized his brother was right. They were all working toward the same goal. They all wanted Amavita Estates to be successful. They weren't out to push themselves ahead, they were looking out for the vineyard. It was a family business, and the family wanted to keep it that way.

For the first time that day, Leo felt like he could actually do the job.

SARA CARRIED a tray of coffee into work, knowing it would be well received by Megan and Adam. She had witnessed more than one argument between them about who was supposed to make the coffee, and while she thought their flirting was funny, running out of coffee was not.

She also had a flyer for Megan, but she wasn't sure how well received that would be.

"You brought coffee," Megan groaned. "I love you."

Sara laughed. "I know. I'll make some more in a little while, but I needed to get my first cup."

"And you knew we'd already drained the pot. I'm sorry. We'll try to do better."

Sara shook her head. "It's fine. I know you guys are here earlier than I am. I don't blame you for being a full pot ahead of me."

Megan laughed and sipped her drink, groaning again. "Just how I like it. Thank you."

Sara nodded and set the tray down. If Adam didn't show up soon, she'd take his coffee to him, but first, she wanted to talk to Megan.

"I saw this flyer at the cafe. Have you heard about this?" she asked, handing over the bright yellow sheet of paper.

Megan glanced at it and shook her head, handing the flyer back. "I've heard of it, but I'm not going to do it."

"Why not? It could be great exposure. You said you wanted to get your name out there a little more."

Megan nodded. "I do, but not like this. I know these people. They turn their noses up at people like me because I use machines to help create my work. They want artists who only use their hands."

"What do you mean?"

Megan sipped her coffee, but the pain in her eyes was clear over the rim of the cup. "A part of me wonders if it's me, but when I've talked about setting up a booth at one of these craft fairs, I was told my work didn't qualify since it's not one hundred percent handmade. They bring in people who knit and crochet and craft jewelry and needlepoint. Stuff like that."

"What about the tire sculptures? And the metal signs?"

"They take a material and change it, they don't craft something with the aid of a machine. That's what they've told me."

"Seriously?" Sara asked, stunned. She thought Megan would be perfect for local craft fairs.

Megan nodded. "Yep. I think it would be great, but they won't even consider it."

"That really sucks."

Megan nodded again. "It does, but it is what it is. Thanks for thinking of me, though."

Sara nodded as Megan disappeared into the studio. She felt bad that she upset Megan, but she believed in her boss. Megan was insanely talented, and she should be able to share her work with more people, especially locals at an event designed to connect people with local artists.

Sara made a mental note to reach out to the organizers and got to work, greeting the new customers who came in and doing her best to sell some new pieces. By the time lunch rolled around, she was starving and ready for whatever Adam made that smelled so good.

"What is this?" Sara asked, joining Adam and Megan in the break room.

"Megan's favorite," Adam said with a smile for Megan. "Beef stroganoff."

Megan hummed. "It's so good. Anna doesn't eat a lot of meat, so we didn't have stuff like this when she lived with me. I kind of got used to going without meat, but Adam keeps me full."

Sara tried to stifle a laugh and failed. When Megan and Adam turned to look at her, she snorted. "You know how dirty that sounds, don't you?"

Megan opened and closed her mouth, not saying anything. Adam just looked at her, desire painted all over his face.

"I'll keep you full of my meat any time you want," Adam said. His tone was teasing, but Sara got the feeling he was completely serious.

Megan brushed him off and said, "You two know what I meant. You'd think you were as single as me with the way you talk about sex."

Sara laughed. "I am as single as you."

Megan shook her head. "You're seeing Leo Young. I know you're not single."

Sara protested immediately. "I'm not seeing him."

"You're just sleeping with him?"

"Yes," Sara grumbled. "And that works for us."

"You should settle down. Leo's a good man. He'd be a good match for you," Megan said.

Sara shook her head. "That's why we're only sleeping together. I don't want to be a good match for anyone. We're not dating, we're not building a future, we're just scratching an itch once in a while."

"How long have you been scratching this itch?" Megan asked pointedly.

"A couple weeks," Sara said defensively. "It's no big deal. He's a nice guy, and he's very talented."

Megan groaned. "Ew, I don't need to hear this. It's one thing hearing second or third hand, but first hand is a little...gross."

"There's nothing gross about sex," Adam argued. "Sex is beautiful and amazing. It's something special shared between two people who care about each other."

"Whoa, there are no feelings," Sara argued. "We're just having sex."

"You show up, drop your pants, and leave?" Megan asked.

Sara laughed. "It's not that bad. And why are we only talking about my sex life?"

"Because I don't have one," Megan said, stabbing a bite of her lunch and shoving it in her mouth.

"And mine is a solo act," Adam added with a glance at Megan.

Megan's mouth dropped, but she recovered quickly. "What do you mean?"

Adam shrugged. "I haven't dated anyone in a while."

"How long is a while?" Sara asked.

"Since I started working here," Adam admitted.

There was definitely sexual tension between Megan and

Adam. Sara again felt like she needed to leave the room to cool off.

"I thought you dated that one girl. Cassie or something?" Megan said.

Adam shook his head. "Cami. I knew her in college, but we split up right after I started working here. I knew she wasn't the one for me, and there was no reason to prolong the relationship when it wasn't going anywhere."

"And you haven't dated anyone else since?" Megan asked.

Adam shook his head again. "No one else measured up. I know what I want. I'm not going to settle for anything less than her."

Megan swallowed audibly, and even Sara felt uncomfortable. If Megan didn't jump Adam after that kind of declaration, Sara was going to seriously wonder if her boss was insane. Hell, Sara wanted to jump him, and she wasn't attracted to Adam like that.

But he only had eyes for Megan.

Lucky woman.

11

———

After the family business meeting on Monday, Leo was feeling better about filling in for Dillon. He still didn't see himself as CEO material, but he could fake it long enough to help his cousins and siblings make the best decisions possible for the vineyard. Most of the time, they wanted someone to talk through an idea, not someone to tell them what to do. Leo was good at listening. He'd been doing it forever, and it was one of his favorite things about the tasting room.

Dillon was leaving in a couple days, and he asked Leo to take the lead on the meeting with Finger Lakes Distribution, Inc. Leo was anxious but prepared. He had a good handle on what to say and had done his research on the person they were meeting with.

Dillon drove to the meeting, chatting the whole time about his trip and everything he and Katherine were planning. "I haven't told anyone, but Katherine and I are thinking about getting married this fall."

"What?" Leo blurted.

Dillon nodded, a goofy grin on his face. "We've been

talking about it forever, and after I asked her to marry me, there's been a ton of pressure. People follow her around and try to get pictures of us. All the paparazzi want the scoop. They ask her if she's pregnant and make her crazy, so we said we might just do it. Not tell anyone."

"Mom'll kill you," Leo said.

Dillon nodded. "I know. But Katherine has to be my priority. If she wants to get married in secret, I'll do it and deal with Mom and Nonna later."

"Oh, shit, Nonna. She'll disown you."

Dillon chuckled, but Leo wasn't kidding. Family was everything to Nonna. She gave up hers to be with their grandfather, and having any of them turn away from family would devastate her. Alyssa already got married three times without the family there. It nearly killed Nonna. Thankfully, none of Alyssa's marriages lasted until she moved back home and reunited with Jake, the vineyard handyman.

"We were thinking of getting married in Niagara Falls when we're there for the concert. Start the tour with our wedding and let it come out while we're gone," Dillon said.

"Why don't you get married at home before the tour starts? That way the family can be there and you know you'll be safe. Plus, you won't be excommunicated."

Dillon laughed. "That's a good idea. I'll talk to Katherine. I'm sure she'll go for it. We could still use the tour as our honeymoon," Dillon said thoughtfully.

"How long will you be gone for the tour?" Leo asked. Apprehension slithered up his spine, putting him on edge. He knew Dillon was going to start the tour with Katherine but thought Dillon would only be gone a few weeks. The way he was talking, it would be a lot more.

"The tour is six months. I probably won't stay the whole

time, but I'd rather not be away from my new wife for that long. You can handle everything, though. I trust you."

Leo nodded, hoping he could live up to that trust. He was silent the rest of their drive, thinking about his future and what he really wanted. He never saw himself as the corporate type, but for the fourth day that week, he was wearing pressed slacks and a button down shirt, this one gray with black pants. He left the top button undone, but he still felt like he was choking, suffocating on his future.

By the time they reached the office outside Ithaca, Leo was freaking out. He didn't want to walk in there and screw up, but he knew he was going to. His feet were heavy as he followed Dillon through the front door. Dillon told the receptionist who they were and she directed them to a seat while she called Darren Walsh, their contact.

Dillon sat calmly in his chair, looking at his phone the entire time, not a care in the world. Leo's leg bounced, his entire body overflowing with pent up anxiety and nervous energy.

Dillon glanced up at him after a few minutes and hissed, "What is wrong with you?"

Leo whispered back. "What if I screw this up?"

"Gentlemen," a man in a navy golf shirt and khaki shorts said. "I'm George Brand, an associate of Darren's. He sends his regards, but he's unable to make your appointment today and asked me to speak with the two of you."

Leo swallowed roughly. All his planning, all his research, all his preparation went up in smoke before his very eyes. He knew everything there was to know about Darren Walsh, but he'd never even heard of George Brand. He had no strategy, and his entire family was counting on him.

He was so fucked.

"Nice to meet you, George," Dillon said smoothly. "We

know how these things go. Thanks for filling in. I'm Dillon Young."

"Dillon, nice to meet you," George said, his loud voice echoing inside Leo's skull.

Did he have a brain tumor? An aneurysm? He couldn't seem to make his hand and mouth work at the same time. He extended his hand, but nothing came out of his mouth. Then he pulled his hand back and opened his mouth, but knew that wasn't right. Finally, he looked at Dillon for help.

Dillon gave him a wide-eyed glared, silently mouthing, "What the fuck is wrong with you?"

Leo shrugged as George turned to Dillon.

"I'm sorry about my brother," Dillon said. "He's never been here before and is a little overwhelmed with it all."

George laughed with Dillon. "Ah, yes. It's an intimidating building. But we're all good people here, so nothing to worry about. Shall we head back to my office?"

Dillon nodded for both of them and followed George down a short, bland hallway, then through a set of glass double doors and into a contemporary space with cubicles in the center and glass lined offices around the edges of the room. They chatted about everything from the weather to the beauty of living in a part of the country that offered so much to do in the summer to family while Leo struggled to pull his head out of his ass.

George's office was one of the ones on the edges. A glass box where he could see out, but small, barely big enough for his large plywood desk and the two plastic chairs across from it. He sank down into his black leather chair, the squeak startling Leo.

"Get your shit together," Dillon whispered as they sat down.

Leo nodded, even though he had no idea how. They

were supposed to be in a conference room, with space to spread out and show Darren what they had and why he should approve Amavita Estates wines for distribution in the area. Instead, they were crammed into a tiny little office with a guy who clearly had no power, whom Leo had never even heard of. They lost before they even pitched.

"So, what do you guys have for me today?"

Dillon glanced at Leo then launched into the spiel they prepared. He talked about the history of Amavita Estates and the popularity of the wines. He had sales reports and data about the volume of production, expansion plans, and detail about each of the wines they made, including how many cases of each would be available for grocery stores.

Leo sat back and watched, listening to his brother and trying to learn. If he wasn't going to close the deal himself, he could learn how so he didn't let Dillon down next time. If there was a next time.

As Dillon continued to share numbers as proof for why Amavita Estates would be a good fit, George's eyes glassed over. He smiled and nodded, laughing even when Dillon said something funny, but he was disengaged. It was only a matter of time before he politely showed them to the door. Rejected by a reject.

Leo wanted to pull Dillon aside and tell him they needed to do something different, but Dillon kept going. He didn't stop talking. For twenty minutes, he droned on and on, leaving Leo and George to do nothing but listen.

With nothing to lose, Leo reached in front of his brother and grabbed the bag of wine they brought. He pulled out the Sangiovese, a wine that was a risk since it wasn't as popular as Riesling in the area, but it was a damn good wine. He quickly stripped the foil aside and uncorked the bottle, setting it on the desk to breathe for a few minutes.

Dillon kept talking while Leo opened the other bottles of wine they brought. A Riesling, merlot, and Gewurztraminer. All bottled in the last few months, and all selling well at the vineyard.

"What are you doing?" Dillon finally asked, hissing at Leo and forcing an apologetic smile at George.

Leo shrugged. "I figured we can tell George all the facts and statistics we want, but what really matters is how good the wine is. Now, George, this first one is our Riesling. It's a little different from the other local Rieslings because it's a little sweeter taste. We don't add sugar to it, but the grapes come through in a strong, crisp flavor that makes it taste sweet. Like most vineyards in the area, we produce more Riesling than anything else, but like Dillon said, we have a variety of wines. Still, we'd be remiss not to bring you a Riesling."

George took the glass and swirled the wine, catching it on the edges of the glass. He watched the legs as it slid down to pool in the tasting sip Leo poured. He brought the glass to his nose and inhaled deeply, then sipped it, bringing in air with the wine to get the full flavor.

George's eyebrows show up. "That does taste sweet. And compared to most dry Rieslings, it's very pleasant. I like that."

Leo nodded and accepted the glass back from George, rinsing it with the bottle of water he packed for just that purpose. He moved to the merlot and poured a taste of that.

"Merlot," Leo said. "It's rich and earthy. Goes great with a bowl of pasta, but is also a good wine to drink with friends. Tannins can get you, but most people don't struggle too much with this wine that we've heard. Our cousin Kristen says it's her favorite and she's never had trouble. Of course, Kristen, like the rest of us, has been tasting wine since she was far too young since our grandparents are from Italy."

George grinned and repeated his swirling process before he sipped the wine. "It has an oaky flavor to it, but light. Some merlot can be very heavy. It even has a lighter color, instead of looking like it's a bottle of ink."

Leo nodded. "That honor can go to the Sangiovese. Ours is heavy, like a Sangiovese should be, but the blackberry undertones give it a fruity flavor that balances out the weight of it."

George finished his merlot while Leo talked about the Sangiovese, then handed over his glass for a refill. His first sip had him closing his eyes.

"This reminds me of a week I spent in Italy. Beautiful country. Have you ever been?"

Leo nodded. "In high school, yes. Our mom wanted to take a trip and see where her parents were from. It was a little insane, but the whole family went back. All seventeen of us. Italy is a stunning country. The area my grandparents lived was in Northern Italy, so we spent most of our time there. Met a lot of distant relatives."

"Northern Italy is beautiful. We spent some time up there and went to the Vatican. We drank far too much wine, and ate far too much pasta, and spent far too much money, but it was the trip of a lifetime." He paused and stared at the bottle. "Would you mind if I kept this? I'd like to share it with my wife."

Leo grinned. "Absolutely. I hope you both enjoy it."

"Thank you." George finished his Sangiovese and handed his glass over for the last wine.

"Our Gewurztraminer. Sweet wine, of course, with lots of fruity flavors. High Brix. We try not to add sugar, but there are years we have to. This particular one has sugar added, but the grapes are sweet to taste right off the vine. We're one of the only local vineyards that are able to produce this wine because of our location on the lake. And we have a good bit of it, enough that we could comfortably stock some shelves."

George tasted it and nodded. "That's definitely sweet. I'm not a sweet drinker, but I can appreciate how good it is."

Leo nodded. "I don't do a lot of sweet wines either. The Sangiovese is my favorite. I keep at least a bottle of that in my home at all times. But all our wines have a customer base."

"And you'd be able to keep up with distribution demands?" George asked.

Leo nodded. "Of course. Like Dillon said, some demands are more easily met than others, but we don't see any issues. We know what we're getting into. And we're looking to expand. It's in the plans for the next three-to-five years. We've started searching for available properties, but are ideally looking for an established vineyard that's looking to sell. One that is in good shape, but maybe a family business that doesn't have anyone interested in continuing with it."

"Isn't that how your family got Amavita?"

Leo nodded. "It is. Our grandparents both worked there for years, but when the previous owners decided to retire, they had no children to pass it on to, so they gave our grand-parents the first opportunity to buy it."

"I'd say that worked out for your family," George said.

Leo grinned. "Absolutely."

George smiled and stared at the bottles for a long moment. Not wanting to push too hard, Leo sat silently, waiting for George to say something.

When George looked up, his eyes went between the two of them. "We'd be crazy to pass this opportunity up. You two clearly love what you do, and your wine is top notch. I don't know why we wouldn't work with you. I'll have Darren draw up a contract and we'll move forward. Hopefully have your wines in the stores by the end of the third quarter, if that works for you."

Dillon nodded and stood, offering his hand to George. "Absolutely. Thank you. We're very grateful for the opportunity."

Leo stood and did the same, thanking George for his time.

"What are you going to do with these bottles?" George asked as Leo slid them back into the bag.

Leo grinned. "You're welcome to them all, if you'd like. And the bag as well."

"Yeah?"

Leo nodded. "Absolutely. Enjoy."

George smiled broadly. "Thanks. I will."

Leo managed to walk out of the building before he lost it. Dillon was calm, cool, and collected, but as soon as they were outside, Leo let out a loud, "Whoop!"

Dillon smiled, scanning through something on his phone. "Holy shit."

"What?"

"George is Darren's boss."

"What?" Leo asked.

"He's Darren's boss. I thought he was an assistant or something, but he's in charge. He's the guy who makes decisions. Darren would have had to go through him to offer us a contract, but you sealed the deal with George directly."

"He's the boss?" Leo asked again. He threw caution to the wind and spouted off whatever he could think of to try to get George to buy their wines. He was himself, selling George the same way he sells customers every day in the tasting room. And instead of sinking, like he thought he would, he sold to the boss.

"I've never met George, and I've never sold anything through the FLDI. Congrats, little brother."

"Hell, yeah," Leo said, pumping his fist. He did it. He actually did it. It felt good to use his bartender skills. To show Dillon how good he was at his job. He took what he'd learned over years of talking to customers and turned it into a new lucrative partnership for Amavita Estates.

"I knew I picked the right one as the next CEO," Dillon said.

"What?" Leo blurted, his euphoria dissipating.

Dillon pulled out of the parking lot and glanced at Leo. "The next CEO. I can't possibly do it if I'm traveling with Katherine. I'll miss too much. That's the only option."

"Why? You do most of your work from your computer. Why would it be any different? And Katherine won't be touring forever. You should keep your title."

Dillon shook his head. "We'll see, little brother, but I think you're the easy answer. You already proved you can do things I can't do. Why stop with this? You're a natural."

Leo wanted to agree with Dillon, but the only reason he was a natural was because he'd been doing the exact same thing for years. It didn't matter who a person was when they sat or stood on the opposite side of the bar from Leo. He looked at a person and knew what they needed, then he delivered it to them. It had nothing to do with training or skills or education and everything to do with practice reading people.

But Dillon still saw the tasting room as a job anyone could do.

"If I take over, what are we going to do with the tasting

room? Kristen's barely in there anymore, and if I'm playing CEO all the time, there won't be any family in there."

Dillon shrugged. "It'll be fine. We don't always have family available to run it."

"Yeah, but when Kristen and I worked there, one of us was always on. Now, I'm still there most days. Without either of us, I worry people won't get the same experience. They come to Amavita because we're a local, family owned vineyard. Not because we're a machine chugging out product. They want us. They want to know who they're buying from. I don't know if hiring people will have the same impact."

Dillon shrugged again. "Maybe, maybe not. But hey, you'll be in charge, so you can make sure they do. You can do the training for new employees. In fact you probably should anyway." He pulled out his phone and recorded a message for himself to have Leo create a training program for all new tasting room employees.

Leo just sat back and watched the lake fly by. It didn't matter what he wanted or what he thought. Dillon was in charge, and Leo would do what he needed to do to help his family. Even if it meant a job he didn't love.

12

——————

Sara was trying to shake her mood all day. It had been building all week, but she was fighting it. There was no way for her to ignore or avoid what day it was.

After she fixed dinner, she sat on her couch and debated going out. The silence was driving her crazy, but going to a bar didn't appeal. It wasn't a night she wanted to be around a lot of people, but she didn't want to be alone either.

She sent a text to Peter, but he was busy. Her next text was to Leo.

What are you doing tonight?

Celebrating my win today.

Oh, okay. Have fun.

Want to come over?

No. Thanks. Sorry to bother you.

Feeling even more alone, Sara drew a deep breath. She

went to her freezer for ice cream and groaned when she found it empty. She slammed the freezer shut and spun around, her gaze landing on the wine she bought weeks ago from Leo.

Across the room, her phone rang, dragging her attention away from the wine and the empty room around her. She knew it was her dad, so she answered without looking.

"Hi, Dad."

"Hi, honey." He sounded like she felt. Beaten, worn, abused.

"How are you doing tonight?"

"Ten years."

"Yeah," Sara agreed. She took another breath, hating how tight her chest felt.

"I went to see her," her dad said.

"What?"

He sighed. "I went to her grave today. I went to see your mom. It's been ten years."

"Why? I don't know why we do any of this. Why we give her this one day to destroy us all over again every year. It's so stupid."

"Because she was your mother and I still love her, dammit."

Sara froze at the anger in her father's voice. He never raised his voice. Not when she was little and not as she got older. She had no memories of him ever yelling at her.

Until that moment.

"Dad—"

"No, Sara. I know I wasn't the best dad. I know I wasn't there for you when she was gone. I tried to be a good father, but I didn't know how to be there for you. And when we found out...I wasn't a good dad for you, and I'm sorry. But

God help me, I still love her. I always will, Sara. And I know you don't understand that, but she was the love of my life. I hope one day you can accept it."

Sara couldn't breathe past the lump in her throat. She tried to say something, but nothing came out. A sob struggled free, catching her by surprise. She clamped a hand over her mouth and tried to stifle the emotion overflowing from her.

"I'm sorry, Sara. I'm sorry I upset you so much. I wasn't trying to."

"It's fine, Dad. I just...um, I have to go. I'll talk to you tomorrow or something, okay? Bye, Dad."

He tried to say something, but Sara couldn't wait for it and hung up. She set the phone down and closed her eyes. She cried enough tears for her mother. She wasn't going to waste any more on a woman who never loved her enough.

Sara wiped her cheeks and stomped to the box in the corner of her kitchen with the wine. She grabbed a bottle, not caring which bottle it was, and set it on the counter. She opened the wine and poured the dark red liquid into a glass, filling it almost all the way to the top.

She took a healthy sip, then another. She would regret it in the morning, but at that moment, she wanted to drink and forget.

A knock on the door startled her. She went to peek out and was surprised to find Leo standing on her doorstep.

"What are you doing here? Did you leave your party?" she asked as she opened the door.

He shook his head and studied her carefully. "There was no party. I was trying to tell you that, but you stopped responding."

"So you came over here?"

He shrugged and stepped inside. "I wanted you to know that I was being sarcastic when I said I was celebrating. I wasn't in the middle of a party. I didn't have people over. I was just drinking a beer alone and wanting to call you."

"You were?" she asked.

He nodded, closing the door behind himself. He moved closer to her. "Are you okay?"

She nodded then shook her head. "It's a rough day."

"Do you want to talk about it?"

She shook her head again, slowly.

"Do you want to do something else?"

She nodded.

He stepped closer until she could feel his body heat. "Do you want me to kiss you?"

She nodded.

He didn't hesitate, sealing his lips over hers and stealing her breath away. She pulled him close, letting herself get lost in him. She needed him. She needed them.

Sara wrapped her arms around his neck and held him close. He guided her back, the two of them moving through her tiny apartment, kissing and tugging on each other's clothes.

They pulled apart to remove her shirt, then came back together again, tongues and lips and hands searching for each other. The kiss was sloppy, uncoordinated, but exactly what Sara needed.

She grabbed the edge of his shirt and tugged it up, dragging her hands over his chest. He groaned and tilted his head, thrusting his tongue deeper into her mouth. He pressed a firm hand to the middle of her back, sealing them head to toe, skin to skin, and heart to heart.

His other hand came up, cupping her breast and teasing

her nipple through the cotton of her bra. She wished, for a second, that she picked something sexier, but she dismissed the idea as quickly as it appeared in her mind. Leo didn't care what her panties or bra looked like. It wouldn't matter once they were on the floor anyway.

She roamed his body with her hands, learning and relearning him. He moaned when she grazed his nipple with her nails, and pressed his body to hers when she cupped his ass and squeezed. He ground his erection into her stomach, almost as if he needed to be close to her as much as she needed to be close to him.

Leo pulled back and looked at her, his eyes searching her face. She didn't know what he was looking for or what he saw, but his gaze softened before he stripped off his shirt and pressed himself to her again.

Skin to skin, they made out like horny teenagers, neither of them in a hurry to move things to the next level. He kissed her like she'd always dreamed of being kissed, like she mattered. For a second, she let herself get lost in him and their kiss, forgetting what sent her into his arms, into his world.

Then it wasn't enough. She needed more. She needed the bliss of oblivion, a bliss she could only get once they were both naked and he was inside her.

She reached for the button on his shorts and worked his zipper down. He kicked out of them and went back to her breasts, cupping them both and teasing her nipples before he slid his hands around her back and set them free.

She dropped her bra to the ground as he teased her closer and closer to her first orgasm. She moaned against his lips, wanting him to get her there as quickly as possible.

He pulled back again, smiling at her as he lowered his

mouth to her breasts. One nipple disappeared between his lips, his open mouth taking all of it in. She watched him work, his lashes sealing off his eyes to her. His jaw twitched with his movements, rolling her nipple around, pressing it to the roof of his mouth, and drawing it out only to take a bite and pull it back in again.

Sara's eyes fell closed, her orgasm racing toward her. She held his head in place, needing, wanting, demanding more from him. He lived up to his end of the bargain and urged her to straddle his leg. The friction was enough to help her up, up, up, and over, and she came with a tremor that made her want more.

"Did you buy a table?" he asked, pulling back just enough that her nipple fell out of his mouth. He kissed her breast, working his way to her other one.

She nodded. "I wanted to make sure sex was on the table."

He laughed and stood, his lips even with hers. "I fucking love that."

She laughed with him, feeling lighter, freer, more alive than she had all day. She'd never known a man who could make her laugh as much as Leo did. Who could distract her from everything going on in her world as easily as him. She needed more people like that in her life.

"You know we have to use it, right?" he said.

She nodded again. "I was hoping so."

He pulled her to the table with him and gave the heavy wood top a shake. When it didn't move, he raised his eyebrows. "Feels pretty solid."

She slid her hand over his erection and nodded. "I was thinking the same thing."

He grabbed her around the waist and tossed her onto

the table. She squealed, laughing at the look on his face. Part annoyed, part amused, and all hot as fuck.

"My dick is solid as fuck. You don't have to worry about that."

She grinned. "I'll take a solid fuck right about now."

He laughed and kissed her again, tilting her head back with a gentle tug on her hair. She felt vulnerable in that position, him towering above her as she perched on the edge of her new table. She hadn't gotten around to buying chairs since sitting at a table alone felt even more depressing than sitting on her couch alone, but she didn't buy the table to eat at. She bought it for the exact reason she was using it.

Sex.

On the table.

With Leo.

~

LEO SETTLED between her thighs and kissed her until he forgot everything outside of Sara. He was consumed by her. Needing her, wanting her, pleasuring her. It was all about Sara.

He threw himself into the task, knowing she was as messed up by the day she had as he was. It didn't matter why. He wasn't going to ask no matter how badly he wanted to. He was just going to give her what he had to give. His body.

Her hard nipples brushed against his chest, making sure he hadn't forgotten about the beautiful, sexy woman making him insane. He toyed with her hair and tilted her head where he wanted it. She groaned when he pressed his cock against her sex, so he did it again, and her thighs tightened around him.

He wasn't going to be able to wait much longer to sink into her, but he wanted to taste her first.

He kissed his way down her body, teasing her by avoiding her nipples and the spot just to the left of her belly button. He kissed her thighs and nipped at the flesh near her knee. He pressed her legs apart, watching her reaction when he settled on his knees in front of her.

"I need these off," he said, running his fingertip along the edge of her shorts.

She nodded and leaned back on her elbows. He tugged at the stretchy waistband and helped her rock from side-to-side so he could pull her shorts and panties out from under her then down her legs.

She sat on her table, her sex bare and open for him. He took a deep breath, watching as she nibbled on her lip and waited to see what he would do. He moved closer, kissing her thighs and massaging her skin. The whole time, she watched him, her gaze never leaving his.

When he reached her center, she drew in a breath and held it. She was nervous, but he wasn't sure why.

"You're perfect," he whispered before reaching his tongue out to run along her slit. "Mmm, so good."

She released her breath with a shudder that said she was on board.

He eased his way in, licking and tasting her, learning what had her hands gripping the edge of the table and what sent her hips right off it.

A lick, a suck, a flick of his tongue, and she was reaching for his head. "More," she whispered.

Leo smiled and did it again, and again, and again. Then he slid two fingers into her and sent her flying. She cried out his name, begging him not to stop.

He added a third finger and repeated the process,

needing to feel her again. His cock ached to be inside her, but he was having far too much fun making her lose her mind. He flicked her clit with the very tip of his tongue until she gasped, all her air rushing from her lungs as she chased her orgasm. Then he sucked hard on her and thrust his fingers deep inside, sending her over the edge.

"Oh, God. Yes. Oh, God. Leo, Leo, Leo. Yes!"

He swirled his tongue around her again, ready for one more, when she tugged at him, dragging him up. He pulled back, loving the blissful look on her face. Her cheeks were pink, her lips wet and plump from her nibbling on them. Her eyes were glassy from the orgasms he gave her, but they were locked on his, asking for more.

"Inside me, Leo. Please. I want you inside. Hard. Now."

He stripped out of his shorts and rolled a condom on. She watched his every move, licking her lips and tugging one between her teeth. When he stood and met her gaze, she drew in a breath.

He could see it in her eyes. She needed him to take control, to make her lose it. She needed him to make her come harder than she ever had before, and she needed it immediately.

He yanked her to the edge of the table, spreading her thighs wide with his hips and thrusting into her all in one move. She gasped and moaned his name, her body trembling in anticipation.

Leo pulled back, drawing her with him so she was perched on the very edge, her ass nearly hanging off the table. He took her hands and set them next to her hips, wrapping her fingers around the edge.

"Don't let go," he said roughly.

She nodded, a flush rising from her breasts to her cheeks at his firm words.

"Let's see how strong this table really is," Leo said, slamming into her.

She moaned, her thighs tightening on his hips. "Oh, yes."

Leo drew back until he almost slid out, then slammed into her again, hard enough to shift the table. He grabbed her breasts, using them as an anchor, and did it again. Draw back, drive home. Draw back, drive home.

Sara held on to the table, her knuckles turning white as he fucked her hard. She watched him, her eyes dark and full of desire. With each thrust, her eyes slid closed, then snapped open as he withdrew.

Leo wanted to last forever, to feel her body pulsing around his for days. But she felt far too good. He wasn't going to outlast her unless he gave her a little help.

"Touch yourself, Sara."

"I thought I had to hold on to the table."

"Use one hand to get yourself off, and the other to hold the table."

She shook her head. "I'm close. I want to feel you. Just you."

"Lay back, on your elbows," Leo said.

She did as he asked without hesitation, holding his gaze with hers. Trusting him to take her where she needed to go.

The new angle let him thrust deeper, hit her where she needed him. She gasped on the first stroke, her body tightening around his cock. He kept going, even as his thighs slammed into the edge of the table and the need to come raced down his spine and settled in his balls. Harder and harder he drove into her, pushing her body until it had no choice but to bend to his will and let go.

"Yes, yes, yes. Oh, fuck me, yes. Leo. Oh, God, Leo. Yes!"

She screamed his name, her sex locking down around

him and refusing to let him withdraw again. Shallow thrusts were all he needed to push himself into the same bliss she was in. A place where his future job didn't exist and all that he cared about was Sara. Sara screaming his name. Sara reaching for him. Sara wanting him when she was lonely.

Sara.

13

When they were both cleaned up, Sara sat on her couch in only her tee, Leo in just his shorts. He did that sexy thing guys did where he zipped them but didn't bother with the button so they hung low on his hips and teased her.

He always looked effortlessly sexy, which drove her mad in the best possible way.

They turned on the TV and let it play, but she had a feeling neither of them were really paying attention. She rested against his side, his arm draped over her shoulders. He absently rubbed his thumb under the sleeve of her shirt while she let her mind wander.

"Thank you for coming over."

He squeezed her arm. "I'm glad I did. This was much better than the pity party I was having."

"Why were you having a pity party?"

He shrugged and hesitated, which about killed her. Just because she didn't plan to stick around didn't mean they couldn't talk and get to know each other.

A rule she wrote but wanted to break.

"I went to a meeting with my brother today. He's the

CEO, but he's...well, long story, but he's not going to be around for a month and wants me to take over."

"And you suck?" she asked.

He chuckled at her blunt assessment, but he shook his head. "The opposite actually. The meeting we had today was with a local distribution company. Dillon's met with them before and always been turned down for distributing into the local liquor stores, but the guy we talked to liked my pitch."

"Wow, that's great news. Um, or not."

Leo shook his head. "It is. It's great for the vineyard and for the long term viability of our wines. If we're established as a local brand, it's better. We've been selling exclusively through our own store forever, but opening us up to sell to stores means we can go through with the expansion plans we've been talking about."

Sara sat up and looked at him. "Okay, I don't know much about running a business, but I'm failing to see why any of this is bad."

Leo laughed softly. "It's not bad. Not for business, not for my family, not for me. But it's not what I want."

"It's not?"

He shook his head. "No. I've been in the tasting room forever, and I love it there. I sell every day to people. I talk complete strangers into trying wines they never would have tried. And I'm good at it. That's all I did today. I talked to the guy like he was any other customer."

"Like me?"

Leo leaned in and kissed her, pulling back just enough to meet her gaze. "You are not any other customer. You never have been."

She smiled, his sweet words warming her.

"My point is, Dillon went all gaga about me landing this

deal, saying he knew he picked the right person to be the next CEO and he can count on me and all this, and I don't know if I can do it."

"I think you can do anything," Sara said honestly. "You're an amazing guy, and there's no reason you can't do this. I think your brother absolutely chose the right person for the job. How could you ever doubt yourself?"

He shrugged. "It's hard to wrap my head around, I guess."

"Do you want the job?" Sara asked.

He hesitated.

"Is that the real problem?"

He shrugged, avoiding her gaze.

"You need to do what's best for you."

He opened his mouth, then closed it again. He stared off. He was still touching her, but he was clearly miles away.

Sara took a deep breath. "My mom died ten years ago today."

"What?" he blurted.

Sara nodded. "She was in Portland, Oregon, in a small town outside the city known for their vineyards. She had a husband and two step-daughters and was on the way home to them from the grocery store when she was in a car accident and killed."

"Wait, what?"

"My mom had a secret family that my dad and I didn't know about until she died. She was raising his kids, his daughters, and living with a man when my dad thought she was on business trips. I guess she was on business trips, but she had a life there, too. One we were in the dark about. When she died, the police found her Montana license first and called my dad. Her other husband found out about her accident and lost it when they told him she had another license and another husband, one who was married to her first and had a kid."

"Holy shit," Leo breathed.

Sara nodded. "Yeah. So, I don't stay put for long because it's easier for me to leave than it is for me to be left behind. I can handle walking away."

"Sara," he said softly.

She shook her head. "It's what's best for me. I don't want to be like my mother and get attached. She couldn't decide between her two families, so in the end, she destroyed all of us. It wasn't fair to my dad and me, but it wasn't fair to her other family either. I hated them for a long time, but she was the one who couldn't choose."

"I'm sorry."

Sara nodded. "Thanks. And I really think if being the CEO isn't right for you, you shouldn't do it. You should keep working in the tasting room. You probably sell more wine in there than you could in meetings."

Leo laughed and nodded. "You're probably right. I just have to find the right way to tell my brother."

"He's your brother. He'll understand."

Leo nodded. "I hope so."

BAILING on Dillon at the last minute felt like a shitty thing to do, so Leo decided to wait until he got back from his month away to tell Dillon he didn't want to be a CEO. That way he could say he really gave it a shot and not feel bad about backing out.

His first official day was Sunday, when they had the picnic. He'd talked to Sara every day since the night she told him about her mom, and they'd gotten together a couple of times, but she still didn't want to go to one of the picnics. She said it felt too much like a couple thing, and if he was working, she'd be sitting by herself anyway. He compromised by agreeing to go to her place for dinner, but he was hoping they could go for a bed instead of the table after. His thighs still hurt.

Leo walked around the picnic in his golf shirt and khakis, feeling like an ass for not helping out behind the bar. Dillon told him he needed to be seen, to greet their guests, since he was the CEO for the next month.

Leo had been attending picnics for as long as he could remember, and most of the locals were people he recognized. The mayor showed up, chatting with Leo about the rain they'd had early in the year and how they were looking for harvest. Good, so far. The volunteer fire chief asked if they'd had all the smoke detectors at the inn checked recently and if they had fire extinguishers on hand in case of an emergency. Yes to both. And the manager of the visitor's center asked if there were new brochures available for the vineyard as they were running low and wanted to make sure they could send people to Amavita Estates. Absolutely.

Most of the guests had eaten and were mingling on the back patio by the time Leo found a seat next to Nonna to scarf down a plate of food.

"You should have eaten before the guests were let in the door," Nonna said, patting his hand. She sipped her wine and grinned at him.

"I was making sure the new tasting room employees were up to speed on everything," Leo explained around a bite of lasagna.

Nonna shook her head. "You can't do everything, Leo. That's why your cousins and siblings are here. This is not a one man show."

"I know, Nonna, but everyone is busy on Sundays. It's always a madhouse around here."

She nodded. "True, but you'll pass out if you don't take care of yourself. Next Sunday, make sure you have a plate of food before the doors open. And keep a glass of water with you so you aren't looking for one all day."

"How did you know?" he asked with a laugh.

She grinned. "You forget I used to do the same thing you are now. It feels like a long time ago, but I was the hostess once upon a time."

"So, I have you to blame for being so exhausted I might pass out?"

She laughed. "Yes, I guess you do. After all, if your grandfather and I hadn't moved here, we wouldn't have all this." She looked around, smiling at the vineyard and the crowd. "I love it here."

Leo nodded. "We all do. I don't know how Dillon is walking away."

"He'll be back. And one day, Katherine will be here, too. She loves it here." Nonna wiped her mouth and set her napkin back on her lap. Her coral dress matched the lipstick she wiped off, making Leo grin. His grandmother was an amazing woman with her own unique style.

"Yeah, but she loves her career, too," Leo said. He loved Katherine, but he was struggling not to resent her career pulling Dillon away from his.

"And she should," Nonna said firmly. "Women should have something that makes them happy. For some women, that's raising kids and running a household, for others it's a career, for others still, it's some combination of the two or maybe something else entirely. There's no one path."

Leo nodded, feeling appropriately chagrined. "True, and I wouldn't want Katherine to give up what she loves."

"But it doesn't make it easier on you."

Leo glanced at his grandmother and laughed. "I'm that transparent?"

She shook her head. "Just to me. I told you, I know you, Leo. You're a kind, wonderful man. But that doesn't mean you aren't human."

Leo took a deep breath. "I'm a horrible person."

She patted his cheek, like she'd done a thousand times when he was younger. He closed his eyes and let the feeling make him feel like a kid again, when life was simple and he didn't have a care in the world.

"You're not horrible," Nonna said. "And you shouldn't feel guilty for being worn out. You need some time for yourself. Where is that girl of yours? I keep hoping she'll come to one of these."

So much for simple. Things couldn't get much more complicated than they were with Sara. Leo shoved another bite of his lunch into his mouth in order to stall while he thought up something that would appease his grandmother so she didn't hate Sara if they ever met.

"Quit stalling," Nonna said firmly.

Leo pursed his lips and swallowed. "Fine. She's not coming."

"Have you invited her?" Nonna asked with a raised eyebrow.

"Yes, but she doesn't want things to get messy between us."

"And coming here for lunch would be messy?"

Leo shook his head. "Coming here for lunch when I'm basically working the whole time and she has to spend the day with my insane family who would pump her for information she doesn't want to share would be messy."

"Why doesn't she want to share information?"

"Because she's a private person. She's only here for a few months, and we're just...having fun. We're not going to get married or be together longer than a couple months. She's just trying to stay distant."

"Distant isn't a good thing, Leo. Are you sure this woman is right for you?"

"I know it's temporary, Nonna. I like her, but she was clear from the beginning that she's leaving soon. It's not worth it to get attached or try to convince her to stay. It'll end badly."

"And you don't think it'll end badly this way?" Nonna asked.

Leo took a breath and fought back the urge to yell at his grandmother. He knew it was going to end badly. He liked Sara. More than he should. But she was leaving. He knew she was leaving. She made it clear, especially when she was talking about her mother, that staying wasn't an option. He wasn't going to push it and have her resent him.

"What will end badly?" Peter asked, joining Leo and Nonna. He kissed Nonna's cheek.

"When did you get here?" Nonna asked.

"I just brought Grandma. She's talking to Aunt Marie," Peter said.

Nonna glanced to where he indicated and smiled. "I'm going to go say hello. We can finish talking later."

Leo nodded, already plotting how he could avoid his grandmother until Sara left town.

"What was that all about?" Peter asked, stealing a meatball off Leo's plate.

"Nothing. Where's the woman of your dreams?"

Peter grinned but it fell flat. "She didn't want to come to a party. I tried to tell her it was a casual thing, but when I mentioned Grandma being with me, she went from maybe to hell no."

Leo snorted. "I know how that goes. How are things with her?"

Peter shrugged and averted his gaze. Leo could tell something was up with his best friend, and chances were good it had to do with his dream woman.

Peter ran a hand through his blond hair. His pale blue Polo shirt made him look like a frat boy, one that couldn't leave the frat and was still hanging out there after ten years. No doubt he was also wearing khaki shorts and boat shoes. Leo nearly laughed, but the pained look in his friend's eyes had him holding back.

"What's wrong?"

Peter shrugged again. "She keeps saying we're friends. We've gone out a bunch, and I think she wants more, but she's scared or something."

"That sucks. Why don't you just cut her loose and move on?"

He shook his head. "I can't. Not with her. I like her too much. And I know she's worth it, but I need to convince her that we should be together."

Leo chuckled knowing he was about to offer similar advice as what he'd just gotten from Nonna. "You shouldn't have to convince her. It should just work. If she doesn't want to be with you, don't kill yourself for it."

"And when did you become the expert in women?"

Leo shook his head. "Nonna just told me basically the same thing."

"Are you seeing someone?"

Leo nodded. "Sleeping with, really. She's amazing, but she's made it clear it's just sex. I kind of wish I had a little of what you have. Although she did open up to me the other day."

"We should get our women together. Sara doesn't know that many people in the area and doesn't seem to want to get too attached to anyone. Maybe seeing you with your woman will make her want to get a little frisky."

"Sara?" Leo asked.

Peter nodded. "Yeah, I told you that when I met her. She just moved here. Only here for the summer, but I'm hoping I can talk her into staying longer. She's great. You'll really like her."

Leo nodded, feeling sick.

"I'm going to grab some food. Then we can talk about how to get our ladies together and make it work out in our favor. I'll be right back."

Leo nodded as Peter left. It wasn't possible, was it? Peter's Sara couldn't be Leo's Sara, could it?

Two women moved to town around the same time. Two women who weren't sticking around past summer. Two women named Sara.

Leo watched his best friend across the room, filling a plate with food and talking to everyone. Peter's family had been a part of Bereton as long as Leo's family. Their grandmothers were best friends.

In all that time, Leo and Peter only liked the same girl at the same time once. It didn't end well, so they always made a deal and one of them always called dibs. Crude, but it worked.

Until they met the same woman the same day and neither realized it. Leo met Sara at the vineyard, and Peter talked about meeting her that night. But Leo didn't say anything to Peter about her. He didn't think he'd see her again.

But now he was sleeping with her while Peter dated her. Both of them had a piece of the same dream woman, but neither got all of her. They were sharing her, without knowing it.

And Leo felt like a first class asshole for it.

The last time he went for a woman someone close to him had a thing for was when he hit on Katherine after she'd slept with Dillon. Leo seriously doubted himself after that. He didn't want a woman to come between him and his brother, and he definitely didn't want one to come between him and his best friend.

Which meant finding out for sure if it was the same Sara. Then choosing. Him or Peter.

14

Sara settled into what had become her chair for lunch at Lakeside Glass. She stopped packing her own lunch after a couple weeks when she realized Adam always had enough food for all of them, and his food was always better than what she had.

She also had gotten into the habit of giving him cash every week to help pay for his groceries. Since they were benefiting her, she thought it was only fair. He argued, every time, but she didn't back down. She was not willing to take handouts. Even from people she considered friends.

"What's for lunch today?" Megan asked, joining them in the small room.

Megan was wearing her boots, but she left her coveralls in the back so she was only in short black shorts and a black tank top. Adam's eyes slid down her body, and Sara averted her gaze to stop invading what felt like a private moment. A private moment Megan was unaware of.

She really needed to talk to her boss again.

"It's Greek chicken pasta salad," Sara said, saving Adam before he got busted.

He looked up at her, guilt in his eyes. She smiled in return, understanding how he felt. She was the same way around Leo. She wanted him, but she didn't know how to tell him. The sex was great, but talking to him about her mom made her want to spend more time with him. She liked him. A lot. And she knew it was dangerous for her to open up, but she couldn't stop the desire to do just that.

"It sounds great. Hot or cold?" Megan asked.

"Cold," Adam said, flashing her a grin. "I'm just getting it dished out so we can eat. It's so hot outside that I thought something that wasn't too heavy would be good."

Megan rubbed her round belly. "I'm heavy enough without the extra food."

"You're perfect," Adam grumbled. "You don't need to change a thing."

Megan looked up at his words, but he wasn't looking at her.

Sara always felt like a third wheel with the two of them. She wanted to tell them to just have sex and get the tension over with, but they both resisted. They both thought the other was going to say no, and it didn't matter how many times she assured them it wasn't the case.

"I always feel full faster in the hotter climates," Sara said. "I think something like this is going to be perfect."

Adam smiled in thanks and handed out heaping bowls of lunch to her and Megan. The three of them sat, digging in.

The feta cheese was the first thing Sara tasted, followed by the Greek dressing. Both blended together in a match that had her diving back in for more before she even finished chewing her first bite.

The fresh tomatoes, cucumber, and orange peppers brought a lightness to it while adding a crispy crunch and sweet flavors. The pasta held the sauce and acted as a vehicle to deliver everything to her palette.

"Wow, this is good," Megan groaned. "I don't ever cook like this. I need to get this recipe from you. It'll impress my parents."

"Your parents?" Sara asked.

Megan nodded. "They're coming over for dinner this weekend. I'm panicking. We don't see them much, but since Anna is finishing up school soon, they wanted to see us."

"I thought she had another semester," Sara clarified.

Megan rolled her eyes. "My parents don't visit us often. My relationship with them was never great, but when I got pregnant, they pulled back even more. They love Anna, but it's hard since they're very religious and feel like I should never have gotten pregnant."

"Ouch."

"Yeah. But it's okay. It's been years. But when they say they want to get together, Anna and I do everything we can to clear our schedules." Megan forked another bite and chewed. "Hey, you guys should come."

"And be the buffer? I don't think so," Sara said. "I have enough of my own family drama."

Megan pleaded, "Oh, come on. Seeing my messed up family will remind you yours isn't so bad."

"Wanna bet?"

"What's so bad about your family?" Adam asked.

Sara realized what she was saying and shook her head. "Nothing. I'm just being overly dramatic. Don't we all have crazy families?"

Adam shrugged. "Mine is pretty great. My parents have always been supportive. I'm the oldest of three, and I get along well with my sisters."

Megan and Sara shared a look. "Never mind," Megan said. "You're not invited."

Adam shrugged. "That's fine. I was going to offer to cook for you."

"Really?"

He nodded.

"Okay, you can come. Sara?"

"I don't cook like this."

"No, but you're funny and kind and will keep my parents from thinking Adam is my new boy toy."

"Excuse me?" Sara blurted, her water nearly coming out of her nose.

"They always think I'm going to end up pregnant again. If it's me, Anna, and Adam, they're going to think I'm sleeping with Adam, but if you're there too, they'll know it's just because I wanted my friends to meet my parents."

"Or they'll think you're sleeping with both of us," Sara said.

Megan laughed. "I never thought of that."

Sara smirked.

"I don't think I'll ever make my parents happy, but at some point I need to stop trying. I need to be happy myself, and if they can't accept that, then it doesn't matter."

"What's not to be happy about?" Sara asked.

Megan grinned. "They want me to get married. Settle down. Stop working so many hours. I had no choice when Anna was younger, but my parents think I need to slow down since Anna's almost done with school. They also think I should have more kids."

Adam was suspiciously quiet during the conversation. Sara glanced at him, noticing his jaw twitching.

"Do you want more kids?"

Megan slid a look at Adam and shook her head. "No. I've raised my daughter. I'm too old to start over with more kids."

Sara finally got it.

"What about you, Adam? Do you want kids?"

He shook his head. "I never saw myself with a family. A wife would be nice, but kids weren't part of my plan."

"Me, too. Although I don't want the wife, or a husband. I'm happy alone."

"Are you?" Megan asked pointedly.

Sara nodded. "Of course."

"Is that why you and Leo have been getting closer?"

Sara scoffed. "Leo and I are just having fun. Like I told you before. He knows what we have isn't going to last forever."

"If you say so," Megan said with a wink.

Sara couldn't admit there was a part of her that wanted to imagine a future with Leo. That wanted to think about settling down and building a life with him. But she couldn't. She wouldn't let herself. She was too afraid of becoming her mother. Wanting more than she could have and not being able to choose. She wouldn't do it. To herself or anyone else.

LEO WAS IN THE OFFICE, nose deep in approving budgets for the next month, when his phone rang. He dug it out of his pocket and saw Ryan was calling him.

"Yeah?"

"You busy?" Ryan asked.

Leo looked at the computer screen, which was stacked four deep, with budgets to review and approve. Busy didn't even begin to explain his day.

"What do you need?"

"We think we have black rot. Two rows near the lake."

Leo was on his feet before Ryan even finished speaking. "I'm on my way."

One of the golf carts was outside, so Leo jumped on it, texting Andie that he took it in case whoever left it there goes looking. She sent him a text back that she was the one who drove it and she didn't need it.

Leo went out to where Ryan said they were and stopped at the end of a row. Ryan and Henry weren't visible down the row, so Leo walked toward the lake until he found his cousins, huddled over a vine.

"What do we have?" Leo asked.

Ryan stepped back so Leo could look at it. The brown patches on the leaves were the death of a vineyard if it went untreated.

"Fuck. How bad?"

"This row and the one next to it. We're checking everything around here," Henry said.

"This could be it?"

Ryan nodded. "We're hoping, but we can't take that chance. We have to treat everything in this area, just in case. Once it's in, we're done. These two rows are scrap. We're hoping the rest is okay."

"How long until we know for sure?"

"We have fungicide on the cart. We're already starting to spray this area to keep it contained. We'll treat the rest of this section today to make sure it doesn't go beyond this," Ryan explained.

Leo nodded. "What can I do?"

"We're going to need more. We don't account for this because of everything we do. We prune the vines and we cut back everything before winter, but we've had such a wet spring and summer that we couldn't control this."

"It showed up today?" Leo asked.

Henry nodded. "We're out here every day. We're walking the vines all the time. I walked this section yesterday and none of it looked like this. I came back today to prune it and found the rot."

Leo ran a hand through his hair and sighed. He stared at the leaves, the spots marring the perfect green leaves, and tried to calm his heart. Black rot was a vintner's worst nightmare. It could destroy an entire vineyard if it wasn't handled quickly.

Dillon was talking about getting certified as an organic vineyard, eliminating the use of chemicals to keep the vines safe. They'd been experimenting with other solutions, but so far, they hadn't made anything work. The section they were standing in had gone all season without any treatment. They thought they finally figured it out.

Until the black rot showed up.

"I need to call Dillon first," Let said.

Henry and Ryan exchanged a glance. Leo stopped and looked at his cousins. They spent all day every day in the field, studying the grapes and learning everything there was to know about how to make them thrive. Leo trusted and respected his cousins' opinions, but the organic project was his brother's baby.

"What?"

Henry and Ryan looked at each other again, then Henry spoke. "We need to start treating this now. We can't wait until we talk to Dillon. If it's this bad in a day, it's moving fast. We need to start treating the rest of the area. We've already sprayed these rows, so we're not organic this year. We can't be. We'll try again next year."

"Dillon is going to be pissed," Leo said.

Ryan shook his head. "He put you in charge. If he didn't

trust you to make the best decision, he would have stayed here."

Leo sighed, nodding once. He knew there was nothing else to do. The rot was in there, and they had no choice but to treat it if they wanted to stop it from going farther. "Let's do it. Treat everything to make sure we're not killing the vineyard."

"You want us to treat the whole vineyard?" Henry asked.

"Have we ever dealt with this before?"

Ryan shook his head. "I haven't. Dad talked about it. When we were little it happened. He spent months trying to save everything, but the chemicals weren't as good back then. He wanted to be organic also, but using copper only gets you so far. Especially in the wet weather like we've had."

"What do you think he would have done? If he had the chemicals, would he have used them?"

Henry and Ryan exchanged a look and nodded. "Absolutely," Henry said. "He knew saving the vineyard was what mattered. The stuff we use is safe compared to some other options. We're not the only ones who use it. It's approved."

"How much is it?"

Ryan told him and Leo almost choked. "Seriously?"

Ryan shrugged. "Yeah. It's not cheap, but neither is starting over."

Leo nodded. "Do it. I'll take the heat from Dillon if he's pissed."

Ryan and Henry jumped into action. Leo followed them around the rest of the afternoon, treating vines and making sure he knew what was going on so he could tell Dillon, in detail.

Ryan and Henry both headed home after dinner time.

Leo offered to grab something for Ryan from The Drunken Grape then headed up to the office to call Dillon.

"Is the vineyard still standing?" Dillon asked when he picked up the phone.

"Yes, I haven't screwed things up that badly yet."

"But you have screwed up?" Dillon asked, his voice rising.

"No, but we have some black rot."

"Where?"

"The organic section."

"Fuck," Dillon swore. "Son of a bitch. Ryan and Henry were supposed to keep an eye on that section."

"They were," Leo said. "Henry walked it yesterday. Everything looked good. Today he went to prune the leaves and found it. It must have been hiding under the leaves."

"That's what it does. It hides in the cool, wet spots. Why didn't he prune yesterday?"

"Because the vines need time to grow."

Dillon sighed. He knew everything Leo was telling him, but that didn't make it easier to hear. Leo understood that. He wanted to be pissed off, too, but he knew Henry and Ryan did everything right.

"What is their schedule?"

"Dillon, they're doing their jobs. We all are. You couldn't have prevented this if you were here, and this would have still happened. The wet weather is killing us this year."

Dillon sighed again. "Yeah, it is. Shit. I really thought this was going to be a good year."

"It will be. We've never had an organic wine, but we got further into the season than we have in the past. This is progress. And I'm guessing we're learning. Like not to go organic with the grapes that are lowest elevation and closest to the lake. Let's start high next year."

Dillon huffed a laugh. "Yeah, that sounds a lot more logical. Did you get all of it treated?"

"Yeah," Leo said.

"How much did we lose?"

Leo drew in a breath. "Forty vines."

Dillon swore under his breath. "That's a lot."

"It could have been much worse. Henry and Ryan are kicking ass."

Dillon blew out a breath. "I know. And so are you. Thanks, Leo."

Leo nodded and hung up. He took a deep breath and let it out slowly. Crisis averted. Mostly. They'd recover from forty vines. And they'd still make plenty of wine. There was no reason to be pissed off about the rot. They just had to deal with it, and Leo was on top of it.

He could handle it.

He hoped.

15

MEGAN TOOK A DEEP BREATH AND SMOOTHED HER HAIR BACK. She had it in a low bun with no tendrils sticking out. Her pale pink sundress was light and soft against her skin, making her feel feminine and beautiful, something she rarely felt in her work boots and overalls.

The doorbell rang, making her heart leap. She'd hoped Adam and Sara would be there before her parents, but her parents were due any minute and were probably at the door. They were always early.

"I got it, Mom," Anna called, rushing out of her room to answer the door.

Megan followed her to the door of the two bedroom cottage she bought when Anna was four. Megan never thought she'd be able to scrape together enough money for a nice house, but she'd found one she loved and saved everything she had to buy it. They'd made a great life there. And even though the house was small, the yard was big.

"Oh, hey," Anna said, reaching out to hug the person at the door.

He stepped inside, giving Megan her first glimpse of

Adam. He wore a black button down shirt and a pair of tan shorts. His hair was trimmed neatly and slicked back from his forehead, making him look even sexier than he did when he was grungy from working by her side all day.

"How's school?" Adam asked Anna.

Anna shrugged. "Not bad. I have some great students, but the teacher I'm working with doesn't seem happy I'm in her class."

"That makes it hard."

Anna nodded. "Mom's in the kitchen. I need to change."

"No you don't!" Megan called out to her.

Anna smiled and nodded. "I do because I look like I'm trying too hard in this dress. I want them to like me for me, and I'm not a sundress kind of person."

"But I—" Megan started, but Anna was already gone.

"She's right," Adam said, taking in Megan's dress, his gaze sliding slowly down her figure. "You should be comfortable."

"I'm comfortable," Megan lied. Although her discomfort had nothing to do with her parents and everything to do with the sexy man looking at her like she was the only meal he showed up for.

"You look amazing," Adam said, his voice low and husky.

"Thank you. It's an old dress. I haven't worn it in years."

"You should wear it more often."

Megan laughed. "Yeah, where? To work?"

"Or on a date," Adam said quietly.

Megan shook her head. "I don't go on very many of those."

Megan headed back to the kitchen. She had partially prepared food all over the kitchen.

"I thought I was going to help you," Adam said, setting a container down on the counter.

Megan shrugged. "I felt bad asking you to come over and then asking you to do all the work."

"And I told you I was happy to."

Megan drew in a breath, trying to convince herself she was worried about her parents showing up, not about Adam being in her kitchen.

Adam made quick work of the rest of the preparations and had food going into the oven in half the time Megan would have. She helped where she could, but she felt wholly unprepared for what she tried to pull off. If Adam hadn't shown up when he did, with more food in hand, she didn't know what she would have done.

"I think we're in good shape," Adam said. "I didn't notice dessert. Did you already have something?"

Megan froze. "Oh, shit. I never thought about dessert."

Adam shrugged. "No big deal. It's lunch so they probably won't expect anything for dessert. We're good."

Megan shook her head. "No, they will. They think it's rude to have people over and not serve them dessert before you send them home. I can't believe I forgot about it."

Adam walked over to her and cupped her cheeks, lifting her gaze to his. His calm, steady eyes and kind smile calmed her before she could think about it. Inside, she was panicking, but looking at Adam, she knew everything was going to be okay.

"Are you good?" he asked.

Megan took a breath and nodded. "Yeah, I think so."

"Are you sure?"

She nodded, not taking her eyes off him. "You being here helps."

"I'm always here for you. Any time you need me."

Her breath hitched at the heat in his voice. He meant more than just as a friend, and she was having trouble separating Adam her employee from Adam her friend from Adam the guy she thought about when she was lonely.

"Megan," he breathed, leaning down.

Their eyes locked and held. She tilted her chin up, meeting his lips for a kiss. His lips were soft and smooth, warm and gentle. He kissed her sweetly, his lips pressed to hers, with little pecks.

It wasn't enough for her. She slicked her tongue over his lips, and he froze.

She started to pull back, wondering if she'd read the whole thing wrong. Then he tightened his hands on her cheeks and tilted her head to the side and plunged his tongue into her mouth.

A groan slipped from her throat, urging him on. He stepped closer to her, one of his hands sliding down her throat and down her body, grazing the side of her breast and drifting to her hip. His fingers dug into her flesh, tugging her closer to him. Close enough that she felt the heat from his body from her lips to her knees.

Adam tilted his head the other way and kissed her again, devouring her, tasting her, teasing her. She wanted more of him. Hands, lips, tongue...and the steel rod pressed against her stomach.

"Adam," she moaned, threading her hands around his neck and holding him close to her. She couldn't get enough of him.

He moved her across the room until her back hit the edge of the counter. He squeezed her waist and lifted her, setting her ass on the edge, and settled between her thighs, pressing his cock to her sex.

The feel of him nestled against her, the thin fabric of her dress and his shorts the only things separating them, and the cold counter biting into the backs of her thighs brought her back to reality.

"Adam," he breathed.

He kissed his way down her neck. "God, I've wanted to do this forever."

"We can't, Adam."

"Can't what?"

"Stop, Adam. We have to stop."

He stopped and looked up at her, his eyes dark with desire and heavy with need. She saw the moment her words registered, when the desire fled and was replaced with regret and frustration.

He took a step back, holding a hand out to help her off the counter, then moved across the room.

"Adam," Megan tried.

He shook his head.

The doorbell interrupted anything else she wanted to say.

Anna didn't say anything, so Megan left the kitchen to answer the door. And of course, it was her parents.

"Are you okay?" her mom asked. "Your face is flushed and you're sweating."

Megan nodded, forcing a smile. "I'm fine. I was just... finishing cooking."

Her mom eyed her, clearly not believing her. "Whose car is in the driveway?"

"Adam's. He works for me."

Her mother's suspicious look became annoyed. "So he's why you're flushed."

"Mom—"

"Gran," Anna said, joining them in the living room. Anna hugged her grandmother and then her grandfather, who still hadn't said anything to Megan.

Megan left them to talk while she disappeared into the kitchen again. Adam was standing in front of the oven, retrieving the chicken Megan put in there earlier.

"I smelled it so I checked. It's done. I hope it's okay that I took it out."

Megan nodded. "Of course. Thank you."

Adam nodded and set the dish on the stovetop. He moved things around and busied himself, ignoring her the entire time.

"Adam."

"Don't, Megan. Not right now. I just can't right now."

She nodded, hating herself for not thinking about how it would turn out before she kissed him. She let herself get wrapped up in him. Let herself enjoy him. But all she did was hurt him in the end.

Adam left the kitchen a minute later. Megan heard Anna introduce him to her grandparents. He made small talk and charmed her parents from what Megan could hear. She knew she needed to go out there, but she didn't have the strength yet.

The doorbell rang again, and the party was complete with Sara there. With her buffers in place, Megan finally left the kitchen, wondering who she needed the buffer for more...her parents or the man she wouldn't let herself want.

SARA SAT between Megan's mom and Adam. Megan's mom, Leigh, was kind and complimentary, but Sara could tell she put Megan on edge.

"This is delicious," Leigh said. "You did a great job with lunch today."

"Adam made most of it," Megan said quietly.

Leigh's mouth pinched, her displeasure clear. "Oh. Well, thank you, Adam."

"Adam's an amazing cook," Sara said. "He brings in food for us at lunch all the time."

"Are you two dating?" Leigh asked.

Sara and Adam both shook their heads. "No," Sara said. "We're just coworkers and friends."

"You two are close to the same age. I'm surprised you haven't dated," Leigh said.

Sara shook her head. "I'm seeing someone else."

"I see. What about you, Adam? Are you seeing someone?"

Adam shook his head. "No."

"How old are you?"

"Mom!" Megan yelled.

"What?"

"Stop."

"I was just trying to make conversation with the people you work with. Since they're here on the one day we're available to see you and Anna."

"I'm sorry, Mrs. Shepherd," Sara said. "We kind of invited ourselves. Maybe we should go."

"No, please stay," Leigh said. "I'm sorry."

Sara smiled and stood. "I'll just clean up."

Megan stood with her. "I'll help you."

Sara and Megan disappeared into the house. When they were closed inside, Megan grabbed Sara's arm. "I kissed Adam."

"What?"

"I kissed him. I think he kissed me. Then I kissed him back. A lot. I didn't want to stop."

"But you did?" Sara asked.

"Of course! I had to. It's Adam," she hissed.

"And?"

"And he's half my age!"

"Hardly. He's older than Anna."

"Yeah, and he should be dating someone like Anna. Or you."

Sara shook her head. "I have enough dating issues. I don't need to compete with my boss for a guy. Besides, he's totally into you."

"He is not."

Sara laughed. "Um, yeah he is. He watches you all the time at work. He loves you, Megan. You have to see that."

Megan shook her head. "He just thinks he does. It's not real love."

"Why don't you let him decide that."

Megan huffed a laugh. "You sound like him."

"Maybe you'll listen to one of us one day."

Megan smirked. "How are things with Leo? Why didn't you bring him?"

Sara couldn't stop her grin. "Leo's good. He's busy right now, but he's good."

"Are you going to a picnic any time soon?"

Sara smiled and shook her head. "No. We're just casual. Meeting his family would be weird."

"But meeting mine..."

Sara laughed. "We're not sleeping together."

Megan nodded. "Good point."

"Why won't you give Adam a shot?" Sara asked.

Megan took a deep breath and put her hand over her stomach. "He makes me feel like I'm someone else. Like I could be doing anything I want instead of needing to be focused on everyone else all the time."

"And why is that a bad thing?" Sara asked. She leaned against the counter and studied her boss and friend.

Megan was older than Sara, but they could have passed for the same age. Megan's dark skin glowed, and her eyes sparkled when she talked about Adam. That was what told Sara Megan wanted all the things she said Adam brought into her world.

"I've spent almost my whole life taking care of other people. When I was a kid, my grandmother lived with us. I helped out as much as I could. In college, my roommate was kind of a mess. And then I got pregnant. Without someone to take care of, I don't know what to do with myself."

"Maybe you should start taking care of yourself then," Sara said.

Megan grinned. "I wish it was that easy."

"It can be. You just have to be willing to try."

"Have you given yourself that advice?"

Sara laughed. "I never listen to myself."

Megan laughed. "I think I have the same affliction."

Sara helped Megan get the dessert Adam threw together. The fresh strawberries had a sweetness that went perfectly with the vanilla ice cream and chunks of chocolate cake. Megan confessed she was binge eating the cake and started to feel sick, thankfully leaving enough for Adam to use for dessert.

Sara would have eaten the whole thing.

"Did you make this also, Adam?" Leigh asked.

Adam smiled and nodded. "I did."

She drew in a breath. "Then I guess it was fortuitous that you came over today. We would have been drinking water and eating raw chicken."

"Mom, I've tried," Megan said, clearly exasperated. "I wanted to make this a nice day. That's why I invited my friends over. I knew if they were here, you would actually enjoy yourself. At least, that's what I thought. I guess it's just being around me that has you pissed off all the time."

"Megan Shepherd, you do not talk to your mother that way," her father boomed, shocking everyone into silence.

Megan turned to her dad. "You know what, Dad? I don't think you should be allowed to speak to me that way. This is my home. And I know I've made some choices you don't agree with, but I wouldn't change anything about my life. I love Anna, and I love my job and my friends and my whole world. And if the two of you are unable to support that, then I think maybe it's time for you to go."

"Megan," Leigh began.

But her father stood. "I think you're right. It was nice meeting all of you. Let's go, Leigh."

Sara, Adam, Anna, and Megan sat still as Megan's dad ushered her mom through the house and out the front door.

Once the door closed behind them, Sara looked at Megan. Her face fell, disappointment written all over it. Then she forced a grin and turned to Anna.

"I'm so sorry, honey."

Anna shrugged. "I've always known who they were, Mom. I love them, but they've never wanted to know me. They pretend they do, but they don't."

"You shouldn't have had to grow up like this."

Anna smiled. "I had the best mom ever, and a pretty great dad, and friends, and there's nothing I feel like I'm missing. I wish they were happy I exist, but I know you are, and that makes everything okay for me."

Sara teared up at Anna's words. She felt the same way about her mother. That anything she did or said could make all the pain go away. Her first boyfriend dumping her, fights with friends, and not getting into the college she wanted to go to. Her mom made it all better. The phone calls when she

was away made up for her not being there. Until Sara realized the phone calls were made when she was spending
time with two other girls. Girls she loved and raised and
treated as her own.

"You're the best part of me," Megan said, wrapping Anna
in a hug. "Thank you for being so amazing."

Anna grinned. "It's all thanks to you, Mom. I love you."

"I love you, too, honey."

Sara wiped tears from her eyes and bit her lip. She
missed her mom. She hated it, but she missed her. She
missed having someone in her corner. Someone who was
always there for her.

She was all alone in the world, and for the first time in
ten years, she wanted to belong to someone.

16

———————

Leo was just finishing his dinner when there was a knock on his door. Since his cousins and siblings would just walk in, and few other people actually knocked on the door, he hoped it was Sara.

His smile fell when Peter was standing on his doorstep instead.

"Damn, dude. Way to make your best friend feel like he's not wanted."

"Why did you knock?"

Peter shrugged. "I'm trying to be a better person. Sara's a stickler for being kind and not acting like an ass."

"She's really good for you."

Peter grinned. "Hell, yeah she is. I just have to convince her I'm good for her, too."

Leo laughed. "What woman could pass up a guy like you?"

"That's what I keep saying. I'm a catch. It's only a matter of time before she falls madly in love with me and decides she can't leave the area unless I go with her."

Leo laughed at his friend's grandeur, wishing it were that

simple. "She should be so lucky. If she doesn't, surely she'll live a life of regret."

Peter clapped a hand to his chest and hung his head. "Poor Sara. Never knowing my love. She'll move to another town and meet another man who won't love her the way I will. I'll find a new woman, a woman who wants to be swept off her feet, and we'll live the life Sara could have had. If only she'd been brave enough to accept my love when she was here."

Leo smiled. He owed it to Peter to ask him about Sara. To find out for sure if they were the same woman. But he couldn't figure out how to do it.

"What does she look like? Maybe I can convince her."

Peter shook his head. "Oh, no, my friend. I'm not giving you a shot with the woman of my dreams."

"We've never gone after the same woman," Leo said.

Peter raised his eyebrows. "You honestly don't remember Victoria Brighton?"

"Victoria...Damn. I did forget about that." Leo laughed, the memory of the girl they both fell for freshman year of high school coming back.

Victoria was new, a transfer student from one of the private schools. She lived in a neighboring town, but she was zoned for Bereton High School, so first day of freshman year, she showed up.

Being the only new girl in class, Leo and Peter both met her that day. They also both asked her out that day. And she said yes to both of them.

When they got together after school, they each went on and on about the girl they met, and at the same time shared her name.

They spent the first half of freshman year fighting over who was going to date her. By the time they stopped arguing, she'd moved on to another boy in their class. They dated all through high school and went away to college together.

"It should have been me," Leo said, pouring two glasses of wine.

Peter accepted his. "It definitely should have been me."

They clinked their glasses, laughing over their shared misfortune.

After Victoria, they never fought over another girl.

Until Sara.

If she was the same Sara.

"I'm not going to steal her from you."

Peter shook his head. "I can't take any chances. She's really skittish. She doesn't even like me going to her work because she's afraid she'll end up with a bad recommendation. She's the most free person I've ever met with so many rules."

Leo doubted they were the same Sara. The woman he knew had a few rules, but nothing like Peter was making her sound. Maybe there were two Saras.

"How long until she leaves town?"

Peter shook his head. "Not long. A few weeks. I spent all those years in Atlanta and never met a woman I liked half as much as Sara. Then I move back, and I'm working with my cousins, giving me zero prospects. And then Sara walks into my world."

"She's really changed you."

Peter nodded. "She has. She's funny and smart and works her ass off. I've never met someone like her. I have to convince her I'm worth it."

Leo wanted to help his friend, but how could he when he still wasn't positive they weren't after the same woman. Obviously, Peter had no clue. He didn't suspect that Sara had been standing where he was a few days ago, giving Leo a look that had him chasing her to his bed and making her come until she begged him to stop. Or that the only reason Sara had a table in her apartment was so they could have sex on it. Or that she was refusing getting too close to him just as hard as she was refusing Peter.

"Would you leave again? If she asked you to?"

Peter nodded without hesitation. "If she wanted me to go with her, absolutely."

"Even though you just got back."

"Yep. She's it for me."

"Have you kissed her?"

Peter shook his head. "I will. When I do, she'll know we're right for each other. She won't be able to resist all this."

Leo laughed with his best friend and wondered if he just gave him advice that included trying to make out with the woman Leo was sleeping with.

He really hoped not.

SARA WAS CLEANING up her kitchen when her phone dinged with a new alert. She finished the dishes, then checked the message.

> We're going out. I'll be there in ten minutes.

She smiled at the text from Peter. He sent it six minutes ago, so she rushed to change out of her pajamas and into something she could wear in public. She was just pulling a pair of shorts on when there was a knock on her door.

Sara hobbled to the door and finished buttoning her shorts then pulled the door open.

"Oh, good. You got my message," Peter said, stepping inside. "You look great. Are you ready?"

Sara laughed. "No. I had four minutes to get ready."

"And you're still gorgeous. Women around the world would be jealous."

Sara laughed again. "You're a charmer. How is it you're still single?"

"Because you haven't admitted you're in love with me yet."

Sara shook her head. "Woman around the world would be jealous."

He threw his head back and laughed. The joy on his face was enough for her to wish, again, that she could fall for him. "Where are you taking me?"

He winked at her. "It's a small town Saturday night. We're going where everyone goes. Have you had dinner?"

She nodded.

"Oh, well," Peter said. "I was hoping to ruin it for you. I guess I'll have to just entertain you instead."

Sara smirked at him and shook her head. Peter was constantly surprising her and taking her out. Him not telling was a part of his charm.

Sara ran a brush through her hair and grabbed her purse, then followed Peter out the door into the balmy night. The sun was fading quickly, just like the summer and Sara's time in Bereton. Of all the places she'd traveled to, Bereton was quickly becoming her favorite. And not just because the town was cute and had more to do than most towns she'd lived in, but because of the people.

Peter went down a road Sara hadn't been on before and

ended up in a line of cars. Sara tried to peek around the car in front of them, but she couldn't see anything.

"Is there a tractor on the road?" she asked. "What's the holdup?"

Peter just grinned, not giving her any clues. He inched forward with the rest of traffic, not saying anything as she rambled.

"This is taking forever. I don't understand it. Why wouldn't you pull over if you saw a line of cars behind you? And it's not like they can't see all of us. The line is so long, I can't even see the vehicle that's causing all of this. What a pain. Are we going to be late? I don't want to miss our... dessert? Bowling? Mini-golf? Come on, where are we going?"

Peter chuckled and zipped his lips up.

Sara scowled, hating that he wouldn't tell her where they were going. She wasn't big on surprises after her mom died, but Peter didn't know anything about that. Only Leo did.

Sara shook her head. She was not going to think about Leo when she was with Peter. It wasn't right.

Sara turned back to Peter just as a sign came into view.

```
Community Drive In
Every Saturday Night
```

"A drive in?" Sara asked.

Peter grinned at her. "I thought it would be fun. Low key, quiet, and we can be out but still be alone. What do you think?"

Sara's smile was slow and genuine. "I've never been to a drive in."

"Lucky me. I get to be your first," Peter said.

Sara laughed. "Not even close."

Peter winked at her. "That's okay. I'd rather be your last."

Sara tried to process while Peter paid for their entry and followed the directions to a parking space. He adjusted the radio to pick up the station playing the movie and backed into a parking space so the bed of the truck was facing the screen.

"Um, shouldn't we be looking at the screen?" Sara asked.

Peter shook his head and grabbed a blanket in the backseat. "We're going to watch from the back of the truck. Best seat in the house. If we stayed in the cab, the roof would get in the way. We're going to have a great view. Trust me."

Sara looked around the lot and found a lot of other people doing the same thing. She peered through the windshield and realized Peter was right. They wouldn't be able to relax if they stayed in the front, but moving to the back gave them space to spread out and a perfect view.

"Well, I'm a drive in virgin, so I'll trust you."

Peter grinned. "You won't be a virgin after tonight."

Sara laughed and climbed out of the truck, impressed with Peter's planning. He had an air mattress in the back, all inflated and ready for them to stretch out on. The blanket he grabbed from the truck would keep them warm, but the pillows strapped to the side would make sure they could watch the movie comfortably.

"I have a feeling you've done this a time or two."

He nodded. "Once or twice." He threw the blanket in the back and reached for her hand. "Let's go grab snacks."

"Snacks?"

He nodded again. "This is a movie. You can't watch a movie without snacks. What are you hungry for? Popcorn, candy, you gotta have a drink."

"Yes, yes, and yes?" Sara said.

Peter laughed. "The woman gets what the woman wants."

They ordered a bucket of popcorn that Sara was sure they wouldn't finish in a week let alone a few hours, more candy than two people should have, and two extra large drinks. Sara was wondering how they were going to carry it all back to the truck when Peter added a hot dog and nachos.

"Where are you going to put all that?" Sara asked, astonished.

He lifted his shirt and patted a mouthwatering stomach, flat with a strip of blond hair that cut off at his waistband. He dropped his shirt, oblivious to her ogling, and paid for their food. The woman behind the counter grinned at him as she ran his card. Sara started to ease away, hoping she wouldn't think Sara and Peter were together. The woman laughed at something Peter said, then he turned to Sara.

"Hey, babe. Come help me carry all this."

The woman's face fell as she found Sara. She smiled stifly at Sara and nodded once at Peter.

Sara was bad for Peter's sex life.

They carried everything back to the truck and set it on the tailgate while they climbed in. The truck was too high for Sara, so Peter helped her. He scooped her up like she weighed nothing and set her on the edge of the tailgate. He winked at her, then held his hand out to her so she could stand and move onto the mattress.

Sara sat on the edge and moved their food onto the bed while Peter closed the tailgate and effortlessly leapt over it and into the bed of the truck.

"Why did you do that?"

"What?"

"Close the tailgate?"

"So we can sit wherever we want and not worry about the mattress sliding out of the truck."

Sara laughed. "That would definitely be my luck. Good plan."

She handed Peter his drink, then his hot dog and nachos. Sara took her candy and the bucket of popcorn and leaned back against the back of the cab.

"So, what movie are we watching tonight?" Sara asked.

"They show two. The first one is family friendly, but the second one is always rated R."

"Do you know what they're playing?"

Peter shook his head. "Nope."

Sara laughed. "Do you come here a lot?"

Peter nodded. "I do. I like to support my community. Every week is a different fundraiser. This week, the money goes to a local family who lost their house over the winter. Burned to the ground. They lost everything. Insurance helped, but it was an older house and to rebuild it is more than the insurance paid out."

"They're not going to buy something else?"

Peter shook his head. "They're on family land, a lot that's been in the husband's family for generations. It's right on the water. I'd be building if I were them, too."

Sara smiled. "Because you stick. You're a reliable guy, steady. I have to admit, I'm surprised you ever left the area. You seem like the kind of guy who'd never go anywhere."

Peter shook his head. "I'd leave for the right reasons."

"Why did you leave before?"

"I was young and stupid. I went away to college and thought I knew what I wanted."

"What was that?"

"Amber Mallone."

Sara laughed. "No."

Peter grinned and nodded. "Yep. I was in love with Amber. She moved to Atlanta, so I moved to Atlanta. She got a job, so I got a job. She married someone else, so I realized I was an idiot."

"And moved home?"

Peter laughed. "Not right away. I'm not that bad. I knew if I ran back home just because my chance with her was gone I would regret it. I needed to figure out who I was and what I really wanted."

"And you decided you wanted to be home, with your family."

Peter nodded. "It was time. I missed my family, and I wasn't happy in Atlanta. I was happy here."

"That's nice," Sara said. "I think everyone should have a place they belong."

"Even you?"

Sara shrugged. "I do have a place I belong. It's just not always the same place. Right now, I belong here, with you."

Peter smiled and put his arm around her. He kissed the top of her head and held her close. "Yeah, Sara, you do. You do belong here with me."

17

———

Sara laughed through the family comedy that played first. She and Peter ate almost all their snacks, and she was stuffed and ready for a nap. And a bathroom.

"Want to take a walk?" Peter asked as the crowd thinned around them.

She nodded. "I could definitely use a walk. I don't want to fall asleep during the next movie."

Peter smiled and helped her out of the truck. He didn't let go of her hand as they strolled toward the bathrooms, avoiding cars leaving for the night and new movie watchers pulling in.

She met Peter outside the bathrooms and he asked if she wanted anything else to eat.

"I couldn't eat another thing if I tried!"

"Really? I was thinking about a slice of pizza," Peter said.

Sara shook her head. "Just thinking about it makes me feel sick. I'm definitely done."

"Your loss," Peter said with a grin.

He walked up to the stand and waited in the short line. Sara hung back since she wasn't getting anything. When he ordered, the woman behind the counter flirted with him again. Peter said something to her that made her laugh. She talked to him another minute, ignoring the growing line behind Peter.

"Sara, will you grab this, babe?" Peter called out to her.

Sara walked over and took the drink he offered. Peter thanked the woman and put his arm around Sara as they walked away.

"You know she was flirting with you, right?" Sara asked.

Peter scoffed. "Why do you think I kept calling you over?"

"She's cute! Why wouldn't you want to date her?"

Sara didn't understand men. The woman was petite with light brown hair tied in a high ponytail. She was pretty and clearly thought Peter was funny, and there was no reason at all for him not to at least get her number. Especially if he was the ladies' man he claimed to be.

"I'm just not looking right now."

"What? Since when? You were hitting on me the day we met."

Peter shrugged. "I'm just a little hung up on someone."

"Who is she? Do I know her? Why haven't you told me about her? Ooh, we should pretend we're together to make her jealous."

He chuckled. "It won't work."

"Why not?"

He grinned. "It just won't."

"Well, she's a fool for not wanting you. She should really have her head examined."

Peter laughed. "I'll have to tell her you said that one day."

"Good."

They fell into silence once the second movie started.

Sara got wrapped up in the plot, guessing along with the characters on the screen as they tried to solve the mystery before them. By the time the movie was over and the bad guy was dead, Sara was exhausted.

"Did you know who did it?" Peter asked.

She shook her head. "No. I was totally surprised."

"Me, too. I thought it was pretty good." He jumped out of the bed of the truck and lowered the tailgate. "I'm going to hit the bathroom before we go. Do you need to go?"

Sara shook her head. "I'm good. I'll wait for you here."

Peter nodded and jogged off.

Sara folded up his blanket and put it in the backseat, then secured the rest of the items in the bed and threw away their trash. Peter was still not in sight. A lot of cars were slowly making their way toward the exit, but plenty were still there.

Sara pulled out her phone and clicked on Leo's name.

How was your night?

Lonely. You?

Good. Went to the drive in.

That sounds like a date?

Sara laughed. If he only knew.

Not a date, just out with a friend.

A male friend or female?

Male.

Definitely a date. Should I be worried?

Not a date. Just a friend.

Didn't answer my question.

No. No reason to worry.

Her skin heated at the memory of Leo's hands on her body. Peter definitely didn't make her feel like that. She liked having a friend, but she wasn't going to fall for him.

Are you going home alone tonight?

Are you jealous?

When he didn't answer for a minute, Sara got worried. She was teasing, but she felt bad if she pissed him off.

Yes. I want to be the one taking you to the drive in and driving you home at night. I want to be the one walking you to your door. I want to be the one testing out that table you bought.

She laughed, caught up in Leo, and didn't realize Peter was right there until he asked, "What's so funny?"

Sara jumped and locked her phone before Peter saw the texts she was trading with Leo.

"Sorry, just texting."

"Texting who?"

"It's no one. Are you ready to go?"

Peter nodded and let it go. "Yeah, I'm good. Want me to take you home or is there something else you want to do?"

Sara thought about the text from Leo waiting for her response and said, "I think I should go home."

Peter smiled. "Sounds good."

The drive back to her house was quick. Sara said good-night to Peter at the truck. He offered to walk her up, but she told him she was okay. He finally relented and Sara rushed up to her apartment and inside to reply to Leo.

Sorry. I'm home now.

Alone?

Yes.

Do you want to stay that way?

She didn't have to think about her answer.

No.

On my way.

~

MEGAN LEANED back in her chair and rubbed her stomach. She was stuffed. "You did it again," she told Adam.

He grinned at her. "Did what?"

"You made me eat it all and now I'm so full I might be sick."

He laughed. The sound sent a shiver through her. She loved it when he let his guard down with her. When they first met, he was formal and polite, but over the years, he relaxed until most of the time, he treated her like a friend.

"I didn't tell you to eat all of it."

Megan shook her head. "I couldn't say no when everything you make is this good."

Adam grinned. "Well, I'm glad you enjoyed it. I like to cook. It's relaxing for me."

"Did you do a lot of cooking growing up?" she asked. He

shared that he helped raise his younger siblings and cousin, and Megan wanted to know more about him.

He nodded. "Once I could reach the stove, I did most of the cooking."

"How old were you?"

He shrugged. "By the time I was ten, I was cooking dinner most nights. I also fixed breakfast and lunch for everyone. I got really good at creating my own assembly line."

"There weren't any adults around?"

Adam nodded. "There were, but my mom had babies. My youngest sister is special needs and she was with her most of the time. She was a great mom, but my sister wanted to be with her. It made it hard for her to cook. She reached up and almost burned herself on the stove when she was around two. She didn't understand, but my mom cried. I started cooking more and more after that until I was the only one who did it."

"That had to be hard," Megan murmured.

Adam drew in a breath and nodded. His chest lifted, stretching the garnet tee he wore. His biceps strained the sleeves. He hadn't shaved that morning and dark scruff covered his jaw. He seemed even younger than usual when he talked about his family. A reminder to Megan he was her student, not her equal. Not her boyfriend or lover or anything other than the man she was teaching.

"It was hard on my mom. She's one of those people who feels like she should be taking care of everyone. Because my sister needed constant attention, we were on our own more than she liked. I'm the oldest, so it was easy for me to help out. My other sister is five years younger than me. She helped out when she got older. That's what families do. They help each other."

Megan huffed a laugh and shook her head. "Obviously, not all families were created equal. Mine clearly doesn't believe in helping and supporting each other."

Adam sat in the chair next to Megan and reached for her hand. "I'm sorry about your parents. I know that bothered you."

Megan nodded. "Thanks. I kept telling myself that they'll come around, but I don't know if I have any hope for that left."

Adam lifted a strand of Megan's hair and wound it through his fingers, tugging just enough to tease her with his touch but not enough for her to sink into him.

"I don't think we should ever give up hope. Even if we tell ourselves we don't have any, I think there should always be hope inside. It's not easy to hope for things that don't happen. To want something so badly that you think you'll do almost anything to get it. In the end, if you had to kill yourself for something to come true, it's never as worth it. Maybe you should hope for something smaller. Maybe hope that your parents are the ones to reach out next. Or hope that they come to Anna's graduation. Or hope that they apologize for the way they acted."

Mortified that her parents were so rude to Adam and Sara, she looked up at him. "Again, I'm sorry for the way they acted. They had no right."

Adam shook his head. "It doesn't bother me. They're not my parents so I can ignore their comments and move on. But I know they upset you, and for that, I'm sorry."

"How are you just okay with it?"

Adam shrugged and released her hair. He stood, carrying their plates and cups to the sink. After a minute he turned to her.

"I'm not okay with the way they treat you, but I don't

matter in their world. Your parents should love you and want to keep you safe, no matter how old you are. They weren't nice to you, but the way they treated me had nothing to do with me. They don't know me. I know who I am, you know who I am. That matters so much more than what your parents think. If we were together, I might feel differently, but your opinion will always matter more to me."

Megan sucked in a breath, surprised at the emotion she felt. Her eyes welled with tears that she struggled to keep at bay. Adam held her gaze, not looking away from her until she stood up and went to him.

His eyes went wide and grew darker. He'd been a steady presence for her over the years. Someone who came in, just like he did for his family, and took care of things. Took care of her. Megan enjoyed working alone before Adam came into her life, but with him standing there, wise beyond his year and giving her advice, she couldn't imagine not having him in her world.

"I sent in an application to one of the craft fairs," she admitted.

"You did?" he asked with a grin. He knew how hard it was for her to let her guard down and try to be accepted by others. For years, she fought against it, choosing to go against the crowd. For her to throw caution to the wind and try for something that would get her broader recognition and put her on level with other local artists, she was taking a huge step.

"I'm scared, but yeah. It'll give me so many more opportunities. If they say yes, it's a long weekend, but I could make some great contacts and it should open me up to a lot of new things."

"I'm so proud of you," he said, pulling her in for a hug. He held her tight, his body pressed against hers.

Megan heated at the contact, wanting to lose herself in him. He was strong and warm and smelled like a man. She tried to keep her breathing even, but every inhale brought his sexy scent into her lungs, turning her on more and more with every second.

Megan ached to let go. To stop thinking about the consequences and the future and just enjoy life for a minute, but she couldn't. She had no one else to rely on. No one else who could take care of anything. If she let go, her entire world could fall apart. She could lose her business, her future, her career. She couldn't risk it.

Megan pulled back slightly, but Adam's arms tightened around her.

"Don't go," he said softly.

She stared up at him. He brushed a strand of hair from her face and tilted her chin up. Her breath stopped, waiting, anticipating. She wanted him to kiss her. She wanted him.

He moved closer slowly, giving her plenty of time to stop him, and plenty of time to think. She felt his breath on her cheeks, the warmth of his body against hers. Her eyes slid closed and she let herself just feel.

His lips touched hers, just enough that she couldn't deny how real the amazing man in her life was. But just like the last time they were locked in an embrace, in the kitchen at her home, Megan froze.

"Stop," she breathed.

Adam sucked in a breath and moved back.

"I'm sorry," she said.

He pressed his lips together and shook his head. "I shouldn't have pushed."

"It's not that, Adam."

"Go out with me."

"Excuse me?"

"Let me take you on a date. Just the two of us. Away from work and life and everything that keeps making you stop us."

"I..." Megan wanted to say yes. She ached to. It was Adam. The only orgasms she'd had for years were at her own hand while thinking about Adam. He was as entrenched in her world as anyone had ever been. She wanted him, and she wanted them. But she couldn't do that to him.

"I can't."

His face fell. "Can I ask why?"

Megan dragged in a breath. She was still in Adam's arms, still pressed against his body. Saying no to him when she could feel every inch of him was torture, but it reminded her why. It told her she had no choice.

"Because I'm not right for you," she forced out. "I'm the single mom with a child who's almost your age. I'm the struggling business owner who also happens to be your boss."

"We've been through all this, Megan. None of those things are issues for me."

"They are for me," she said forcefully.

He finally took a step back, his hands falling to the sides. "Wow. So, it's not that you're too old for me, it's that I'm too young for you. I'm not your equal. I don't measure up."

"That's not what I said," Megan argued.

Adam shook his head. "Maybe not in so many words, but that's what you meant. You don't want me. You don't want to be with me. I'm not enough for you, so you're making excuses and making it all about what's better for me."

"That's not true," Megan argued again. She didn't want Adam to think he wasn't enough. He was everything. If she was twenty years younger, she'd let herself fall hard for him. She'd date him and love him and marry him and have a family and a life with him. But she wasn't twenty years younger. She was fourteen years older than him, and it wasn't fair to him that she steal those years from him.

"Maybe it's not true. Maybe it is. At the end of the day, it doesn't seem to really matter. You don't want me. Not in your bed at least. Maybe you'll still want me to work with you."

"Of course I do," Megan said immediately. "You're so close to finishing your apprenticeship. I wouldn't ask you to leave and start over."

"And what about after?" Adam asked. "Are you going to ask me to stay on and work with you? Then I would be your equal. Or closer to it. We make a great team, Megan."

She nodded. "We do. And that would be great, but we're going to have to see. If the fair thing works out, it'll be great for us. If not...I'm not sure."

"And maybe if you give me a shot here, you'll give me a shot here," he said, tapping her chest right over her heart.

The traitorous organ thumped at his touch, trying to get to him. Not that Megan blamed her heart. It was his anyway. He owned her. And that more than anything else terrified her.

18

Leo was finally hitting his stride as the CEO. The tasting room was running smoothly without him, but he checked in on them regularly. The black rot was under control in the fields, and Sean was starting to run the bottling lines for the wines they bottled at the end of summer.

All was going well, which was not what he expected after the first week on the job. But things came together and he was feeling a lot more relaxed being in charge.

He leaned back in the desk chair and waited for his video chat with Dillon to start. He took a sip of water just as the call came through, and choked.

Leo was still coughing when he answered the call. Dillon's face filled the screen. "Are you okay?"

Leo nodded. "Just choked on my water. Sorry."

Dillon shook his head. "Katherine said hi. She was pissed I didn't tell you that last time we talked. And she said thank you for covering for me so I could be here with her."

"No problem. I'm happy to help out."

Dillon smiled. "You look a little more relaxed than last week. How's everything going?"

"Good. We're harvesting a new batch of grapes and starting up bottling. The black rot seems to be gone now, which is good. We're running with the grapes, just to see how they are, and will be processing and bottling them separately. We've never tried it, but Henry and Ryan wanted to give it a shot since they think they got it early."

Dillon's face twisted like he ate a lemon. "I don't know if I agree with that decision."

Leo shrugged. "It was their call. You told me to trust them, and I am."

Dillon sighed and nodded. "Okay. I'll let it go, but we're not going to throw too many resources into this and risk losing money. More money."

Leo nodded. "We already talked about that. Henry and Ryan are on top of it. Sean's up to speed with everything. It's going to be watched very carefully until we decide either it's good or we need to scrap it."

"Do you think this is a good idea?"

Leo shrugged. "The rot didn't appear to get to the grapes themselves. Henry spotted it on the leaves, not the fruit, so he thinks the fruit is still good."

"That's not what I asked you," Dillon said.

Leo drew a breath and let it out slowly. "Yes, I do. It might not work, but it's something we should try. If it doesn't work, we will know for next time. We'll watch the expenses and keep track of everything from extra time monitoring them to the price of separating those grapes into another area and then we can quantify it. If it's a loss, we know going into it if this happens again. But if it ends up working out, we know that also."

Dillon raised his eyebrows and nodded. "It sounds like you really thought this through."

Leo nodded. "Of course I did. This is my home, too. I'm not going to make a decision that might hurt the longterm viability of Amavita. None of us are."

Dillon grinned. "Thank you, Leo. I'm not sure if I said it, but thank you for doing this."

Leo felt guilty accepting his brother's thanks. He still had every intention of telling Dillon he was done filling in after this, and that he didn't want to be the next CEO, and that he couldn't handle being away from the tasting room for long periods of time again. It was a good experience and gave Leo a new respect for the place he's always called home, but that didn't mean he wanted to be in charge. Not forever, and not even for now.

Leo filled Dillon in on the rest of the news from Amavita and they hung up. Leo leaned back in his chair and rested his head. He covered his eyes with his palms and tried to breathe deeply.

"You doing okay?" Sara asked from the door.

"Hey," Leo said, opening his eyes and forcing a grin for her. "I didn't know you were coming here tonight. Or did I forget about something?"

She shook her head. "Andie told me you were in here. Is this the CEO's office?"

Leo looked around and nodded. He wondered if Sara saw the place as the same prison he did. One door, one window, dark furniture, and the weight of his family on his shoulders.

"It's nice. Doesn't strike me as your style."

He grinned. "Not exactly. It's been like this forever. I don't think it's ever changed."

Sara laughed and moved into the office. "I have to admit,

I've always kind of had a thing for a guy in a suit. There's something seriously sexy about unwrapping every piece and knowing I'd find something amazing underneath."

She nibbled her lip as Leo tried to swallow. He grew hard watching her walk toward him.

"I could direct you with the tie, dragging your lips up to mine when I need a kiss or down when I need something else. I've always wanted to yank a shirt apart and send buttons flying. And the coat, watching it slide to the floor. I've never dated a guy who wore a suit."

Leo stood and walked past her. Her gaze tracked him to the door, where he closed, and locked, the door, then turned back to her.

"I've never thought of myself as a suit kind of guy, but right now, I want to memorialize this thing."

She stepped closer to him and ran her hands up his chest, stroking over the thin fabric of his shirt. Her hands slid under the coat, shifting it over his shoulders and pushing it off until it slipped from his arms and fell to the floor in a soft thud behind him.

Sara grinned. "That was kind of hot."

Leo smirked. "You're hot. I like this side of you."

Sara's hands went to the buttons on his shirt. "Will you be pissed if I ruin your shirt?"

Leo locked his arm around her back and pressed her to his throbbing cock. "If you don't, I think I'll be more pissed."

She yanked hard, sending buttons pinging around the room. His tie kept his shirt closed at the top, and his pants locked in the bottom, leaving his middle exposed from the ripped shirt.

"That was so sexy. I almost came just doing that," Sara moaned. She slid her hands into the gap she created and smoothed them over his heated flesh.

Leo wanted to pick up her skirt and bend her over Dillon's desk, but he was letting her decide how the night was going to go.

She leaned forward and tongued over his nipple. He groaned and threaded his fingers through her hair, holding her there for a minute, then dragging her up to kiss him.

She wrapped her hand around his tie and held him there, kissing him and rubbing against him. His head spun as she arched into him and nearly made him come.

"I'm not gonna last long, Sara."

"Then we better make it count," she said softly.

She stepped back and reached under her skirt, sliding her panties down her legs. Leo rushed to drop his pants and put on a condom. When she moved over to the desk and put her hands on the surface, he almost wasted the condom.

"Jesus Christ, Sara."

She peeked back over her shoulder at him. "Are you going to help or do I need to do this all by myself?"

He didn't have to be told twice. He grabbed her hips and lined himself up, sliding into her slowly as they both moaned.

Leo palmed her ass and slammed into her, unable to take her slowly. She pressed back against him with each stroke, moaning louder and louder with each thrust.

"Sara, we have to be quiet," he hissed.

"Then fuck me harder so I can come."

Leo bent his knees just enough to shift how he entered her and lifted as he filled and stretched her. Sara gasped and stilled. He did it again, then felt her tighten around him.

"Oh, God. More. Yes. Fuck, Leo, yes," Sara moaned. She was trying not to yell, but Leo had very little doubt anyone walking by wouldn't know exactly what was happening behind the locked door.

"Fuck, Sara," he grunted, stroking hard into her and coming. He stayed buried inside her as she trembled and pulsed around him.

Leo finally pulled away, hating the feel of sliding out of her. He wrapped up the condom and threw it in the trash under the desk then pulled his pants up.

He tucked in his shirt and laughed.

"What?"

Leo turned to her and held his arms out. His shirt gapped the entire way down. "Think anyone will notice?"

She snickered and walked over to him. "They'll all be jealous because they didn't get hot sex in the office."

Leo cupped her ass and pulled her to him. "Especially if they get a look at you. Men all over will be jealous of me. Because I got a hot woman like you to lose control and rip my shirt."

Sara giggled. "I did lose control. It was awesome."

"You're awesome," Leo said. His stomach rumbled. "And now I'm starving. I was going to order a pizza tonight. Want to join me?"

Sara nodded. "Sounds good."

Leo did his best to hide his torn shirt, but they didn't run into any of the family on their way out. Once they got outside, Sara drove the vineyard roads to his house.

"Ryan's home," Leo said when they pulled up. "Is that okay?"

She nodded. "Yeah. I don't mind meeting one or two people, just not the entire family all at once. Or your parents. At all. I don't think I should meet your parents."

Leo chuckled and nodded. He'd love to introduce Sara to his parents, and his grandmother, but he understood her reluctance. He was in a different place than she was.

"I just need to text them really quickly so they don't stop by," Leo teased, pulling out his phone.

"No," Sara said, fear in her eyes. "Did you tell them to come over?"

Leo laughed and shook his head. "I'm just kidding. Besides, it's not my parents you should be worried about. It's definitely Nonna. My grandmother."

"Your grandmother?"

Leo nodded and let them into the house. "She's a pistol. My grandmother is the judge and jury in this family. If she doesn't approve, it's over."

"She sounds tough."

Leo nodded. "She's had to be. She left her family behind in Italy when she fell in love with my grandfather. When they got here, she found out she was pregnant with my aunt. They had four girls, all raised on this land. When they were grown, just after my brother was born, my grandfather died. Nonna pulled the aunts together with their significant others and told all of them they needed to make it work. And they did."

"She sounds amazing," Sara said.

Leo grinned. "She is. She knows about you."

"Should I be worried?"

Leo shook his head. "Nope. She just wants to meet you one day."

Sara froze, her face panicked.

"Don't worry, I told her you're not coming to a picnic. If you meet her, you meet her. If not, no big deal. What do you like on your pizza?"

Leo knew Sara needed a subject change, and fast. She jumped on it, picking out her favorite toppings. Leo called in the order, adding a pizza for Ryan, then gestured at his torn clothes.

"I'm going to change real quick. Help yourself to anything here. You can open a bottle of wine if you want, or whatever. I'll be right back."

Sara nodded, and Leo took off up the stairs.

"Welcome home, boss," Ryan teased when Leo bounded up the stairs.

"Funny," Leo said. "I just ordered a pizza if you're hungry."

"Sausage and onions?"

"Yep," Leo said. "Sara's here."

"Sara? I get to meet Sara?" Ryan asked, leaving his room to talk to Leo. He noticed Leo's shirt and raised an eyebrow.

"Don't ask."

"Now you know I have to know. Should I ask Sara? Or did you get attacked by a wild animal on your way home today?"

Leo smirked. The wild part definitely fit the bill.

"Nice," Ryan said with a grin. "I like this girl already. Wait, in the vines?"

Leo shook his head. "The office."

"Dillon's office?"

Leo laughed.

"Dude, I love this girl. If she won't stay for you, maybe she'll stay for me."

"Hands off," Leo said, pulling a clean tee over his head. He tossed his dress pants aside and grabbed a pair of shorts. Only then did he realize Ryan stopped talking to him.

The hallway was empty, and the murmur of voices drifted from downstairs. Leo tried not to rush, but he didn't want to leave Ryan alone with Sara long. Women had a tendency to fall for the work-hardened guy who also happened to be a firefighter.

"He never told me that," Sara said, a laugh in her voice.

"Oh, that's a good one. Leo, tell Sara about the time you tried to pick up Kate Maddox."

Leo glared at his cousin. It definitely wasn't his finest moment. "Do we have to talk about that?"

"Yes, I have to know. I love her music." Sara flashed him a grin that said she was having a great time. "Where did you see Kate Maddox that you didn't recognize her?"

Leo sighed and told Sara how Dillon and Kate met, and how Leo flirted with her before he knew she was involved with his brother.

"Wait, I totally forgot about that. She went public with her name here, didn't she?"

Leo nodded. "She did. She's the one Dillon's with right now."

"Now it all makes sense. You're filling in while he's with her. Wow, I can't believe I never pieced that together."

"It's definitely a little crazy," Ryan said. "But Katherine's cool. She's a regular kind of person. You'll meet her if you're here for a while. When are you leaving?"

"A few weeks."

"Oh, well, maybe you won't meet her then. Unless you come back some day. This guy is pretty irresistible," Ryan said, nudging Leo.

Leo shook his head, but Sara smiled and said, "Yeah, he is."

SARA, Leo, and Ryan ate pizza and talked. Ryan shared embarrassing stories about Leo that had Sara laughing. Leo just sat there looking like he was going to kill his cousin.

"And then there was the time that he went skinny

dipping in the lake and his sister's friend caught him," Ryan said.

Leo groaned. "Oh, my God. Do not tell that story."

"Now you have to tell me," Sara said, laughing.

Leo leaned over and covered her ears. "Nope. You don't need to hear it."

Sara laughed and struggled to her away from him. Ryan watched them and laughed.

"He had the biggest crush on Andie's friend," Ryan said.

Leo glared at him. "Do you want to find another place to sleep tonight?"

Ryan shrugged. "Wouldn't be the first time. They always need people at the fire station."

"You're a firefighter?" Sara asked.

Ryan nodded. "I am. Bereton only has a volunteer company, and I help out as much as I can."

"That's awesome. Dangerous."

Ryan nodded. "It is, but we have to go through a lot of training before we can be on the team. It's a great group of people. Men and women."

"I'm impressed."

Leo sat next to her, absently rubbing the back of her neck and listening to their conversation. When she thought he'd forgotten about the skinny dipping story, she said, "Finish the story."

Leo gasped, and Ryan laughed.

"I told you I like her. She's amazing," Ryan said.

Leo tugged her onto his lap. "When she's not trying to learn all my secrets, yeah. I'm not so sure right now."

Sara wiggled on his lap and settled against him. "You still like me. I'm hard not to like."

He grinned. "You definitely are."

"Why don't you want me to know the story? Are you still hung up on this girl?"

Leo laughed. "Not even a little bit. Should I call your dad and ask him about all your embarrassing moments from your childhood?"

Sara grinned. "You can, but my dad doesn't know about most of the stupid stuff I did."

Leo smiled and leaned in, pressing his lips to hers. "Why don't you tell me?"

Sara shook her head, their noses rubbing together. "I don't want you to know all my embarrassing moments."

"And I don't want you to know mine."

"Yeah, but Ryan does."

Leo tickled Sara until she was gasping for breath. He kissed her again, holding her close to him. It felt like they were in their own little world. Ryan disappeared while they were cuddled together, and Sara found herself happy to be alone with Leo again.

"I'm really glad you showed up in my office today," Leo said.

Sara nodded. "Me, too. Best work visit ever."

Leo groaned and suckled her neck. "Absolutely. Any chance I can talk you into coming upstairs with me? I don't have a table."

Sara grinned. "We don't need a table for sex to be on it."

Leo chuckled and stood with her in his arms. He let her feet slide to the floor but kept his arm around her. He leaned down and kissed her, pressing her lips apart.

Sara sighed, loving the feel of him surrounding her. Her world was complete with Leo Young in it. She just hoped she could walk away without feeling like she lost a piece of herself.

She was really starting to doubt it was possible.

19

———————

SARA WAS SEARCHING FOR JOB OPPORTUNITIES DURING A LOW point at work. It was after lunch, and the showroom was quiet. She took advantage of the silence. She didn't have long before she was leaving Bereton, and she had to find something else.

The only problem was, Sara didn't know where she wanted to go. She couldn't search for jobs without a destination, and every time she started to put a new city in, she hesitated. She wasn't ready to leave Bereton. Which meant it was past time for her to go.

She typed in Sanibel Island, Florida and waited for the results to load. She never went to the same place twice, but she was feeling the need for something familiar. Maybe it was the ten year anniversary of her mother's death, or maybe it was Sara getting closer and closer to thirty, or maybe it was the people she met in Bereton, but moving on to a new place and starting over from scratch held less appeal than usual.

There were a few jobs she could do, but nothing really

caught Sara's eye. She searched a few more places she'd been, and it was all the same. Nothing exciting. Nothing she wanted to do. Nothing that promised more than she had around her at the moment.

She slammed the computer shut and sighed heavily.

"What did that computer ever do to you?" Adam asked.

Sara jumped. "Sorry. I didn't realize you were here."

Adam shrugged. "I've been trying to stay quiet lately. Keep out of everyone's way."

Sara felt for Adam. Megan told her he asked her out and she told him no. Sara was definitely on Adam's side and thought Megan should give him a chance, but Megan wasn't listening.

"You don't have to stay out of my way," Sara said.

Adam gave her a questioning look. "I saw what you just did to the computer. I think I do need to stay away."

Sara chuckled. "I'm just trying to find another job."

Adam groaned. "It's the worst, isn't it?"

"Are you looking?"

Adam nodded. "Megan isn't going to keep me."

"Why? I thought you were almost done with your apprenticeship."

"I am, which means I will start creating on my own. I've been doing a lot on my own already, but after a certain number of hours training with a professional like Megan, I can charge higher prices for my work and know I'm worth it. It makes me more legitimate."

"Wouldn't it be good for Megan to have you stay?"

Adam shrugged. "I'm hoping she'll keep me on, but I have my doubts."

"I think you need to have faith. She's going to realize letting you go is a big mistake."

Adam met her gaze and held it. "I don't have much hope for that either."

Sara sighed. "Have you ever told her how you feel?"

Adam nodded. "She knows. She doesn't want me. If she did, she wouldn't have said no when I asked her on a date last week."

"No," Sara breathed.

Adam nodded again. "It's always the same thing about me needing to be with someone younger who wanted kids and all the things she couldn't give me."

Sara wanted to throttle her boss. Megan was going on and on about all the things Adam needed, all the things he should want. Not once in all of that did she stop and think about what Adam actually wanted. If he wanted a wife his age or kids, or if he just wanted the woman he loved to love him back.

"What did you tell her?"

Adam shrugged. "The only thing I could. That I wanted a date with her. She didn't want to hear it."

"So you're leaving?"

Adam drew in a breath and looked around. It was clear by the look in his eyes that he loved being at Lakeside Glass as much as Sara did. Her gaze followed his, taking in the beauty that surrounded them every day. The only thing that made the place more amazing was the wonderful woman who made it what it was.

"I don't want to go, but I can't sit around here and do nothing. If she hasn't offered me a job, I can't count on one being there. I need to work and I need to pay my bills. I have things I need money for. And I've worked my ass off in order to get to where I am. I'm not going to sit back and let Megan decide I can't have a career."

"I'm sure she's not—"

"I know," Adam interrupted. "I don't think she's trying to sabotage me, but I need to take over my career. I need to find something else, just in case she doesn't want me to stay here."

Sara shook her head, her blonde hair dancing around her shoulders. She hated that they were both leaving. She knew Megan wouldn't handle it well, even if she was afraid to admit how much she wanted Adam.

"Adam," Sara tried, "don't give up on her."

He forced a smile. "I can only take so much rejection, Sara."

She nodded. "Trust me, I understand."

~

"Hey, welcome back!" Leo said as he walked into his office. Not his office. Dillon's office.

"Thanks," Dillon replied, looking up from the desk. "It's good to be back."

"Is Katherine with you?"

Dillon nodded. "For a few weeks. She's taking some time off before the tour starts. We're going to visit her parents next week sometime and mostly just hang around."

"It sounded like you had a good trip."

"We did. It was good to get away. And I knew things here were running well thanks to you. I appreciate it."

Leo grinned. "Any time."

"That's good to hear," Dillon said.

"Why is that?" The hopeful tone in Dillon's voice made Leo anxious. He was going to tell Dillon he didn't want to be the next CEO, but the way Dillon was talking, it wouldn't be long before Leo was.

"I realized getting away for a month was a good thing for

me. I was a lot less stressed out, and I was able to spend time with Katherine instead of working myself to death. I need to do more of that. Take time off. Enjoy life."

Leo nodded. "Everyone does. We all work too much."

"I agree. For the most part, it's seasonal. Henry and Ryan are swamped over the summer, but have time off through the winter. Sean is busier when we're actively bottling, but the rest of the time is easier. Andie, Kristen, Alyssa, you...the winter is quieter. Even Zach. Everyone has downtime in the winter. Except me."

"What are you saying?" Leo asked, his nerves getting the better of him.

"I'm saying I need a break. I need to be with my new wife after we're married. I want to have a honeymoon. Katherine and I talked a lot about it and I'm going to go on tour with her. For six months."

Leo thought he was going to pass out. One month was hard enough on him, but six months? He wasn't sure he'd survive.

"Will you think about it?" Dillon asked before Leo could respond. "I know it's a lot to put on you. But I need to have this time with Katherine. We're getting older and we want a family, which means starting to try for kids as soon as we're married. But if she's on tour for six months, we can't do that."

"I didn't know you were going to go for that long," Leo finally said.

Dillon nodded, ducking his head. His dark suit was neatly pressed, making him look like the professional he was. His short, dark hair didn't move, and the five o'clock shadow he had gave him a slightly relaxed look. More chill than the Dillon Leo had gotten used to.

Dillon looked up, his hazel eyes meeting Leo's own.

There were similarities between the brothers that always made Leo want to be more and more like his big brother. Dillon was a smart, good man. He always seemed to have his life pulled together, but looking in Dillon's eyes, Leo saw how badly he wanted this. How badly he needed the time off to be with Katherine once they were married.

A month had been good for Dillon. He had more color in his face and he looked happier and more rested. Leo couldn't take that away from him.

"I'll think about it," Leo finally said. "But I can't make any promises."

Dillon nodded. "I understand. And thank you. I'll do everything I can to support you. Maybe Katherine can introduce you to a friend of hers."

Leo snorted. "And have us both go off on tour? I doubt that will work."

Dillon laughed. "Probably true. Plus, Sara might not be too happy about that."

"How do you know about Sara?" Leo blurted.

Dillon smirked at him. "How do you think?"

"Amavita grapevine," Leo groaned. "Who told you?"

"Andie."

"I should have known."

"She also told me Sara won't come to a picnic because you're always working and she doesn't want to be left alone."

Leo nodded.

"So invite her to come while I'm here."

"I'm still working. I'll be in the tasting room."

"So take a weekend off. You deserve a break, too."

Leo thought about it. He wanted Sara to meet his family, but she was adamant that she not meet his parents, or his grandmother. He knew they would descend on her if she showed up at a picnic.

"I still don't think she'd come."

"Why not?"

Leo shrugged. "We're temporary. She's leaving in a few weeks, and we agreed that would be it."

"Where is she going?"

"I don't know. She doesn't know yet. She was only here for the summer, and then she's going somewhere else. She does this all the time. Finds a temporary job somewhere, works for a few months, and then moves on."

"Why would anyone want to live like that?"

Leo's back stiffened at Dillon's mocking tone. "She has her reasons."

Dillon's eyebrows rose toward his hairline. "Protective of her? She sounds like she's good for you. From what Andie said you're happy with her."

Leo nodded. "I am, but it doesn't matter."

"Would you go with her?"

Leo shook his head. "She won't ask. That's the whole point for her. She doesn't want to get attached. To people or places. So she moves on, cuts ties. I doubt we'll even keep in touch after she leaves."

"Wow, seriously? That's kind of harsh."

Leo drew in a breath. He agreed, but he couldn't be pissed at Sara for it. He understood it, even if he didn't like it. She was allowed to live her life the way she wanted to live it. Leo just had to find a way to get over it once she was gone.

"I knew what this was going in. I know what it is. It's fine."

Dillon held up his hands. "Okay, sorry. I'm not trying to piss you off. I just worry about you."

Leo nodded. "I know. I'm sorry. It's not easy because I really like her, but I'm not going to push back on this. It's too important to her."

"Are you sure she doesn't want you to ask her to stay? Katherine felt that way. She wouldn't ask me to go with her, but she hoped I'd ask her to stay."

Leo shook his head. "Your situation was different. With Sara, she's not sticking. Anywhere. I'm not going to ask her because I know that. It wouldn't be fair to either of us."

Dillon nodded. "As long as you know what you're doing."

Leo nodded. He sure hoped he did, but he wasn't sure of anything when it came to Sara. All he knew was he wanted to spend as much time with her as possible before she left. Store as many memories as possible. And find a way to move on and forget her once she was gone.

If only it were that easy.

SARA'S TIME in Bereton was running short. She had to figure out where she was going next, but she wanted to enjoy every last minute of her time before she left also.

She met Peter at a new food truck in the middle of town. It was a new company trying to generate enough income to buy one of the vacant storefronts along Main Street in Bereton. Peter wanted to support them and invited her along.

"This is so good," Sara said, taking another bite of her barbecue sandwich. "This tastes like the barbecue I had in North Carolina."

"It's supposed to be similar to Carolina Barbecue from what they told me. It's great. I hope they get the money and can open up the restaurant. This will be a good addition to Bereton. One more reason for you to stick around."

Sara smiled. If he knew how badly she wanted to stay, he

wouldn't joke. She was dragging her heels on finding some-place to go because she really wanted to stay put.

"Or you could just admit you're really in love with me and just stay for that reason," he teased.

Sara chuckled and kept eating.

"Are you okay?" Peter asked after a minute. "I was just kidding. I know you're leaving, and I'm not going to be one of those assholes who tries to talk to you into staying some-where you don't want to be."

Sara shook her head. "You're not being an asshole. It's always hard to leave a place I fell in love with. There are so many things around here that I'm going to miss. And people."

"Including me?"

She laughed again. "Stop fishing for compliments. You know I'll miss you."

"Maybe I can come visit you wherever you go next," Peter suggested.

Sara nodded. She always cut ties when she left a place. Maybe followed her former employer on social media, but she didn't stay in touch. It was too hard to see everyone she cared about moving on without her. Living their lives and seeing the things she missed by not being there.

But walking away from Peter and Leo and Megan and Adam was going to be almost impossible. Sara didn't know how she was going to do it. Megan and Peter had become close friends of hers. Adam was someone she enjoyed spending time with and wanted to see him happy.

And Leo? There was no one like Leo.

"Have you looked at jobs yet?" Peter asked.

Sara drew a breath. "I don't really want to talk about where I'm going after this. I just want to enjoy today. With you."

Peter grinned and nodded. "Sounds good to me."

They finished their food and thanked the owners then Peter invited her back to his house for a movie. Sara said yes without any hesitation, wanting to be somewhere with just Peter where she could be herself with her friend.

They sat on the couch together, watching the opening credits of one of the Avengers movies. She'd seen them all, and was as big of a fan as Peter was.

"Ooh, I love this part," he said halfway through.

Sara was barely paying attention to the movie. She just wanted to talk to Peter. To know they could stay in touch after. She needed that.

"Are you going to be one of those people who says he'll stay in touch and then never does?" she blurted.

"What? No. Why would I do that?"

She shrugged. "I don't know. I think I'm one of those people. I've always ignored messages from former friends and coworkers once I left a place. It was too hard to stay in touch. But I don't think I can do that this time."

Peter paused the movie and turned to her. He brushed her hair off her shoulder and squeezed it. "I promise you, I'll stay in touch. I'll come visit. Whatever you want, Sara. I'm not letting you go."

She smiled. "Thank you."

"If you're having this much trouble leaving, why don't you stay? For real. I'm sure your job would love to keep you, and you can move in with me if you need a place to stay."

Sara shook her head. "I wouldn't do that to you. I know you don't need me crashing here and ruining any dates you have."

Peter smiled at her. "You don't have to worry about that. I promise."

She huffed a laugh. "I would feel bad if you brought

someone home and she ran into me. That might be awkward."

He shook his head. "I'm not going to bring someone home, Sara. You're the one I want. You're the one for me. I'm just waiting for you to say you feel the same."

20

———

"I..." Sara didn't know what to say. She couldn't form words. If Peter knew about Leo, he wouldn't be saying that, but she kept them separate. She wanted the two men in her life to be apart. One to hang out with, one to sleep with. One as a friend, one as a fuck buddy. Neither was jealous of the time she spent with the other because neither knew about the other. It worked for her.

Until now.

Peter squeezed her shoulder again and leaned closer. She drew in a breath, unable to move away from him. She wasn't scared, but she felt paralyzed.

His lips brushed hers gently. They were fuller than Leo's, and didn't feel as normal against hers.

Immediately, she brought her hands up and pushed him back. "I can't, Peter. I'm sorry. I...There's someone else."

Peter dropped his head and sat back against the couch. He forced a smile for her and said, "I'm sorry. I shouldn't have done that."

"It's fine," Sara said, even though it really wasn't. They were friends. She thought they were friends. She felt like she'd led him on or something. If he knew about Leo all along, that wouldn't have happened. It was her fault for not telling Peter.

Not that it gave him the right to kiss her, ever, but she knew Peter wasn't a bad guy. He was just confused.

Like her.

They finished the movie and Peter drove her home. He didn't say much, and she didn't blame him. Sara apologized again, but Peter told her it was all his fault and that he was sorry.

"Are we okay?" she asked him before she got out of his truck.

He nodded. "We are. If you're okay, I'm okay."

She nodded. "I'm okay."

"I won't do anything like that again, Sara. I promise you."

She smiled. "I know. I'm not worried about you. I just hate that I don't feel the same way."

He huffed a laugh. "Me, too."

ADAM WAS RUNNING out of time to make a decision. He'd hoped Megan would have offered him a permanent job already, but for some reason, she hadn't. He needed to come out and ask her about it again so he could make the best decision possible.

Adam was in the studio before Megan. He cleaned up and laid out the work for the day. It would be a few hours before Sara came in, so Adam had Megan all to himself. Just the way he liked it.

Megan showed up an hour after Adam. He already had the furnace ready and the pieces from overnight out and ready for her inspection and approval. He was excited to get started on their work for the day.

"Good morning," Megan said, offering him a fresh cup of coffee. She wore a pair of gray biker shorts and a purple, loose-fitting tank top. Her hair was tied up in her signature ponytail, but a few stray pieces curled toward her face.

The coffee was black with four sugars, exactly how he liked it. She knew him. And as much as he counted on her, she counted on him. They were a team, and a damn good one.

"Morning. I think we're set up for today."

Megan nodded. "Thank you. It's so much easier when you're here first. Then I can come in and just start working. What's our plan for today?"

Adam laid out their work to maximize furnace usage. They had a busy day, but it was possible for them to get everything done.

"Here," he said, handing over his plans. "It's an ambitious day, but we've done it before. I'm ready if you are."

Megan studied his notes and nodded. "I like it."

Her words were right, but something in her eyes had him stopping. "Are you okay?"

Megan forced a smile and nodded again.

"What happened?"

She shrugged. "It's stupid."

Adam shook his head and said, "Nothing is stupid. Not if it's bothering you. What happened?"

She pressed her lips together. "Do you remember that craft fair Sara told me about? The local one?"

Adam nodded. "The one you applied to display at?"

She nodded. "Yep, even though I knew they'd reject me. I thought maybe it was different. Maybe they wouldn't be so strict on things since the machines don't actually create the pieces, but they still said no. I was really hoping it would give me some exposure."

"Screw them," Adam said firmly. "Your work is amazing, and you need to find a place where they'll love to show it."

Megan shrugged, and Adam could see it was a blow to her confidence that this group deemed her not worthy.

"Did I ever tell you why I came here? Why I asked you if I could work with you?"

Megan shook her head and turned toward Adam. He had her full attention.

"When I was finishing up school, I talked to one of my professors. Do you remember Mr. Robbins?"

Megan grinned and nodded. "I do. He was my favorite professor. Always pushing us to expand our minds."

Adam nodded. "Absolutely. I loved the idea of doing new things. Trying something everyone else wasn't doing. When I told him I was looking for an apprenticeship, he helped me find a lot of options. But none of them felt right until I met you."

Megan smiled.

"I know it wasn't easy for you to take me on, but it was an easy choice for me to come here. You were sensational. The way you see things and how easily you go from thinking about something to trying something. Look at the sculpture you made for Sara. I've never seen anything like that. That's why I came here. Because I wanted to do things like that. I wanted to learn to push myself. And I have. I can't wait to see what else we can come up with over the years."

Her smile faltered with his last words. She avoided his gaze and started wringing her hands together. She only did that when she was really nervous, which put Adam on edge.

"Just tell me," he finally said.

She drew in a deep breath and looked up at him. "Adam,

I'm sorry, but without something new, I don't have the money to keep paying you. Not what you should be making. It wouldn't be right to keep you here and continue to pay you the salary you're at."

"I don't mind."

Megan shook her head. "It's not right. I was hoping I could get into this fair and it would bring in some new work, but without it, I have nothing."

"What about other fairs? Or something else? Maybe I can update the website and increase online sales."

Megan shook her head again. "You want to be a glass-blower, not a money manager."

"I'll do whatever I need to do so I can keep working with you. Please, Megan."

She looked as defeated as he felt. "I'm sorry, Adam."

His head spun as the world around him crumbled. He thought he was set. That he was going to stay put. He'd been looking at buying a house and asking Megan out again once he was no longer her student. He was building a life, and even building a clientele.

And like a dropped sculpture, it was gone in seconds.

"Is money the only thing holding you back from hiring me?" Adam asked.

Megan hesitated then nodded. "Of course. That's what I said."

Adam held her gaze. "Are you sure it doesn't have to do with us?"

"Us?" Megan squeaked.

Adam nodded. "Us. You know I want you, Megan. Is this your way of pushing me away so you don't have to deal with the way you feel? So you don't have to admit to yourself that you want me?"

Megan shook her head, her gray curls bouncing with the movement. "No. There is no us. We're not together."

"Because you're too scared to hold on to something that could be wonderful. I've always admired you because you take risks. You aren't afraid to try something new with work. And it shows. Your showroom is stocked with spectacular pieces, pieces that delight the buyers and make them want to come back for more and more. But you're afraid to do the same thing in your personal life."

"I haven't been allowed to have a personal life! I got pregnant when I was barely an adult, Adam. I had a child to care for. She had to be my focus, not some guy who wasn't going to stick around for the long haul."

"Is that what you think? That I'm just going to sleep with you then leave?"

Megan smirked. "Why wouldn't I? It's what happens. People sleep together, then one of them gets bored. I haven't had sex in so long I'm not even sure I could do it."

"Megan."

"No, Adam. Don't try to sweet talk me. I like you. We work well together. I haven't been willing to jeopardize that. Like you said, my work is the only thing I have. It's my life. I have Anna and I have Lakeside. If we got involved, I could lose Lakeside."

"How would you lose it?"

She drew in a breath. "Things like that happen."

Adam shook his head, defeated. "Do you really think I'm that kind of person? The kind who will lie and steal from you and take your life's work?"

She breathed a sigh. "I never thought my parents would turn out to be people who were disappointed by everything I've ever done. Before I got pregnant, we got along well enough. They supported me even if they didn't always agree with me. I don't think they understood why I wanted to be a glassblower, but they didn't tell me I couldn't do it. As soon as I found out I was pregnant, they cut me off. I was dead to them. The people you met? That's after more than twenty years of me trying to get back into their good graces. I can't do it again."

"Not everyone is going to be disappointed in you."

"Aren't you? Right now, can you honestly tell me you're not disappointed?"

Adam knew he walked right into that one. He sighed and looked at her. Her amber eyes sparked fire, but fear was hidden in the depths. Her shoulders were tense, drawn up around her ears. Even her breathing was off, tight, strained.

"Yes, I'm disappointed, but not in you."

She huffed a laugh. "It's only a matter of time."

"Megan, you don't need to protect yourself from me."

"But I do, Adam. I do. Because I don't have space for you in my world. Working with you has been great, but when you're done, you'll be my equal. You'll be a glassblower, and if people come in here, they'll see you and want you to do their projects. You'll be earning more money than me, because that's what happens. You'll want a piece of my business. You'll want a piece of me. And I can't spare all that. I can't give more of myself away. I need to keep some for me."

"I won't do all that," he said firmly. He wanted to know where her fears were coming from, but it didn't seem to matter. She didn't trust him. That was what it boiled down to for him.

"Adam, I just can't. I'm sorry, but I can't take these risks. I can't give up my business. I can't give up my heart."

"You can, but you're scared. I never thought I'd see Megan Shepherd scared."

She smiled sadly. "I'm scared every day. You've never

seen me not scared, Adam. And you not knowing that just proves my point."

"What point?"

She pressed her lips together. "I think we need to get started on our day."

Adam wanted to push her for more answers, but it wouldn't matter what else she said. She was done with him. He had to find a new job. He needed to move on. He had to go somewhere that didn't have Megan.

And he honestly wasn't sure if he could handle being without her. He'd try, but she was everything to him, and without her, nothing made sense.

~

Sara debated telling Leo about Peter's kiss all day. It felt like the right thing to do, but she didn't want to fight with him for her last couple weeks.

As soon as it happened, she pushed Peter away and told him they were just friends, so Leo couldn't be mad. Sara did nothing wrong. But she wasn't willing to risk Leo not seeing it that way.

She knocked on his door and waited for him to answer. There was a cool breeze coming off the lake, bringing the earthy scent of the vineyard toward her. She really could stay there forever, enjoying the heat of the fading sun and the beauty of the vineyard. And of course the incredible man who made her feel like she actually did belong.

"Hey," Leo said as he opened the door.

"Hi," Sara said, turning back to him.

"Do you want to go for a walk?"

Sara looked back at the vineyard and nodded. "Yeah. That would be awesome."

Leo stepped outside and reached for her hand. His yellow tee almost matched the bright sun. His hazel eyes sparkled in the afternoon sun. It was his sweet smile that had Sara wishing she could burrow into him and never leave.

He led her closer to the water, walking silently side-by-side for a while. Sara simply existed. Being there with Leo felt natural. There was no pressure for her to be one way or another. She just got to be Sara.

Leo squeezed her hand, drawing her attention to him. He pointed to the water where a family of ducks was swimming under the low trees hanging over the edge of the water.

"They're so cute," Sara gushed.

Leo nodded. "They live on the property. We have a good number of animals out here."

"Do they mess with the grapes?"

Leo shrugged. "Some do, but it's hard for us to monitor every area all the time for animals. We don't see a significant loss of product because of them."

"We had a lot of wild animals on the farm where I grew up. Those were problematic, though, because they were usually wild dogs or cats that would try to pick off the cattle."

"Ouch," Leo said with a laugh. "Rough place."

Sara chuckled. "It could be. I think that's part of why my mom didn't always like it there."

"What did she do for a living?" Leo asked.

"She sold cosmetics. She was always perfectly made up when she left the house, even if it was to help on the farm. When I was little, I got into her makeup bag and tried everything. She kind of freaked out."

Leo laughed. "I would hope so. My sister did the same to my mom. I'm sure my cousins did, too."

Sara smiled. "I don't think I was always an easy kid. I wanted to be like my mom, but I was always more like my dad. I loved playing in the fields and being outside. I've always wondered if that's part of why my mom had another family. If I wasn't girly enough for her."

Leo stopped and faced Sara. He cupped her jaw and shook his head. "You can't think that way. Whatever her reasons were for having another family, they weren't your fault."

"But—"

"No," Leo interrupted. "I've seen it with my brother and his daughter. You can't dictate who a person is going to be, and you can't be disappointed in them if they're not who you want them to be. Your expectations are yours, not theirs. My brother thought he was going to raise his daughter with his wife, but she lied to him and hid her cancer. It took him more than ten years to forgive her for that. She wanted to protect their daughter, and she knew he'd choose Angela over the baby. She kept her illness from him, and I think a part of Sean resented Emily for being there and taking Angela from him, but it was Angela's choice. Just like it was your mother's choice to have another family. You can't take that responsibility on."

Sara struggled to nod in agreement, but a part of her knew he was right. She was nineteen when her mother died. Her mother lied to her and her dad for years, living with another family as though they were her only ones. She lied to all of them.

"I just don't want to end up like her. I don't know if I'll ever have kids, but I don't want to treat a man the way she treated my dad. Unable to choose one life."

"I can't see you doing that."

Sara shrugged. "I hope not. Right now, I love my life. I get to do different things and see the country. I have no permanent ties to anywhere, which means I won't hurt anyone. It's definitely for the best."

Leo nodded, turning and walking toward the water again.

Sara caught up to him and slid her hand into his. "What did I say?"

He gave her a sad smile and shook his head. "I'm just going to miss you when you leave. I'm trying not to think about it."

Sara smiled. "You'll be too busy running this place to worry about me."

Leo turned to her. "I don't think I'll ever be so busy that I forget about you."

Sara pressed her lips together in a smile, trying to keep the tears away. She knew how he felt, but she had to go. She couldn't stay. If she stayed, she risked hurting him because she was like her mother somewhere inside her. And she'd hurt him if she didn't let him go.

21

———

Leo watched Sara out of the corner of his eye. She stared out at the lake, lost in her own thoughts. Leo wanted to ask her about Peter, or ask her to stay, or say something that would make her feel better, but he kept his mouth shut.

Sara didn't open up often, but when she did, Leo liked to listen to her. She'd done things he'd only dreamed of doing. The idea of leaving Bereton behind permanently scared him, but to go on a trip, to explore the country and the world, appealed to him. Being one of the youngest, he never had an opportunity for that. He had to jump into work quickly, barely taking a vacation.

"Have you thought about where you're going next?" Leo asked. If he couldn't take his own trip, he could live vicariously through Sara.

She shook her head. "I haven't figured it out yet. I've been looking at a few options, but I'm not sure what I want to do."

"Well, are you looking for someplace snowy going into winter or someplace sunny?"

Sara grinned. "Definitely sunny."

Leo laughed. "I can't say I blame you. Texas? California? Florida?"

Sara nodded. "I've been to all of them. Nice, but I always go someplace new. I was thinking New Mexico or Georgia."

"Have you found anything?"

She hesitated then shook her head. "I don't know what I want to do."

Leo could feel her apprehension, so he changed the subject to their date. "How about tonight? Do you want to eat dinner outside? We have a patio."

Sara nodded. "That sounds good. Can we sit here just a little while longer?"

Leo nodded. "Absolutely."

Sara snuggled up to him and rested her head on his chest. Leo kissed the top of her head and breathed in the scent of her shampoo. He wasn't looking forward to a long, cold winter without Sara in his life.

It was his fault, though. She was clear from the start that she was leaving, but he got sucked in by her. He couldn't say no to her. Even at the beginning. She made him laugh and took him away from the struggles of being CEO.

A part of Leo wondered how Dillon survived in the role for so long. When he met Katherine, Dillon finally seemed settled. Like nothing bothered him. Before that, his brother was constantly on edge.

Leo was always the laidback, casual brother. Sean ended up somewhere in between, but being a single dad made everything harder for Sean. Seeing his two older brothers uptight pushed Leo to let things go, to roll with the punches.

He'd always been able to do it, but with Sara, he found himself wanting to fight back. To keep her in his life.

After a few minutes, Sara's stomach grumbled. She laughed, and they stood and headed back to Leo's house. He heated up the dinner he grabbed from The Drunken Grape and carried two plates outside to the patio behind his house.

"Your cousin cooked this again?" Sara asked with a smirk.

Leo laughed. "Yes, he did. I wouldn't survive on my own."

She chuckled. "You really need to learn how to feed yourself."

"I know how to feed myself. I go to The Drunken Grape and ask for food."

Sara laughed again, throwing her head back and exposing her neck. Leo leaned forward and pressed his lips to the column of her throat. Her laughter turned into a soft moan. "Leo."

"You taste good."

"You feel good."

He kissed his way down her neck and across her collarbones until her stomach growled again.

"Sorry. Eat your dinner."

She pulled him back in for a kiss full of tongues and teeth and need. Leo struggled to let go of her again, wanting to lay her out and make love to her until she decided to stay. He forced himself to withdraw from their kiss and eat his food.

Sara followed suit. They sat and listened to the soft sounds of the impending night with they ate dinner.

When the food was gone and the wine glasses were empty, Leo pulled Sara to her feet and wrapped his arm around her back, taking her hand in his other one. Soft music played from his phone as he danced her around the patio, their bodies pressed together.

With each shift of her hips against his, Leo wanted her more and more. He grew hard between them, a fact he did his best to ignore. He wanted her, but he wanted her to know it wasn't just sex for him. It was her. He wanted Sara. The woman who'd swept into his life and made him see everything in a new and exciting way. The woman who made him want new things. The woman who challenged him in new ways.

He wanted everything with her. But until he could convince her to stay, he wasn't going to get it.

"Should we go inside?" Sara asked softly.

Leo shook his head. "Not yet. I like having you in my arms."

She laughed softly. "I like it, too. Usually I have less clothes on, though."

Leo laughed. "I've never danced under the stars before. It's beautiful out here and I wanted to share it with you."

Sara nodded and leaned her head against Leo's chest. They swayed together, their steps slowing until neither was moving their feet. They stood still, clinging to each other and shifting their body weight side-to-side in unison.

Sara tilted her head back at the same time Leo dipped his head down, bringing their lips into contact. He struggled for control so he didn't strip her down and take her right there on his patio for all the world to see them.

"Let's go inside," Sara murmured against his lips.

Leo wasn't willing to wait another second to have her and nodded in agreement. They carried in their dirty plates and wine glasses, leaving everything in the kitchen before they rushed to his room.

Leo closed and locked the bedroom door, then pressed Sara against it. She squirmed against him as though she was trying to get closer. His hands ran up and down her body, needing to touch all of her at once.

Her hands moved with the same urgency, sliding up

under his shirt and across his back, her nails digging in to his skin and leaving their mark on him just like she left her mark on his heart.

In that moment, he knew without a doubt that he was in love with Sara and that there would never be another woman like her.

He just hoped he was wrong.

SARA COULDN'T GET CLOSE ENOUGH to Leo. She wanted to make up for kissing Peter, even though he kissed her. She felt guilty, and the guilt was destroying her.

Leo's hands felt magical as they moved over her body. She needed to feel the heat of his skin, the press of his body. She wanted to be closer to him. As close as she could get.

Leo leaned back and tugged his shirt off, throwing it to the side. Sara did the same, wanting his bare skin against hers. They came back together quickly, both searching for the other with their mouths and hands, needing the connection.

They kissed like they had all the time in the world. Sara told herself they did, even though she was leaving soon. In less than a month, she would be gone. Moved on to a new place with new people and a new job and no Leo. It felt empty already just knowing he wouldn't be there. But it was the life she chose so she didn't hurt anyone else.

So she didn't get hurt.

Leo brought her back to the present with a pinch of her nipple. He unclasped her bra and drew it down her arms, letting it trap her wrists together while he teased her breasts with gentle fingertips on her skin.

He kissed down her neck and lifted one breast to kiss.

His lips against her skin felt amazing, but looked even better. Sara watched him, eyes closed and bliss written all over his face, and memorized the way he looked.

He pulled back and kissed his way to the other one, tonguing her nipple before he sucked it into his mouth and rolled it against the roof. She moaned and let her head fall back. He lifted both breasts together, biting her nipples at the same time, sending heat and need straight to her sex.

"Leo," she murmured, wanting him inside her.

"Tell me what you want, Sara."

"You. Inside me."

"My hands, my tongue, or my cock."

"Yes. All of them."

He rose up and kissed her hard, his fingers fumbling with her shorts as hers fumbled with his shorts. She got the button free on his the same moment he gave up and plunged his hand inside her shorts.

Sara moaned and spread her thighs to give him access. His fingertips brushed against her, but he wasn't close enough. She struggled to help him, to kick her shorts off while he continued teasing her.

When she was finally naked, he thrust two fingers inside her. Her knees gave out, nearly dropping her to the floor. She caught herself on his shoulders as he stroked her. With her arms around his neck, she couldn't touch him, and that just wasn't going to work for her.

She backed up, bringing him with her, until her legs hit the side of his bed. She scooted to the center, smiling at him. He made quick work of the rest of his clothes and crawled onto the bed, covering her body with his. She spread her legs, welcoming him in against her as he kissed her.

His hands never stopped moving, caressing and pinching and teasing all over her until she was wiggling with need. He kissed her throat, her breasts, her stomach on the way down to her sex. Her settled between her legs and stared up at her.

"I love the way you look at me," he said, his voice deep and husky.

Sara chewed on her bottom lip, ready for him to dive in. She knew he would when he was ready. She loved that he teased her, kissing her thighs and slicking his tongue through her folds before he centered on her sex and drove her crazy.

Her hips came off the bed with the first flick on his tongue. Her core flooded, ready for him, waiting for him. He teased her entrance with his fingers, barely entering her as he tasted her, bringing her right to the edge of her sanity.

Sara panted through her first orgasm, a second one already on the heels of it. Leo finally thrust his fingers inside, sucking hard on her and sending her flying again.

"I need you," Sara breathed, reaching for him. She tugged on his hair until he lifted his head and looked up at her.

"I was enjoying myself," he said with a sexy grin.

"Me, too, but I need you inside me."

Leo wiped his mouth on the back of his hand and climbed up her body. He sat back and reached for a condom, rolling it on before he lined himself up.

She watched him, not wanting to miss a second of the look on his face as he filled her. His jaw clenched, his eyes slammed shut, and his body twitched. He stilled once he was fully seated inside her, giving her a chance to run her eyes down his body.

Her mouth watered at his chest and perfect pecs. She licked her lips at his abs. His hands had her pulse spiking, thinking of all the times those hands had taken her to heaven. And then there were his arms, his sexy shoulders, and that beautiful face. The smiling lips and the sparkling eyes. Yeah, he was watching her watch him.

"What?" she asked.

"Like what you see."

She clenched her channel and smiled when he groaned.

"You're going to fucking kill me."

She laughed. "You love it."

"I...do," he said, his words falling on each other like he was about to say something else.

Sara's pulse kicked up again, but with fear that time. He couldn't love her. They barely knew each other, and she was leaving in a few weeks.

No, he was just caught up in the moment. That's why he sounded funny. Not because he was going to say he loved her but because he knew he didn't.

He stroked in and out slowly, giving Sara time to get out of her head. When she looked up at him, he was watching her.

"You with me?"

She nodded. "Always."

He slammed hard into her, and her eyes slammed shut. Her core clenched around him as her channel flooded. She was already on the edge, ready to come again.

"You feel so damn good," he moaned. "Amazing, Sara."

"You, too," she breathed.

Their bodies moved in sync, her legs coming up as his hand moved to cup her knee. He shifted the same time she did, and he sank deeper into her, hitting her just right.

"Oh, God," she moaned, the rapid pace of his thrusts demanding she come even as she fought it. She wanted to feel him, to focus on how he felt inside her, but he felt too good and she couldn't hold back.

"Come, Sara. I'm almost there. Come."

She stopped fighting it and let her orgasm wash over her, dragging her down until she stopped breathing and all that was left was Leo. Leo and Sara. Sara and Leo.

For now.

THEY GOT CLEANED up and Leo waited for Sara to grab her clothes and make a run for it. She never stayed the night, and always made sure he knew she didn't want him crashing at her place either.

But after the connection they shared, Leo wanted to keep her in his bed. At least for a few more hours. Preferably naked.

"I don't think I can drive home yet," she said. "I'm still trembling."

"I finally figured out how to get you to spend more time with me. Fuck you senseless."

"I think you fucked me boneless."

Leo smirked. "I took care of the bone part."

She snorted. "Yes, you did."

Sara climbed into his bed, still completely naked, and snuggled under his covers. "This is a really comfortable bed."

Leo nodded and joined her.

"Hey, I didn't say you could come in here."

"It's my bed," he argued with a laugh.

"And I'm your guest. Aren't you supposed to sleep on the couch or something?" she asked.

Leo shook his head and wrapped his arm around her, spooning against her back. "Then I wouldn't be able to do this." He kissed her shoulder. Then he kissed her neck. Then he ran his tongue along the shell of her ear.

"Don't stop," she murmured.

He laughed and kissed her lazily, teasing and tasting her body until they were both ready to go again.

"You really are trying to get me to stay, aren't you?" she asked after their second time. She was stretched out on his bed spread-eagle, her eyes closed.

"You need to come over tomorrow night and we can do this again. Then you can meet my family at our picnic."

Her entire body tensed. "I don't think that's a good idea."

"Why not?"

She shrugged. "I just don't. I'm not staying here much longer, and I don't want your family to think I might be."

"Why does it matter what they think?"

"Because you love your family," Sara said softly. "And I love that you do, but my family is different. My dad...I don't talk to him, and now that I know he's still in love with my mom...And well, I told you about my mom."

"What about your step-sisters?"

Sara shook her head and laughed. "They're not my step-sisters. They're the girls my mom raised when she didn't want to be with me. They're both pretty girls. Into fashion and makeup and all the same stuff my mom was. They're the daughters she should have had."

"I'm sure she never felt that way," Leo said.

Sara shrugged. "I'll never know for sure, but that's how it feels."

"Then maybe it's time for you to make your own family."

"I'm not getting pregnant," Sara said adamantly.

Leo chuckled. "I didn't mean that. I just meant find your own people. Friends that become family."

"Do you have that?"

Leo shrugged. "Some. I have a big family, but I have a best friend who's like a brother to me. We're close, and he's the person I talk to about everything."

"Does he know about me?"

Leo nodded. "Yeah, he does."

"Do you think he'll like me? If we ever meet?"

Leo looked sad as he nodded again. "I'm sure he'd love you."

22

———

Leo felt like the lowest of the low. He had to tell Peter at some point that he was sleeping with Sara. That they'd been together for almost two months. It wasn't fair to him that Leo kept it a secret.

As Leo laid in bed the night before, wrapped up in Sara, he knew why he waited so long to confront Peter or Sara. He didn't want things to change. He wanted his best friend, and he wanted Sara. But he couldn't have both of them in the same world, which meant he had to come clean.

Because he was in love with Sara, and he was going to ask her to stay.

After the picnic, Leo was going to confess everything. Tell Peter about Sara, that he didn't know she was the same person until after they'd been together a month, and that he was sorry. Peter would be pissed, but eventually he'd get over it. They were friends, and they wouldn't let a woman come between them.

Leo was in the office, going over more paperwork. Dillon was pushing for him to make a choice about taking over, but he wasn't ready to choose yet.

"I'm still partly amazed you didn't burn the place down while I was gone," Dillon said from the doorway.

Leo looked up and found his brother watching him, leaning against the door jam. Dillon looked relaxed in a pair of jeans and an Amavita Estates tee. He even wore sandals, which were not on the Dillon Young approved fashion list for a CEO.

"I love this place. Why would I want to see it burn?" Leo asked.

Dillon shook his head and pushed off from the jam. "I didn't mean it like that. I knew you weren't on board with this from the start. I figured you'd do something to screw it up so I had no choice but to go back on asking you to take over."

"Thanks for the vote of confidence, big brother."

"I don't mean it like that. I just meant I'm proud of you. You've really risen to the occasion with this. You've worked your ass off this past month. Unfortunately, we see it in decreased sales in the tasting room, but we're up overall thanks to the deals you made with Finger Lakes Distribution."

"That was luck," Leo argued.

Dillon grinned. "It was skill. I've been going to them for years, and Dad before me. We both have plenty of luck, but we never managed to get a contract. One meeting with you, and they're practically begging us to work with them. That's on you. You're going to kick ass at this job. Better than I ever did."

Leo wanted to let the praise wash over him, but it felt like a bitter pill being shoved down his throat. Dillon was buttering him up, trying to talk him into doing what Dillon wanted.

"What does Katherine think of you walking away?" Leo asked.

Dillon cringed just enough for Leo to know he hit a nerve. "She doesn't want me to leave. But we're about to get married. I don't want to be away from my wife for six months while she's on tour."

"And me taking over is the only option?"

Dillon shook his head and sat in one of the visitor's chairs. He leaned forward, his hazel eyes staring behind Leo at the wall of awards Amavita had won over the years. They made damn good wine, and they earned every bit of praise they'd gotten, but none of it had been easy.

Leo couldn't imagine walking away. He didn't want to think about what would happen if Sara refused to stay. He considered following her to wherever she decided to go next, but the idea of leaving gutted him. He wanted to be there. He wanted to stay at Amavita forever. It was home.

"Putting you in charge isn't the only option, but it's the best one. If I decided to run things from the road, stuff would fall through the cracks. There are always things that come up that need immediate attention, or close to immediate attention. I can't do that to you guys."

Leo nodded, knowing Dillon was right. Most days, he spent his time answering emails, fielding calls, and making decisions that needed to be made immediately. If Dillon tried to do that when he was gone, he'd never spend any time with Katherine, which defeated the purpose.

"You're the best one for the job, Leo. You have the degree, you've been doing the job, and you're damn good at it."

"What happens after her tour?" Leo asked. It was one of his big questions. If he took the job for six months, then what? Would he just be out? Would he be pushed into whatever else was needed? Would he stay on and Dillon would be a kept man? Leo needed to know his future, at least partially.

Dillon ran a hand through his hair and leaned forward, resting his elbows on his knees. "I don't honestly know. I haven't thought that far ahead. Right now, I'm just trying to get things together so when I leave in two months, you're not treading water off the bat."

Leo nodded. It didn't help, but it was the only answer Dillon could give him. Until they were in it, Dillon wouldn't know, which meant Leo wouldn't know.

Leo stood and walked around the desk. "Well, for now, the desk is yours. I'm due in the tasting room for a couple hours today."

Dillon nodded. "Good. We'll sell some wine then."

Leo grinned and waved, heading to his happy place. Or what used to be his happy place. His new happy place was becoming anywhere Sara was.

Leo walked into the tasting room still wearing his goofy grin, but it fell when he saw Peter sitting on one of the stools.

"Hey," Peter said brightly. "Where have you been? I thought you were in here today."

Leo nodded and took his place behind the bar. He tied an apron around his waist and washed his hands. "I was working with Dillon for a while. I didn't know you were coming here today."

Peter shrugged. "I didn't have anything else to do. I invited Sara out to lunch, but she said she has other plans."

"So I'm the consolation prize?"

Peter laughed. "Something like that."

"Did you already start a tasting? Want something else?"

Peter nodded to his glass. "Izzy's taking care of me."

"Okay, then I'll—"

"I kissed her," Peter blurted.

Leo froze. "Izzy?"

Peter scoffed. "No! Sara. I kissed her the other night. We went out to dinner and she came back to my place. We were watching a movie, and I just went for it."

Leo's entire world froze. Peter told him they were going to dinner a couple nights ago, but Sara still hadn't mentioned Peter. He knew she was with a friend, but that was all she said when he saw her the night before. When he slept with her. When he almost told her he loved her.

He was falling for her and she was kissing another guy.

"What did she do?"

Peter shrugged. "She told me she saw me as a friend."

"Did she kiss you back?"

He huffed out a breath. "I don't know. I thought maybe, but then she just said she couldn't and that we were friends and we needed to stay friends and...get this. She said she liked someone else. I mean, she didn't have to lie to me. I understand she didn't want me, but why lie? She doesn't know that many people here, so she can't be seeing someone."

"Maybe she is," Leo said.

Peter shook his head. "There's no way. I'd know."

"You don't spend all your time with her. Maybe she met someone else."

Peter stopped and looked closely at Leo. Leo worried he said too much, but Peter said, "I just don't see it. She kept talking about wanting to leave. Maybe she's still hung up on her ex."

"Her ex?"

"Yeah. She dated this guy in college. When her mom died, he started pulling away and eventually ended up cheating on her with her best friend. It kind of makes sense why she wouldn't want to get attached, but still. It's hard to believe she'd want him. She has a good friend from growing up, but I think she said he's married. She hasn't ever mentioned anyone else."

Leo nodded absently, thinking about all the information Peter knew about Sara that he didn't know. She never told him about her ex boyfriend, even though he knew about her mom. He also didn't know about her married guy friend from Montana. What else didn't he know about her?

And would she ever tell him who she really was? She was hiding her friendship with Peter, her ex, and her childhood friend. What else was she hiding?

SARA WAS SMILING when she got out of her car. It wasn't easy for her to make the leap to go see Leo, especially when she knew the chances were good she'd run into some of his family.

But she was feeling less anxious about it than she expected. She'd already met Andie and Ryan. She'd heard enough about Dillon that she felt like she knew him. Same with Leo's grandmother.

Andie was at the front desk, so Sara stopped to see how she was feeling.

"I'm beyond ready to give birth."

"Is your husband ready?"

Andie nodded, a genuine smile showing her love. "He is. He's so excited. He can't wait for the baby to get here. I'm just ready not to feel like an elephant anymore."

"You're excited about the baby, too," Sara said with a wry

grin. She didn't know Andie well, but she knew enough to know she was going to be a great mom.

"I am," Andie admitted. "I've wanted to be a mom forever, and I'm lucky I have such a wonderful guy to do it with."

Sara smiled. Andie was lucky. She had a great guy, and a baby on the way. Her life was exactly what she wanted it to be. Sara was a little jealous that Andie seemed to have everything figured out.

"There's another great guy around here who will make a great dad one day. He's a little taller than me, same dark hair, hazel eyes, kind of looks like me..."

Sara laughed. "Yeah, yeah. Leo's amazing."

Andie laughed. "I know how things go, though. I didn't jump right in with Cody. It took us a long time to get together, then we both had doubts and I thought he was going to leave me when I found out I was pregnant. Relationships aren't easy, but the right ones are worth it."

Sara nodded and took a deep breath. She was hoping Andie was right because she'd never taken a risk like she was going to take with Leo.

They talked a few more minutes, then Sara left to look for Leo. She heard his voice in the tasting room and smiled as she headed that way.

Then she heard another voice. One she knew almost as well as she knew Leo's.

Sara stopped short when she walked into the tasting room. Leo was talking to Peter. Both of them, together. And the look in Leo's eyes said he knew everything.

She wasn't sure how she felt about that.

No, that wasn't true. She was terrified.

"Hi," she said cheerfully, hoping both men bought it.

"Hey!" Peter said with his trademark grin. His eyes lit up

like they always did, and he hopped off his stool and went to her. "I didn't know you were going to come here. I thought you had other lunch plans. But this is good. You can meet Leo. He's awesome. You two will get along great."

Peter turned and grinned at his buddy, the friend he'd mentioned a few times. Sara couldn't believe she never put two and two together, that she never realized Peter was talking about Leo. He never mentioned his name, but he said his friend's family owned a vineyard. Sara felt so stupid for not figuring it out. If Peter only knew just how well she knew Leo, he wouldn't be introducing them.

"Uh, I already know Leo."

"You do?" Peter asked. His eyebrows drew together, confusion plain on his handsome face.

Sara nodded. "Yeah, I—"

"She came in here a while ago for a tasting. It's nice to see you again. Have you gone through all the wine you bought?" Leo said smoothly, holding her gaze.

Sara's heart sank. He didn't want his best friend to know about them. About her. She was his dirty little secret. She was the only one falling. The only one who thought they could be more than casual sex on a temporary basis.

"This guy is a spectacular salesman. How much wine did he talk you into buying?" Peter asked. His grin was back. He shook his head at his friend, laughing like he was in on the joke.

But the joke was Sara. She never saw people for who they were, just took them at face value. And ended up hurt for it.

She wasn't going to let it get to her this time. If Leo didn't want Peter to know what they were, she wouldn't tell him. She pasted on a grin and said, "A whole case."

"Jeez, dude. That's insane," Peter said, laughing at Leo.

Leo forced a grin, his eyes hurt. He wouldn't look at her, which made her want to reach out to him and explain everything.

"Um, so, why don't you guys go ahead and get a table. I might not be able to join you, but you can enjoy your lunch without me," Leo said.

Peter slid off his stool and turned to Sara. She was watching Leo, silently begging him to meet her gaze and let her know she could talk to him later. She didn't ask Peter to be there. She didn't tell him where she was going to be. She went there to see Leo.

"Wait," Peter said slowly. "I never told you I was coming here. I decided to come here when you told me you had plans. Why are you here, Sara?"

Sara closed her eyes knowing she couldn't deny the truth to Peter. She had to tell him.

"I came here to have lunch with Leo."

"Huh?" Peter asked, looking between the two of them.

Leo held his friend's gaze steadily, not hiding from him.

"You...two...are together?"

Sara nodded.

"Wow," Peter said. "Wow." He spun on Leo. "You let me talk about her for two months, telling you how much I liked her, and the whole time you were together?"

"It wasn't like that," Leo started.

"Really? What was it like? I'd love to know."

"I didn't know who she was. When you met her, I didn't know her name. She came in for wine that day, but I never thought I'd see her again."

"Then what? You chased her down?"

"I came back here to see him," Sara interjected.

Both men swung to look at her. Leo's eyes held distrust, but Peter's just had pain in them.

"I liked him, and I wanted to see him again, so I came back here a week after the first time we met."

"Was that before or after we went out?" Peter asked harshly.

"After," Sara admitted.

Peter nodded. "Well, I get it. I mean, really, what woman would say no to Leo Young. Not only is he handsome and funny and rich, but...No, wait. That's enough."

"It wasn't like that," Sara said loudly.

"Then tell me what it was like, Sara. Tell me about how I asked you out and got to know you and made it clear I liked you and you decided you'd rather be with my best friend."

"I didn't know you two knew each other," Sara confessed. "Not until I walked in here."

Peter narrowed his gaze at her, then spun to Leo. "But you knew, didn't you? You were trying to tell me she's seeing someone because you're seeing her."

Leo opened his mouth, then snapped it shut. He took a breath and nodded. "I'm sorry."

"Sorry? You're sorry? That's really fucking great. My best friend is fucking the woman I'm in love with and lying to me about it."

"Hey! Don't you dare. I'm not just fucking her," Leo said harshly.

Peter took a step back. "You're in love with her? Are you kidding me?"

Leo glanced at Sara. Her breath froze in her lungs, the world around her stalling as she waited for his answer. She didn't know what she hoped he'd say.

"Of course not," Leo finally said. "It's sex. She's leaving. And I didn't tell you because it wasn't worth blowing up our friendship over someone who isn't going to be here much longer."

Sara's eyes stung with the burn of tears. As soon as the words were out, she knew what she wanted him to say. She wanted to hear that he was in love with her. That they were building something. That he cared about her and didn't want to mess it up. Not that she was less than nothing to him.

Too bad her story never changed. She was never good enough.

23

Leo stood still while his best friend stormed off, leaving him there with Sara. Sara that he thought he loved, right up until she kissed someone else.

"I didn't know," she whispered.

Leo nodded. "I figured. I'm sorry, but I'm just not really feeling like lunch right now."

Sara nodded. "Yeah, me either. I guess I'll see you later."

He nodded again, ignoring the tears in her eyes as she turned and ran off.

Leo took a deep breath and pasted on a grin. He had a job to do, and it didn't involve cheating, lying women who were only going to break his heart anyway.

Leo worked the rest of the day in the tasting room, laughing with customers and selling wine. He pushed all thoughts of Sara and Peter out of his head. It wouldn't do him any good to think about either of them, so he didn't.

By the time the tasting room closed, Leo's stomach was growling and he was getting frustrated by everything. He was ready to go home, find some dinner, and have a few drinks. Sara was supposed to come over, but he had little hope that would happen. He really didn't want her to show up. He needed time to think.

Ryan was there when Leo walked in, rinsing a bowl in the sink before he set it in the dishwasher. "Hey," he said without turning around. "You hungry? Or are you going out with Sara?"

"Nope," Leo said with a pop.

Ryan finally looked at him, his eyes narrowing. "What happened?"

"She kissed Peter."

Ryan's eyebrows shot up. "Your best friend? Your girlfriend kissed your best friend?"

Leo shook his head. "Yeah. I'm...I don't know."

"Why?"

Leo took a breath and blew it out. "They're friends. They've been hanging out for months, but he's had a thing for her."

"And she kissed him?"

"Yes, well, no. I guess he kissed her, but she didn't tell me."

Ryan sighed and rolled his eyes. "If he kissed her, you can't be pissed at her."

Leo nodded. "Yeah, I can. It doesn't matter if he kissed her or she kissed him first, their lips touched, that's a fucking kiss. And she never told me she kissed another guy."

"She probably didn't want to make it weird between you and Peter."

"She didn't even know we were friends."

"How is that possible?"

"She's not from here. She doesn't know everyone. They met right after she moved here and struck up a friendship. He told me about her, but I didn't know it was her until a few weeks ago."

"Weeks?" Ryan asked.

Leo nodded and rubbed his neck. "Yeah, and I didn't know how to tell him. I asked her a few times if she met anyone else or had any other friends, but she never mentioned him. Just like she never mentioned her ex boyfriend or some guy she grew up with."

"What are you talking about?"

Leo shook his head. "I don't know. I just...I was going to talk to Peter tomorrow. After the picnic. I wasn't expecting him to show up today when she was here for lunch."

"Are you pissed at her or at him?"

"Both. No, that's not fair. Peter did nothing wrong. I was the ass who didn't tell him we were both involved with her. I should have told him the truth once I figured it out."

"Why didn't you?"

Leo drew in a breath and let it out slowly. He hated admitting the truth, even to himself. Saying it out loud was going to cost him. "Because I was afraid I'd lose them both."

"So what if you did? If Peter couldn't handle that you both fell for the same chick, then fuck him. You didn't steal his girlfriend."

"He feels like I did."

"Why?"

"Because they got to know each other first. I met her before he did, but I didn't know her name. By the time she and I hooked up, they'd gone out a few times. In his mind, I swooped in and stole her out from under him."

"He was sleeping with her, too? You two need to quit fighting over her and walk away."

Leo shook his head. "They weren't sleeping together. Peter kissed her the other day for the first time. She stopped him and said they were just friends, but it still happened."

"All right, back up. I'm so confused here. She met you,

then she met Peter. The two of them became friends, but he wanted more. She started sleeping with you, then he kissed her and she said they were friends. Where's the problem?"

"She didn't tell me he kissed her."

"Ah, so what else is she hiding?"

"Exactly! If she's not going to tell me about a guy kissing her, whether she knows I know him or not, then what else is she going to keep from me? Peter told me she has some ex from college that he thinks she's still hung up on, and some guy she grew up with. All these other guys I know nothing about."

"Did you ask her?"

Leo shook his head. "Peter just mentioned all this today. I haven't talked to her."

"Maybe you should then. Maybe it all makes sense."

"And maybe she's a liar."

Ryan nodded. "Maybe, but until you talk to her, you won't know."

Leo nodded, hating that he needed to talk to her but knowing there was no other choice. He had to see Sara.

Sara was surprised when Leo sent her a text asking her to come over. She planned to give him a few days then ask if he meant what he said about them not being anything more than sex.

She decided to give him the benefit of the doubt since his best friend was her good friend. It was strange to her that they both spoke about the other, but neither ever used a name, so she never pieced together that they were friends. Not until she walked in and saw them talking.

Sara parked outside Leo's house and knocked on his

door. She heard him call out from inside and let herself in. He met her near the kitchen on her way inside.

"Hey," he said.

"Hi."

Awkward didn't begin to describe how she felt.

"I—"

"Do you—"

They both stopped and he gestured for her to go first.

"I didn't know you and Peter were friends."

Leo nodded. "I picked up on that."

"Are you mad at me?"

"Why didn't you tell me you two were friends?" he asked, not answering her question.

Sara shrugged. "It didn't feel important."

"What about your ex from college? Was he important?"

"Who?"

Leo shook his head. "Peter mentioned some guy from college that you dated. And another guy you grew up with. Three men in your life I knew nothing about."

Sara was agitated, hating that she felt like she was being attacked and had to defend her choices. Not to mention, she really didn't want to tell the guy she was falling for about her last boyfriend who cheated on her with her best friend.

"None of them mattered. There was no reason to tell you about them."

"Just like there was no reason to tell me that you kissed Peter?"

Her breath stopped, frozen in her lungs. The anger and hatred in his voice told her that was unforgivable for him. She didn't blame him. Her ex boyfriend slept with her best friend. She didn't approve of cheating. She wasn't okay with it. But she didn't see that as cheating. She pushed Peter away as soon as he kissed her. She didn't kiss him back. And she definitely set the record straight with Peter.

"I didn't kiss him," she said softly.

He nodded, walking away. He went to the kitchen and opened the fridge, then slammed it shut.

"You should have told me you kissed someone else."

"Why? So you could be pissed off at a random guy and hate me? It wasn't a thing. It happened. I told him I only thought of him as a friend, and that I was involved with someone else."

Leo sucked in a breath, still not meeting her gaze. He was so pissed off he couldn't even look at her. She'd only experienced that kind of anger once in her life. When she met her mother's other family and had to pretend she didn't hate them even though she did. She blamed them for her mother's death, just like Leo blamed her for Peter kissing her.

"I didn't lead him on. From the beginning, I told him we were friends."

"And if that's all you were, why didn't you ever tell me? I asked you, point blank, if you met other people here. If you had other friends. And you always said no."

"So you were trying to trap me? You knew and you were questioning me?"

He shifted his feet and moved around the kitchen, grabbing a glass and filling it with water. "I was trying to figure out if Peter and I were dating the same person. You never mentioned him, so I thought we both just happened to be seeing someone named Sara."

"I wasn't dating him! We were friends. Are friends. Not anything else."

"Secret friends."

"Yeah, well, you weren't all that forthcoming either. You

talked about your friend, but you never told me his name or where he worked or who he was."

"Because I didn't think you knew him. You're not from here, so there was no reason to assume you knew each other."

"So me omitting his name is an issue, but you omitting it just makes sense."

"You didn't want me to know you were seeing someone else."

"I wasn't seeing him! Friends. Just friends. Nothing happened."

"Except that kiss."

She groaned and threw her hands up in the air. "I don't know how to talk to you right now. You're not listening to me. Peter is my friend. We ate dinners together and saw movies and hung out. I never slept with him."

"It's all clear to me," Leo said. He finally looked up at her and his eyes were blank even though he smiled. "I don't know why I didn't see it before. I guess I just didn't want to."

"See what?" Sara asked.

"This. Us. You're just not as into this as I am. You don't want this."

Sara shook her head. "I told you from the beginning that I was leaving. That this was temporary. That doesn't mean I don't care about you."

He laughed mirthlessly. "Care about me? Really? Well, that proves it."

"Proves what?"

He leveled her with a glare she felt to her toes. He was good and pissed off now. "You have no clue, do you?"

She shook her head again. "Obviously not."

"You're dating him and fucking me. You got the best of both worlds."

"What are you talking about?"

He drew in a breath. "It doesn't matter." He snatched his glass from the counter and shoved it in the dishwasher, then left the room.

Sara scrambled to follow him, chasing him up the stairs to his bedroom where he pulled off his shirt and threw it into the hamper in the corner of the room.

Sara paused, watching him. He was beautiful, even though he was pissed off. He stalked to the window and stared out, his back to her. The vineyard was bathed in a soft pink glow, the sun barely lighting up the endless sea of vines. The lake was barely visible, the water reflecting the setting sun.

"This matters to me," Sara said softly.

He stood there for a minute, not looking at her, just staring out the window. She took him in, the muscles of his back, the faint scar she never had the courage to ask him about. His hair was longer than when they met, something she'd teased him about more than once. He liked to wave it in her face, and truthfully, she loved the soft feel of it on her thighs when he settled between her legs.

Leaving Leo was going to be harder than leaving anywhere she'd ever been, but she would leave, just like she planned. But that didn't mean she wanted to leave when he was mad.

"You never felt the same way about me as I did about you," he finally said, his voice soft, as though he could barely stand to push the words out.

"What are you talking about?"

He turned and met her gaze, his full of all the emotions she never knew he felt.

"No, Leo. No."

He took a step toward her. "I love you, Sara. I have for a while, but you're not there, and you're never going to be."

"You don't mean that, Leo. Don't do this."

He shrugged. "I do mean it, but it really doesn't matter. You're not interested in more than a few more days here. We had our fun. You told me it wasn't anything more than sex, but it was for me."

"Leo, I can't. I never asked for this."

"No, you didn't. And trust me when I say I didn't want this. I wanted to fall for someone who was available. Who wanted me. Not someone who's barely able to have a conversation about the way she feels."

"That's not fair," Sara said softly. She knew he was upset, but she was always careful not to lead him on. She never got close, with anyone.

He walked by her and back downstairs to the fridge. He grabbed a beer and twisted off the cap. "You know what, Sara? It's not fair that you showed up here, fucked up my friendship with my best friend, and then you walk away. I'm left here to clean up the mess you made."

"I didn't mean to do that. I wasn't trying to."

Leo scoffed. "No, but you never mentioned us to each other. You wanted both of us, the best friend to hang out with and the other guy to fuck. Joke was definitely on me for that one."

Sara choked back tears, refusing to let them fall. He was hurt. He could lash out at her. She knew it wasn't really him. And she could take it. She'd taken worse.

"I know you don't really want to leave. And that's what pissed me off the most. You want to stay here. You want this life. A tiny little town where everyone knows everyone else, a place where you can be yourself and be happy. You want this life, with me. But you won't even admit it to yourself. You're too damn scared."

"I'm not scared! I don't want this, Leo. Don't you dare tell me what I want."

"Like you told me I don't really love you? I know you, Sara. You might not want to admit it, but I know you. I know you'd rather stay up all night long than get up early in the morning. I know you love being right and will suffer to prove that you are. I know you'd rather run out that damn door right now and never see me again instead of being vulnerable and admitting how you really feel about me."

"Leo."

"No, Sara. Don't. Don't tell me again that I don't love you, because I do. But you know what else? I deserve better than this. I deserve someone who's going to have a chance at loving me back. Someone who isn't so scared shitless that she's going to be like her mother that she becomes her mother."

He couldn't have hurt her more if he'd hit her. She took a step back. Tears slid down her cheeks.

Leo's chest heaved with each of his breaths, his face firm and unforgiving.

"I'm not like her."

He laughed. "Yeah, you are. You're scared. You don't know what you want. Why do you think you don't stay in one place longer than a few months? Because you know you'll get attached. You'll be happy. And God forbid you're actually happy. That would just be the worst thing ever if you were happy. If you met someone. If you let yourself love someone back."

"You don't know what you're talking about."

"Yeah, I do. Because I know you. I love you. But we're through, so you should just go. It's what you want to do."

Sara tried to take a breath, but her chest was too tight. She couldn't believe he said all that to her. She was nothing like her mother. Her mother lied to everyone. She manipulated them. She kept secrets and deceived. She destroyed Sara's life, and her father's, and probably her other family's.

Sara was nothing like her. It's why she didn't get attached. It's why her relationships were temporary, and so were her jobs. She couldn't get attached if she wasn't there long. And when she left, everyone moved on.

"I'm serious, Sara. Get out," Leo said, drawing her attention. He was angry. But beneath the anger was hurt. Hurt that she caused.

"I'm sorry, Leo."

He turned away from her, ignoring her. Dismissing her. He was done.

She walked away, just like she always planned. Just like she always did. It was good. It was right. It was for the best.

It hurt like fucking hell.

24

———

MEGAN WAS IN THE STUDIO DRAWING UP A NEW DESIGN WHEN Adam walked in. She already missed him and he hadn't even left yet. But he was going to. She didn't blame him. She didn't know if she'd ever have the money to pay him what he deserved. She couldn't offer him what he wanted, and it was better if he moved on.

Then maybe one day she could, too.

"What is that?" Adam asked, peering over her shoulder.

"Just something I've been toying with."

"It looks...kind of erotic."

Megan covered up the drawing and stacked her papers together. She was thinking of Adam when she started drawing, but she couldn't tell him it was erotic. It was an abstract idea of the way he made her feel. Sexy, confident, worthy.

All the things she normally didn't feel.

"What was it?" Adam pressed, trying to grab the papers to get another look. "Was it erotic?"

"No," Megan argued. "It was just something I was working on. If you think it's like that, then obviously I'm on the wrong track."

Adam stopped fighting her, giving her a chance to regain some of her composure. Her cheeks burned with embarrassment and her body heated with desire from fighting him off. He was freshly showered and smelled like a man should. A hint of soap, a dash of sweat from the summer heat, and the musk of a man. It made her blood hot and her body hotter.

"Are you okay?" Adam asked, putting his hand on her forehead. "You're flushed."

She shook him off and turned away. "I'm fine. Just trying not to get made fun of."

Adam took a step back, putting distance between them. She wanted to be grateful for it, but she wanted him to come closer. To put his arms around her and tell her he wanted her for her.

Adam nodded. "Sorry. I'll get started for the day."

Megan immediately felt guilty for hurting him. He was more and more sensitive to her moods lately. Or maybe he was just holding back less. She thought he would brush off her dismissal of his feelings, but instead he was hurt and confused.

Kind of like she was. All the time.

They worked side-by-side for the morning, like they always did. Sunday was a day they were always able to get a lot done. No one else was ever there, so they worked and talked and laughed.

They used to.

They finished one of their standard plates and put it in the annealer to cool. Megan was sweating and ready for a break. She pulled the top of her coveralls off, revealing her white tank top, and tied the sleeves around her waist, noting how they barely tied anymore. That was the only thing she wouldn't miss when Adam left. His cooking. She'd gained weight over the last few years with all the delicious foods he brought in because she couldn't say no to him. Most of the time.

"Do you have to torture me?" Adam said from behind her.

"What are you talking about?"

He shook his head, his gaze locked on her tank top. Megan glanced down, wondering if she had a rip in her shirt or a stain, but she saw nothing.

He was still staring at her. "You know I want you, Megan. I've been telling you that for months, but you ignored it. I made myself perfectly clear, and you still strut around here in barely there clothes showing off your sexy curves."

"I am not!"

He nodded, his gaze straying down her body to her toes then back up. When his eyes met hers, she was bowled over by the look of desire he gave her.

"Yes, you are. You're turning me on just standing there in that tank top plastered to you." He shook his head. "I just want to know why you don't want me."

She shook her head and turned away. "We work together."

"So?"

"It wouldn't be right. I'm your boss."

"Want me to report you to HR?" he teased.

She spun back to him. "This is what I'm talking about. What if you do feel pressured and you don't think you can say something because you'll lose your job? I mean, not that I'd fire you for breaking up with me, but you know what I mean."

"So you're worried I won't know how to end things with you. What if I don't want to?"

She scoffed. "Of course you will. You're young and good

looking. You're the kind of guy all the young women will be chasing. You should have a family and a life, not be saddled with some old lady."

"You're not old. And I don't want kids. I told you that."

She shook her head. "You're just saying that because I don't want kids. You'll change your mind one day."

"No, I won't. I have a bunch of cousins and siblings, and I love them, but I've helped raise enough kids. I don't want my own. I'd do my best to be there for Anna, but I wouldn't ever really be her dad. She has one, and she's old enough that I wouldn't really have much to offer."

Megan still shook her head. "I—"

"I think you're scared to admit you want me as much as I want you. That's why you hid that drawing earlier. You don't want me to see how you feel about me."

"That wasn't you," Megan protested.

He shook his head and moved closer to her. "I don't believe you. I think you were drawing something that made you think about me. I think you want me. I felt it when I kissed you. You might be scared, but you kissed me back, Megan. Your body trembled in my arms. This isn't one sided, no matter how much you want me to believe it is."

"I..."

"Show me the drawing, Megan."

She shook her head.

"I want to see how you feel about me."

"I can't," she whispered.

"Yes, you can. I love you, Megan. I want to be with you. Not just sex, although I want that, too. I want to work with you every day. I want to share your life. I want to love you the way you deserve to be loved. Every day."

"What are you saying?"

"I'm saying I'm not going anywhere if you'll let me stay. But if you really don't want me, I'll leave."

"I thought you had another job lined up."

He shook his head. "I don't. I couldn't bring myself to do it. I wanted to, but I kept playing our kisses in my mind and knew I couldn't leave you. Not until I knew for sure you didn't want me."

"I told you—"

"Those are words, Megan. Words only mean so much. Your actions tell me a whole lot more. Like the way your eyes sparkle when I get closer to you. And how your pulse flutters right here in your neck. The way your breath hitches when I touch you. That lip...you kill me when you bite that lip. I want to taste it. To nipple that lip and draw it into my mouth. I want to kiss you and touch you and hold you, Megan. And I know you want the same."

She wanted to deny it, but she couldn't. She nodded slowly then turned away from him. She stood at the table with him behind her, close enough that she could feel his heat. He didn't touch her, just stood there, not moving.

Then he stepped away.

"I'm sorry I pushed," he said sadly. "I'll get out of your way."

"Wait," she said. "I wasn't...pushing you away. I wanted to show you this."

She handed him the drawing she was working on. The one of a woman, head thrown back in passion, fire burning from her sex and licking flames at the rest of her body. Hands circled her from behind, a slightly different color. One low and one high.

Adam studied the drawing intently while Megan nibbled her lip. It was abstract, intended to let the viewer see what he or she wanted to see. She hoped he saw passion and love and desire, because that was what she felt.

He finally looked up at her and shook his head. "You can't make that."

"Why not?"

"Because I don't want any other man to ever see you like that. Fuck, I've never seen you like that, Megan. It's making me crazy. Those are my hands on you. Making you feel like that."

She nodded.

He moved closer, forcing her to tilt her head back to meet his gaze. "You're going to offer me a job."

She huffed a laugh.

"And you're going to take me home tonight."

Her breath hitched.

"And you're going to tell Anna not to come over."

She pulled her lip between her teeth.

"And we're going to do that. And anything else we want to do."

She nodded slowly.

"I'm yours, Megan. I'm all yours. I'm not going anywhere."

She reached up, threading her arms around his neck. "I'm yours, too. Always."

He devoured her with a kiss that said he'd been waiting just as long as she had for those words. But the actions were even better.

SARA STARED at her empty suitcase and tried not to cry. It wouldn't do her any good. Leo made it clear he was done with her, and she had no choice but to move on.

She always planned to leave. She'd interviewed for a job in California and another in Alabama. Both jobs were temporary, of course. She would be there until just before Thanksgiving, which was perfect because there were always tons of places looking for holiday help.

Sara turned away from her suitcase and went to her kitchen. Maybe that would be easier to pack. Instead, her gaze fell on the table she bought. The one she only got so she could have sex with Leo on it. She never even bought chairs.

Sara couldn't go anywhere in her apartment without seeing him. He was haunting her, driving her crazy. She thought about reaching out to him, but she didn't know what to say. That he was right and she was scared. That she should have told him about Peter. That she was like her mother.

That was the hardest to admit.

But after thinking about it for three days, she knew he was right. She did the same thing her mother did. She toyed with two men instead of two men and three daughters, but she did the same thing. She couldn't choose between her friendship with Peter and her relationship with Leo. So she chose both, and all three of them ended up hurt.

A knock on the door had her heart leaping. She rushed to it, hoping it was Leo. She flung the door open, a smile already on her face, and saw Peter.

"Hey," she said, trying to hide her disappointment.

"Ouch," he said with a wry grin. "And I thought finding out you were sleeping with my best friend was hard."

"What do you mean?"

"You're disappointed I'm not him."

She shook her head. "No, I'm not."

Peter nodded. "Yeah, you are. But that's okay. He's always

been that guy. The one who women can't seem to get over. Who has everything."

"Yeah, so you said," Sara said, remembering Peter's hurtful words.

He took a breath. "I was an ass. I was hurt, and I felt betrayed. I said all that more to hurt him than you. I know you aren't like that."

"How? How do you know I'm not?"

He smiled and tugged on a strand of her hair. "Because if you were, you wouldn't be this upset."

She pressed her lips together and took a step back, letting her friend inside. Peter wrapped her in a hug, pressing her cheek to his chest. The tears she held at bay for days pushed forward, demanding to be let free.

She cried against his chest, letting go of all the pain she'd held on to for months and years. She cried for her mother and the woman Sara never knew. The scared, confused woman in love with two families. Sara cried for her relationship with her college boyfriend and her lost friendship. And she cried for Leo. For what could have been with him. What would never be.

When she finally calmed down, Peter brushed her tears away and led her to the couch. He got her a glass of water and pressed it into her hand. "Why didn't you tell me about him?" he asked.

Sara shrugged. "I don't know. I think I wanted to keep Leo in a bubble."

"Why?"

Sara thought back to the first time she saw him. "I knew if I let him too close, I'd fall for him. I didn't want to. I wanted to leave without feeling like this. I wanted to walk away like I always did. Telling you, or anyone, would have made Leo real."

"And hiding him?"

She smiled. "Still hurt like hell when I lost him."

Peter's eyes narrowed. "What do you mean lost him?"

She shrugged. "He's done with me."

Peter sighed, closing his eyes. "Because of the kiss."

Sara nodded.

"Shit, Sara. I'm sorry. I was talking to my best friend about the woman I was falling for. I didn't realize—"

"I know," she said firmly. "You weren't trying to ruin anything. I took care of that all on my own."

"Leo's a stickler for faithfulness. And loyalty. If I'd known—"

"Don't," Sara said. "Don't blame yourself. I was the one who kept all this a secret. I should have told him about you. Then I would have known you two knew each other. It's not on you that this happened. None of it."

Peter nodded, giving her a smile. "I'm still sorry. I shouldn't have kissed you."

She smiled up at him. "All this would have been so much easier if I'd fallen for you instead."

He huffed a laugh. "Yes, it would have been. For all of us."

Sara hugged him, wishing with all her heart she'd seen Peter the way she saw Leo. She never would have gone back to Amavita to find Leo. She would have just starting dating Peter and none of the mess she was in would have happened.

"He'll get over it eventually, you know. He'll realize it was my fault for kissing you, and he'll forgive you."

She pulled back and shook her head. "No, he won't. He hates me. We're over."

"For now, maybe."

"For good," Sara said firmly. "I leave this weekend."

"I thought you were here a couple more weeks," Peter said.

Sara shook her head. "I can't stay here. I can barely be in this apartment. And I can't sit around hoping he'll forgive me."

"Were you going to tell me?"

Sara looked at him and shrugged. "I thought you hated me, too."

Peter paused for a second, then shook his head. "I could never hate you, Sara. I'm sorry all this happened, but I don't hate you."

"I...I still only think of you as a friend. I'm sorry."

He grinned. "I know. And I'm good with that. What do you say we watch a movie and forget all about Leo Young for a couple hours."

Sara chuckled and nodded. The movie would distract her, although she knew she'd never forget about Leo. He was a part of her, and he owned a piece of her heart. She wanted to take it back, but it was forever his.

Peter chose a movie about aliens invading and a group of people fighting them off. Sara half paid attention, smiling when Peter laughed and trying not to remember when she and Leo started watching the same movie and got distracted halfway through and ended up in bed.

It was going to take her a while to get over Leo Young. Maybe forever. But no matter what, she was leaving. She was giving him the freedom her dad never had. She was making a choice. And her choice was to let both Leo and Peter go. It was the best for everyone.

25

LEO THREW HIMSELF INTO HIS WORK AFTER THINGS ENDED with Sara. He stopped resisting becoming the CEO and just went for it. He worked more and more hours with Dillon and picked up shifts in the tasting room as often as possible. Anything so he didn't have to slow down and think about everything he was missing.

Sara.

Her voice whispered through his mind at night. Her scent still clung to his pillows. He told himself to wash his sheets, but he didn't want to lose her yet. It was only a matter of time before she left town and he'd never see her again, but for a few more days, he wanted to cling to her.

Leo was in the tasting room for a late Saturday shift when Ryan walked in and sat down at the bar.

"Hey," Leo said, pulling out Ryan's favorite wine and setting the glass and the bottle in front of his cousin.

"You're not going to serve me?" Ryan asked.

Leo shook his head. "You always say I don't pour you enough."

Ryan grabbed the bottle and nodded. "It's true. A wine glass should be used, not stared at."

"Don't let Nonna hear you say that."

Ryan grinned. "She knows it's true."

Leo laughed, agreeing. Their grandmother drank more than the rest of them. She loved her wine, almost as much as she loved her family.

"You haven't been home much," Ryan said as he lifted his full glass.

Leo nodded. "Working. Dillon is trying to make sure I'm up to speed on everything before he leaves. I can't screw this up."

"So you're really going to do it? You're going to take over for him?"

Leo shrugged. "He's leaving. Someone has to. Do you want it?"

"Hell no. I like my job, and I like that I have a few months off and can do a little more volunteering when the weather sucks and people run space heaters and fireplaces. I'm not changing my world."

Leo nodded. Everyone had their lives figured out. Ryan had two careers he loved, all the rest of his cousins and siblings were set with their jobs and their significant others. Some having kids or getting married. He was floundering, getting involved with a woman he knew wouldn't stick around even though that was what he hoped for. He was the guy who thought he could change his girlfriend instead of loving her for who she was.

He deserved to be left.

"If you don't want to fill in for Dillon, don't," Ryan said.

Leo shook his head. "I have to. No one else is going to do it and Dillon asked me. It doesn't matter what I want. He's my brother."

"It always matters what you want."

Leo laughed. "Not lately. It didn't matter to Sara."

"Sara is a different story. I still think you should have gone after her."

"Why? So she can tell me I'm an asshole and to leave her alone?"

Ryan shrugged. "Yeah, maybe. But you're going to beat yourself up over her, and throw yourself into working, and you're going to hate it. You're going to pine for her for months, if not longer, and find yourself one of those creepy stalker dudes who looks up his ex online to see if she ever got married. Don't be that guy. Go see her before she leaves. Give yourself that closure."

Leo shook his head. "I don't want to see her."

"Why? Because she kissed Peter? You and I both know that's not a good enough reason to push her away."

"Are you saying I should be okay with her cheating?"

Ryan shook his head and leveled Leo with a hard look. "No. But she didn't cheat on you. She didn't kiss him. She didn't sleep with someone. She didn't do anything. She couldn't help that he kissed her, and she ended it right away. You're just looking for an excuse."

"Screw you, Ryan."

He nodded. "Sounds about right for you. Unable to really admit that you're pissed off at yourself for not being honest about what you really want. You're letting Sara go because it's easier than asking her to stay and risking her saying no. And you're letting Peter be pissed off at you because it's easier than admitting you're hurt that he had a part of Sara you didn't have. And you're letting Dillon force you into being the CEO even though you don't want it because you're afraid to not live up to your big brother. All your life, you've been doing what everyone else told you to do. One of these days, you're going to wake up and realize you don't know who you are or what you want because no one is telling you. And you're going to be fucking miserable."

Ryan grabbed his glass and the bottle and slid off his stool and left the tasting room.

It was only after he was gone that Leo realized Dillon was standing there, watching him.

"How much of that did you hear?" Leo asked.

Dillon crossed his arms over his chest. "All of it. We need to talk. Now."

Dillon turned and left, heading back toward his office.

Which meant Leo was in trouble.

"Fuck," he muttered, then followed his brother. Leo was not looking forward to the conversation, or to having to kiss his brother's ass so he could keep the job Dillon gave him.

"Close the door," Dillon said, taking the large leather seat behind his massive desk.

Not since Leo was a kid and he got in trouble for fighting at school had he felt so small. Back then, he was facing his father over the desk. Years later, his older brother was no less intimidating than their father.

Leo took his seat across from Dillon and looked up at his brother. He refused to back down or hide from what Ryan said. He had to face it.

"Was Ryan right?"

Leo shook his head. "Not about all of it."

"About the job."

Leo drew a breath. "Not entirely."

Dillon ran a hand through his hair and sighed heavily. He was silent, leaving Leo to panic as his brother processed.

"Do you want to be the CEO?" Dillon asked patiently.

Leo took another breath and held it. "I just don't know if

it's right for me. Long term, I mean. If you're gone for a few months, I'm okay covering for you and all. But what about what happens when you're back full time. When the tour is over or Katherine decides she doesn't want to be away from here forever? Do I just step aside and give you the job back? And if I do, where does that leave me?"

Dillon looked at Leo for a long moment, then closed his eyes and sighed. "I'm sorry, Leo."

"What? Why?"

Dillon shook his head. "I never thought this all through. I was selfish. I wanted to follow Katherine around and just convinced myself that you were the easiest one to pick for the job."

"Easiest?" Leo asked, feeling more than a little hurt that he was just an easy pick, not a smart one. He'd been telling himself Dillon wanted him for the job because he was the best person, not because he was the easiest one to choose.

"I didn't mean it to sound like that."

Leo stood, pacing away. "No, it's fine. I understand. I'm not really that important to the business. I'm just standing in the tasting room and pouring drinks. I don't really contribute. You can hire other people to work there, so I'm easy to replace. I can just come in here, answer a few questions, be the figurehead until you come back, and then get shoved back to where I don't really matter again."

"That's not true, Leo," Dillon said firmly.

Leo scoffed. "That's exactly what it is."

Dillon shook his head. "No, Leo. I'm selfish and an ass, but that has nothing to do with you. You matter, and you know you do. I apologize for making you feel otherwise."

"It's fine," Leo said, not feeling it at all.

Dillon stood and walked over to him. He put his hand on Leo's shoulder. Leo wanted to let his brother's strength fill him and give him confidence, but it wasn't working. Leo felt betrayed by all the people in his life.

"When Katherine and I got together, I knew she was the person I was going to spend my life with. I didn't know how we'd make it work, especially when I found out who she is, but I knew she was worth it to figure it out. When this opportunity came for me to travel with her, I didn't think twice about it."

"You shouldn't have," Leo said.

Dillon nodded. "I know. But the reason why is because of you."

Leo took note of that. He met his brother's gaze and waited for Dillon to explain.

"Every time I'm not around or available, you are. Forever. You've always been the one people go to, the one who's a sounding board. You deal with everything, and it's easy to count on you. But I've taken advantage of that."

Leo shook his head. "You haven't—"

"I have," Dillon said firmly. "You see yourself as the baby, but you're not. Well, you are, but only because you're the youngest. You hold everything together, so asking you to take care of it when I'm away made sense. But that's not because you're not valuable in the tasting room."

Leo absorbed everything Dillon said. He was right. Leo did see himself as the baby. As the one everyone looked at as incapable of contributing. He told himself Dillon didn't believe in him running the tasting room so he forced him into the CEO role, but there's no way Dillon would have asked him to take over the most important role in the vineyard if he didn't trust him.

"I, um...Thanks, Dillon."

Dillon nodded. "I should have thought more about you. I'm sorry about that."

Leo shrugged. "I should have talked to you."

"You don't want this job, do you?"

Leo shook his head slowly. "I don't. Not forever. This is you. This office is you. I never wanted to do this, but it was always your dream."

Dillon looked around the room and nodded. "It was. And honestly, walking away is tough."

"But it's not forever."

Dillon shook his head. "It's not. I'll be back. Katherine wants a family, so after this tour, she's done."

"Done?"

Dillon nodded. "No one knows yet, but yeah. She'll probably record once in a while and sing duets or be featured, but she's achieved everything she ever wanted to achieve, and now it's time to have a life. Her words, not mine."

"And she wants to be here?"

Dillon nodded again. "She's inspired to write when she's here. She might move into songwriting. But she wants to be here. We both do."

"So, how do we handle this?"

Dillon took a breath and moved back to his chair, studying the calendar. "I don't know."

Leo sat across from his brother. "Okay, you've left before. One day or even a week is no big deal. For a month, I couldn't be in the tasting room, but there were a lot of things I handled that I didn't really need to do. What if I spent my mornings in here, but went to the tasting room for four afternoons and Saturdays."

"You won't have a day off," Dillon argued.

Leo shook his head. "I don't need a day off. I'd rather be working."

"And this is about Sara. What happened?"

Leo closed his eyes. "She kissed Peter."

"Whoa, what?"

Leo sighed. "She and Peter met around the same time we did, but they became friends. He really likes her and thought she felt the same even though she kept saying she just wanted to be friends. He kissed her, and before you say that's not her fault, she didn't tell me."

"Shit," Dillon breathed. "That's a mess."

Leo nodded. "Yeah."

"Did you know they were friends?"

Leo nodded again. "I was pretty sure, but neither of them came out and said so."

"Well, she wouldn't know you two knew each other. Why didn't he tell you?"

Leo shook his head. "He said her name was Sara and she had just moved to town, but it didn't connect."

"Wait a minute," Dillon said, examining him closely. "He told you about her, and she had no way of knowing you were friends, and you're mad at her?"

"And him. He shouldn't have kissed her."

"And you shouldn't have kept it a secret that you were with her."

"I didn't see the point in telling him. She was supposed to be leaving."

"So that means Peter didn't need to know you were both in love with the same woman?"

Leo took a breath.

"Listen, I get it. All three of you made assumptions. My question is, why are they the only ones to blame? It sounds like you were the only one who knew everything that was going on, but you're mad at both of them for not being honest with you. Did you ask Sara why she didn't tell you Peter kissed her?"

"She figured it wouldn't matter that much."

"Kind of like you figured it wouldn't matter that much if your best friend never found out you were sleeping with the woman he wanted to sleep with?"

Leo opened his mouth to argue but snapped it shut. Dillon was right. He made just as many assumptions as Peter and Sara did, except he blamed them. He was mad at them for not telling him the truth. Peter was pissed, but he was hurt more. And Sara...

"Fuck."

"You need to go apologize to her. Just because she's leaving doesn't mean you don't owe her an apology."

"But we—"

"Can talk later. Go see your woman, baby brother. We have time to figure out work. You need to see Sara before she goes. Spend her last weeks with her."

Leo jumped up and rushed to the door. With his hand on the knob, he turned. "Thanks, Dillon."

Dillon nodded. "Any time."

LEO RUSHED into Lakeside Glass ten minutes later and stopped short. The showroom was full of sunshine with colored light bouncing off all the bright white walls, but Sara wasn't in sight.

Leo checked his phone, but it was too late for her lunch break. She always worked on Saturdays, so she should be there. Where was she?

"Hello?" Leo called out, hoping someone would answer him. He wandered around the room and was about to give up when the door to the studio opened.

"Leo Young. I didn't think I'd see you here today," Megan

said firmly. Her arms were crossed over her pink tank top. Her cheeks were flushed, but her eyes flashed with anger.

"I need to talk to Sara."

"She's not here," Megan said.

"Come on, Megan. We've known each other for a long time. I want to apologize to her. Please let me."

She shook her head. "If she was here, I'd definitely protect her if she wanted me to, but I'm not lying. She's not here. She couldn't stand being in the same town as you for another day and know you hated her, so she's leaving. Going away like you told her to do."

Leo's heart fell to his toes. He thought he was going to pass out. She couldn't leave. Not without him seeing her and telling her he loves her and wants her to stay. He had to.

Without another word to Megan, Leo took off. He jumped in his SUV and tore across town, not caring if he was going to get a ticket. He had to catch her.

Five painful minutes later, his tires skidded to a stop behind her car, blocking her in so she couldn't leave without talking to him. He flew out of the vehicle, leaving his door wide open in his rush. He didn't care. He just wanted to see Sara.

He made it up to her door, which was also wide open, and stopped short. She was in her living room, wrapped up in Peter's arms.

He was too late. She was gone. His best friend was there for her when she needed someone. Leo was too busy being mad, and Peter was the better man, helping her to move on.

Peter pulled back and kissed her cheek. Leo wanted to leave, but his feet were rooted in place, keeping him there as he watched them together. Peter said something softly to her, something Leo couldn't hear, and she smiled up at him.

Only then did Leo notice the tears on her cheeks.

Peter swiped under her lashes, catching her tears. He smiled at her the way Leo always did with love in his eyes, and Leo hated himself.

He could have stepped back and let them be together, but he wanted her. He could make all the excuses he wanted, but that was the truth. He wanted Sara for himself.

Peter looked up and caught sight of Leo standing in the open doorway. His face hardened, and he tucked Sara behind him, protecting her from Leo.

"What do you want?"

Leo drew in a breath. "I want to talk to Sara." He paused and met his best friend's gaze, then added, "And you."

Peter turned to Sara, lifting his eyebrows and letting her answer. When she finally nodded, Leo felt relieved. Until she grabbed Peter's hand.

26

Sara needed Peter's strength to face Leo. Her heart ached at the sight of him, but she wasn't brave enough to face him alone.

He moved forward, into her apartment. The sun shining behind him highlighted the man she loved, making him look like a dream. For Sara, he was. For a little while.

"What do you want?" Sara asked softly. She didn't trust her voice, or herself.

Leo took another step, and Sara resisted the urge to step backward. If he got too close, she'd forgive him. She had to keep her distance.

"I'm sorry for the way I treated you. Both of you. I had no right to get upset with either of you."

Sara nodded. Peter just stood next to her, his body positioned slightly in front of hers, shielding her. She put her hand on his back, taking his strength.

"Sara, I was wrong to be pissed off at you. And the things I said about your mom...I'm an asshole, and I don't blame you if you hate me. You should, but I wanted you to know that I'm sorry. I should never have said what I did. You're nothing like your mother."

Her throat tightened. She could feel Peter's anxiety through his shirt. She never told him anything about her mother, except that she died. She shared things with Peter, but not deeply personal, highly emotional things. She talked to him, but she only told Leo about her parents.

Leo continued, "I'm sorry I'm running you out of town, but I actually went to talk to you today to ask you to stay. I want you to stay. I've been afraid to say goodbye, and that's a big part of why I was such an asshole. Saying goodbye meant you didn't want me, and I couldn't face that. Knowing Peter had a piece of you I didn't have killed me. And I lashed out. I had no right to say any of the things I said to you. Except when I said I loved you. That part was the truth. That's what I should have said. I love you, Sara. I want you to stay here, with me. I'm sorry it took me so long to say so."

Sara tried to swallow around the lump in her throat, but it wouldn't budge. Leo stared at her for a long minute, then nodded and focused on Peter.

"I was a dick to you. I should have told you as soon as I figured out your Sara was my Sara. I told myself I was doing what was best for you, but I was watching out for myself. I didn't want to blow up our friendship, but I did anyway. That's on me, not you. And you kissing her...if she was single, I wouldn't have thought twice about you kissing her. I was pissed because I love her and wanted her all to myself. I was jealous of your friendship. I was wrong to be, but I was. I still am. And maybe one day we can work past this."

Peter nodded. "We've been through worse."

Leo shook his head. "I'm not sure we have. We've always been up front about the women we were with and avoided going after the same one at the same time. I screwed this up.

The good news is, I won't be dating for a long time. There's this amazing woman I'm going to be pining over for a while. But she's not mine."

Peter nodded again, reaching for Sara's hand. Sara let him take it as tears streamed down her cheeks.

Leo met her gaze and gave her a small smile. "I'm sorry. And I love you. Thank you for letting me for a little while."

Then he turned and left.

Sara stood there, watching the empty doorway for a minute. She couldn't breathe or think or move, just stare. He had to come back. That couldn't be it.

Then she heard his SUV start, and she jerked out of her trance.

"I have to get to him. He can't leave," she breathed, letting go of Peter and rushing out the door.

Leo was backing up, pulling out of her driveway into the street. She raced down the stairs, hoping she was fast enough to catch him.

He stopped and looked at his dashboard, then up at her, a smile on his face. Sara didn't stop, just ran, not taking a chance he wasn't looking at her.

Leo was out of the vehicle before she reached him. She leapt into his arms, letting him catch her.

"I'm so sorry, Sara," he whispered against her cheek. "I'm so sorry. I'll never keep things from you again. Just don't leave me. Stay. We'll figure it out. Don't go. Please."

Sara pulled back and shook her head. "I have to go."

He let go of her, his face falling.

She enjoyed that a little too much and grinned. "But I'll come back."

"What?"

"I'm going to visit my dad. It's been a long time since I've seen him, and I want to go back to Montana for a little while."

"And then?"

Sara shrugged. "I haven't been able to make a new plan. I was having trouble letting go of this place. And these two amazing men I met. A great friend, and one who might be more."

Leo stepped closer to her and slid his arm around her waist. "I'll be whatever you're willing to let me be."

Sara nodded. "Are you okay with being the man that I love?"

He tried to fight him grin and failed. "Hell, yeah."

Sara tilted her chin up and accepted his kiss, knowing she was finally where she was supposed to be. She found her home. With Leo.

SARA CAME BACK two weeks later, and the whole family was excited to meet her. While she was gone, Leo and Dillon talked to the others about everyone helping out while Dillon was with Katherine on tour. Dillon would manage what he could, but the day-to-day stuff would be handled by all of them. Whoever was off would take the lead, and if everyone was working, Leo was willing to fill in.

Leo knew he'd end up working like crazy, but it was worth it to help his family. He still managed the tasting room, scheduling the employees and training new people. He was getting their new hires up to speed and looking forward to a few quieter months after the summer rush was over.

Months he was planning to spend with Sara.

Since she gave up her lease, she was trying to figure out

where she was going to stay. Leo wanted her to just move in with him, but Sara was resisting. She said they needed time to get to know each other, and that she wanted a little bit of independence.

Leo just wanted her in his bed every night. And every morning.

"Hey," the woman of his dreams said as she rolled over. She agreed to stay with him while she looked for another place.

He was doing his best to show her staying with him was the only place she needed to be. "I thought you might be hungry after last night."

Her cheeks pinked at the mention of their aerobic love-making the night before. Ryan was working all night, so they took advantage of having the entire house to themselves. Full advantage.

Sara sat up in bed and tugged the sheet up to cover her bare breasts. Leo tugged it back down, feasting his eyes on her perfection. "You're so damn beautiful."

"You're good for my ego."

He grinned and held up her mug. "Coffee?"

She nodded. "Thank you." She took a sip. "Are you going to bring me breakfast in bed until I agree to move in with you?"

He shrugged. "Maybe."

"And after?"

He shrugged again. "I guess it depends on what your answer is."

"Ah, so if I say yes, breakfast in bed is over?"

Leo shrugged. "Maybe. Or maybe I need to keep convincing you."

He moved the tray to the side and kissed her, leaning her

back on the bed. She pushed at his chest to get him up. "I'm going to spill my coffee!"

He let her up, then reached for her coffee and put it on the nightstand, then kissed her again. He teased her lips and tested her willingness with a gentle swipe of his tongue. When she groaned and wrapped her arms around his neck, he knew he was in and climbed on top of the woman he loved. Nothing was better than that.

SARA'S CHEEKS heated as they walked into the family picnic late. Leo said they were supposed to help set up, but he distracted her in bed, then again in the shower, and once more on their way out the door.

He claimed it was because Ryan wasn't home and they could have sex wherever they wanted, but Sara was starting to think he was just using all his tools to convince her to move in with him.

It wasn't that she didn't want to. She loved Leo. But she was still scared. There was a big part of her that worried it wouldn't work out. She didn't know if she'd ever get over that fear. She was starting to think she needed to just jump in with both feet and trust in them.

"Are you ready?" Leo whispered in her ear once they had plates of food.

Sara nodded even though she was anxious. He led her to a table in the corner where his grandmother was sitting with Andie and Cody.

Leo leaned down and kissed his grandmother's cheek before holding out the chair next to her for Sara. Sara smiled at him and took the seat, shaking Tina's hand.

"It's so nice to finally meet you," Sara said.

"Likewise," agreed Tina. "I was starting to wonder if Leo was telling the truth about you."

"What do you mean?"

Tina looked at him as he sat. "He's been talking about you for so long, but we'd never met you, so I thought he could be making you up."

"I've met her," Andie argued.

Tina waved her hand at Andie. "You have pregnancy brain. You can't be trusted."

Andie scoffed. "I can, too."

Tina shook her head. "Nope. I've been there. I know how it goes. Talk to me when that little one is in college. Then you might get some of your mind back."

Andie looked panicked. "I really hope it doesn't take that long."

Tina just grinned at Andie then turned to Sara. "How was your trip to visit your father?"

"It was good," Sara said with a smile. She and her dad talked more than they ever had. He was honest with her about her mother, and how he felt, and she was honest about how much it hurt that her mother had another family. For the first time, Sara felt like she was able to let go of that pain, though, and start to move on.

And she had Leo to thank for that. He was the one who encouraged her to talk to her dad while she was there. It was definitely the best thing for her. And for him. Her dad mentioned a woman he knew from town that he was thinking about having over for dinner. It was time for both of them to move on.

"What does he think about you being here?" Tina asked.

Sara grinned. "He was happy to hear I'm settling in one place. And he's hoping Leo will come with me next time I visit him."

"I'm sure he will. And maybe your dad can come out here sometime. We would be happy to put him up in one of the rooms in the inn for free. He's family after all."

The words made Sara's breath hitch. She wasn't family, but the idea of being a part of it one day made her feel all warm and gooey inside. Her throat clogged with emotion and she nodded.

Tina seemed to understand and leaned over to give Sara a hug. "We're thrilled to see Leo so happy with you. Thank you for that."

"Thank you," Sara whispered. It didn't get any better than that.

"Mind if we join you?" Megan said from behind Sara.

"I didn't know you were coming today," Sara said to her boss. She was thrilled when Megan said she could keep her job after she decided not to leave Bereton.

Megan nodded, her hand linked with Adam's. Anna was right behind them with her new boyfriend. "We wanted to be here for your first Amavita Estates picnic."

"Moral support," Tina said. "They probably figured we'd tie you up and never let you leave."

Megan laughed. "They do have a tendency to draw people in around here. There have been times I've hoped they'd tie me up and keep me here forever."

Adam leaned over and whispered something to Megan, something that had Sara's boss blushing.

"I don't want to know," Anna said. "I need to get my own place. Sara, are you going back to Tom's?"

Leo squeezed her leg, drawing her attention. He smiled at her, but she could tell he was anxiously waiting for her answer.

"I don't think so. I'm pretty sure I'm not going anywhere."

Leo's hand rose up and cupped the back of her neck. He drew her to him slowly, emotion filling his gaze. "I love you," he whispered for only Sara to hear.

"I love you."

"So you're staying?"

She nodded. "There's nowhere else I'd rather be."

"Thank God for that."

RYAN WAS OFFICIALLY the last man standing. He stood off to the side and watched his family. He was the only single one of the cousins. The last one to settle down. The last one to have any interest.

He was too young to be wrapped up in one woman. He was busy, insanely so at times, and a woman would only take his focus. He couldn't lose focus in a fire or in the field. Not when they were looking to expand the vineyard. He had to keep his head on straight and make sure everything was going according to plan.

Ryan's brother, Henry, joined him on the fringe. Henry was happily in love with his best friend from childhood. Ryan loved that his brother and Cynthia found each other after so many years apart. They definitely belonged together.

"You doing okay?"

Ryan nodded. "Yep. Just taking it all in."

"Taking what in?"

Ryan gestured to the family. "All of it. Everyone is paired off and smiling. Babies and spouses and new careers. When we took over a few years ago, I never thought all this would come of it."

"You sound like Dad," Henry said.

Ryan nodded. "I've been thinking about him lately."

"It's hard to believe it'll be two years in January."

Ryan sucked in a breath. Losing their father had been the hardest thing Ryan ever went through. His dad was his confidant, his best friend in many ways. He knew his dad was the same for so many people, but Ryan felt cheated. He was only twenty-six when his dad died.

"I still look for him in the fields. I expect him to walk around the end of a row."

Henry nodded. "Me, too."

"I wonder if that'll ever go away."

Henry shook his head. "Probably not. He was the pulse of this place. I don't think it'll ever feel right that he's not here."

"I wonder if that's how Nonna feels about Nonno," Ryan said, looking at his grandmother and the sad smile on her face.

Henry followed his gaze and nodded. "Probably. I wish we'd gotten to know him."

"I wish your future kids had gotten to know Dad."

"And yours," Henry added.

Ryan shook his head. "Nah, I don't think kids are in the picture for me. I'm happy being single."

"That doesn't mean you'll always feel that way."

Ryan shrugged. "Maybe, but I'm not like the rest of you. I don't have a best friend to fall for, or a superstar, no exes to pine over, or anything. I've never fallen in love. I don't see that changing now."

Henry chuckled. "That's exactly how I felt. I loved Cynthia, but I thought I was over her and didn't see how I'd ever let anyone else in. Then she was there, and I couldn't keep her out of my heart."

Ryan smiled. "I'm happy you found her, but I'm not like you. I don't see love coming for me."

Henry shrugged. "You never know."

"What I do see is Perry, though. Son of a bitch. What is he doing here?"

Henry turned with Ryan to face off against the man who stole from their father and tried to ruin the vineyard. He wasn't welcome on their property, and they weren't afraid to remind him of that fact.

"You need to leave. Now."

Perry grinned. "I paid my entry fee. I'm going to get some food."

"We'll refund your fee," Henry said. "Let's go."

Perry's grin faded. There was something in his eyes that almost made Ryan let him stay. Then it was gone and the evil man was pushing once more.

"I don't want a refund."

"And we don't want you here. Time to go."

They escorted Perry to the door and stood as he drove off the property. Henry scoffed and went back inside, but Ryan stared after the man who was a thorn in their side and wondered if he was losing his mind or if there was something there.

Because he recognized the look in Perry's eyes. It was one Ryan saw in his own once in a while.

Loneliness.

THANK you so much for reading Leo and Sara's story! I loved them, and Peter. I really want to see Peter get his happily ever after. Hopefully one day!

The series continues with Ryan's story. It's been two

years since his father died, but Ryan is still dealing with the loss. When a late night encounter with a mysterious woman makes him smile, he wants to know more about her. Until he finds out Bella is the daughter of his father's enemy. Read Love Is Thicker Than Water now!

KAPENA HAS ALWAYS HAD a thing for his little sister's best friend, but he's not the man she says she wants. Actions speak louder than words, though, and Ada's actions definitely say she wants him. Start Better vs. Worse today.

LEXI NEVER WANTED LOVE. It did too much damage to her growing up to allow it to mess with her life as an adult. She was happy with her friends with benefits relationship with Mike. But when he becomes her boss, and refuses to back off, she has to decide if there's more to life than work. Pick up your copy of Shapely & Stunning now!

ABOUT THE AUTHOR

USA TODAY Bestselling Author Mary E Thompson spent most of her childhood wishing she had a few less curves. She hid in the pages of books because her favorite characters never cared what size her clothes were. Now, neither does Mary, and she writes stories that celebrate women like her. Real women who have curves, chase dreams, and find love, because we should all be happy, no matter our dress size.

Mary spends her non-writing time with her husband and two kids, watching too much TV, cheering for her hometown football team (Go Bills!), and hiding chocolate from her family.

Visit https://MaryEThompson.com/ to sign up for Mary's newsletter, **Romancing the Curves**. Subscribers get free ebooks and other fun stuff, like exclusive, members only content and giveaways, plus are the first to know about new releases and sales!